West Valley Homicides

A Donald Carter Mystery

John Buchak

ISBN: 978-0692540183

Printed in the United States of America

For the reason of any type of litigation the following
statement has been included in this novel: This novel is
a work of fiction. Names, characters, places and incidents
either are the product of the author's imagination or are
used fictitiously. Any resemblance to actual persons,
living or dead, events, or locales is entirely coincidental.

Cover Design by Karin Buchak
Photos by www.dreamstime.com

ACKNOWLEDGEMENTS

To my family, thank you for all your support and ideas.

To my daughter who somehow finds the time in her busy life to put the single pages into book form along with a color cover, thank you Karin.

To my good friend P. Chester Daley, wherever he may be.

My thanks to Rick Rofman for all his editing and suggestions.

PROLOGUE

The property value in the west San Fernando Valley, located in Los Angeles County approximately twenty miles north of downtown Los Angeles, California has been on the fast-track since the early 60's. The once beautiful orange groves, expansive ranches, and farm land that stretched out as far as the eyes could see were disappearing at the hands of land developers.

In most cases the land developers were honest business men who purchased the properties for extremely inflated prices leaving the sellers with full pockets and new dreams for their sudden wealth.

But there were, unfortunately, the unscrupulous land developers who would cheat, swindle, and in some cases strong-arm land owners in order to procure their property.

If everything else failed, there was that never spoken order that was carried out where a property owner might have an "unforeseen accident."

The evil men and women who used to carry out these unspeakable tasks also had to be careful walking that fine line of, in some cases, knowing where the bodies were buried or who the puppet master was pulling the strings.

Accidents could happen to anyone, even to evil people, possibly a drug overdose, a hit-and-run while crossing a street, or even possibly a fall from a high-rise building that's under construction.

Power, money and greed, are the driving forces and when you are in control of all three, you can sometimes get away with murder, and then again, sometimes you can't.

1

1993

The office of Donald Carter Security and Investigations in North Hollywood, California, was located on the second floor over a truck and auto repair shop in a commercial area of the San Fernando Valley. Carter was an ex-US Army Vietnam veteran and also an ex-Los Angeles Police Department Detective, who only lasted eight years in law enforcement before calling it quits. Once a respected investigator, he was now on a rapid slide from respectability to becoming a full blown alcoholic, in his mid forties.

On many mornings, Carter's part time secretary, Annie Dugan, would arrive at the office to find her boss sleeping off the result of the previous night's heavy drinking. It was only a few years earlier, that his biggest case of locating several very expensive jeweled eggs that were missing, gave him the notoriety and exposure his new company needed. Now, Carter appeared to be a beaten man heading for bankruptcy or early demise.

As the phone in the office continuously rang, it echoed through the sparsely furnished space. Carter, hungover again, ignored it as he lay on the over-stuffed old leather couch, with his head buried under a pillow. When he finally felt he couldn't take the annoying sound any longer, he yelled out, "Annie, would you answer that damn phone please?"

Annie Dugan had been with Carter Security on and off for ten years. She was a smart twenty-eight year old who first started working for Carter right out of high school. Most of the time the red-headed five-foot two wise cracking woman kept the office afloat, but with times as bad as they were, she was ready to throw in the towel and call it quits. Sharing her time with the repair shop on the first floor, she was starting to feel like it was time to move on.

After spending a few minutes on the phone with the caller, Annie walked into Carter's office. As she walked, she sniffed at a smell that seemed to be a cross between a sweaty gym locker, an overflowing ashtray and a nasty bar rag smelling from stale beer. Annie opened the window blinds and the window so the air could hopefully surge in with accompanying sunlight, and said, "Mr. Carter, there's a man on the phone who needs to speak with you."

"Annie, can't you just get his number and tell him I'll call him back?"

"No Mr. Carter, he needs to speak with you now; he wants to hire you. You need the work Mr. Carter, so you can pay some of your bills. I'm sorry, but I think you need to speak with him now."

Sitting up slowly, Carter brought his stocking feet around and placed them on the floor, then asked in a slurred voice, "What's his name, what does he want?"

"His name is Robert Stearns and he wants to hire you."

Even with the window blinds fully opened, Carter's office was a little dark with the old faded brown knotty-pine walls and dirty dark gray carpeting. With his hands rubbing his face and eyes, Carter slowly lifted himself up from the couch and said, "Tell mister what's his name, 'I'll be with him in a few minutes.' Annie, I got to use the can first."

"I'll tell him you're on another call and you'll be with him in a few minutes."

"Thanks Annie."

Writing the caller's name on the note pad next to Carter's phone, Annie then picked up the receiver and said, "Mr. Stearns, Mr. Carter will be with you in a few minutes, he's just finishing up a call on the other line."

After taking care of business and splashing some cold water on his face in the restroom, Carter sat at his desk and picked up the receiver and said, "Hello, this is Donald Carter, how can I help you?"

"Mr. Carter, my name is Bob Stearns. I would like to come in and talk to you about possibly helping me track down a murderer and turn him over to the police."

"Whoa, Mr. Stearns, you need the police, not a private investigator."

"I have already spoken with someone from the LAPD, Mr. Carter. They told me they couldn't help me, that's why I'm calling you."

"Murder is serious business sir and it's something I'm sure I can't help you with."

"Mr. Carter, your name was given to me by a man who read about you years ago and believed you were the right man for the job. Can we at least meet so I can explain the details and maybe you will reconsider?"

"I don't know, Mr. Stearns."

"I'll pay you for your time and maybe you might be able to recommend another investigator if you can't help me."

Carter looked up and saw Annie standing in the doorway with her hands clasped together in a praying stance. He shook his head a little and then asked, "Mr. Stearns, do you have my address?"

"Yes I do, and please call me Bob, I feel more comfortable with that."

Looking at the wall clock, Carter asked, "Okay Bob. Are you free this morning, around ten?"

"Yes sir, I can be there at ten, and thank you."

Hanging up the phone, Carter said, "Sweetheart, that man wants me to get involved with a murder investigation, one that the LAPD wasn't interested in. Well at least I'll get a consultation fee out of him for my time."

At 9:45 Bob Stearns walked up the old metal staircase on the side of the building leading to Carter Security. Carter shared the second floor for the past ten years with an exterminating company located at the rear of the building. The large metal door at the top of the stairs was being held open by a bungee cord tied from the banister to the door knob. Following the sign nailed on the dirty knotty pine wall, pointing to the right, that read, "Carter Security," Bob walked to the door and knocked. Annie called out, "Come in please, the door is open."

Walking into the outer office, Bob Stearns introduced himself to Annie and looked around at his surroundings. The walls of the office matched the hallway being knotty pine in a lighter finish that reflected light from the window on the right side of the room. Annie's desk sat in the middle of the room on a dark gray carpet and on the left, next to a closet door, stood three filing cabinets and a small table and one chair. A copy machine sat on a second table next to the open door behind her desk that led to Carter's private office.

When he saw a man walk into the office, Carter said, "Sweetheart, please send Mr. Stearns in, and would you join us also and bring your notepad."

Carter's oversized oak desk belonged in an office twice the size, but it gave him a feeling of power, at least that's what he jokingly told his friends. The one window directly behind the desk gave off just enough light to brighten the room a little. The large worn-out black leather couch was against the right wall and on the left wall was a door leading to the rest room. The rest room was shared with the exterminating company next door and it was accessed by a second door leading from their office.

After introductions, Carter asked, "So Mr. Stearns, please tell me what it is you would like me to help you with?"

"First off Mr. Carter, please call me Bob. I *really* do like it better. Well, everything started about a year ago, when my brother-in-law died in what we thought was a terrible accident. He was working for a construction company in the West Valley when he fell or was pushed off a fourteen story building under construction."

"Hold it, excuse me Bob, but why do you think he might have been pushed? Did the police investigators come to that conclusion also?"

"I'll get to that shortly. After a rushed investigation by the LAPD and the insurance company investigators, it was determined that the death was accidental and my sister was paid two hundred thousand dollars. My sister reluctantly took the money, sold her house in Reseda, and moved to Texas to be near our ailing mom. Before she left for Texas, she gave me her husband's old car that he was restoring before his death, a 1954 Ford. Since I was out of work and had plenty of time on my hands, I

8

decided to finish the restoration and sell the car for her."

"Bob, I hope you're not getting off track here about the car, is all this about the car important?"

"Yes it is, it's very important. Now where was I? Oh yeah. I started to do some of the body work by banging and prying out the smashed-in rear quarter-panels from inside the trunk. I pushed a large pry bar between the trunk floor and the inner fender but hit some kind of package. When I pulled the package out and brought it to my work bench to cut it open, I found four packs of money, $40,000 in all, and a note from my brother-in-law Teddy."

Carter sat fiddling around with a pencil and listened, but seemed to have other things on his mind, as Bob Stearns continued with his story.

"The note said if anything happened to him it was because he had helped kill a man named Nathan Fishman and the old man's private nurse whom Teddy was fooling around with. I checked and found out that Mr. Fishman owned a large piece of property in the West Valley. A land development company run by a man named Carson Burnhart wanted it real bad."

Carter sat up in his chair because Bob Stearns finally got his attention. "Bob, did I hear you correctly? Did you say your brother-in-law helped *kill* a man named Fishman for someone named Burnhart?"

"That's correct, and his nurse."

"Did you tell the police this story Bob?"

"There's more Mr. Carter. As I stood there at the bench counting the money and reading the note over a second time, someone came up behind me and hit me on the head. When I woke up two days later I was in the hospital."

"How did you wind up in the hospital Bob?"

"Lucky for me, my neighbor found me and called the paramedics."

"Did the police pay you a visit in the hospital?"

"They never came to see me Mr. Carter, but I went to see them when I left the hospital a couple days later. The detective I talked with told me he didn't know of any report that was filed. So I told him about how I was hit on the head and about the money and the letter."

"Whom did you talk with at the police station Bob?"

"It was a homicide detective named Croft, who wrote down a few notes and told me he would check it out, but that was two weeks ago, and when I didn't hear from him I called back. He told me other than my head injury, there was no evidence. Without the note or the money, there was no way the police could do anything about it. I thought about it a couple days and called my sister. She told me to hire a private investigator to look into Teddy's death."

"Bob, what exactly is it that you and your sister want me to do?"

"We want you to find Teddy's killer and turn him over to the police, also the guy who cracked me on the head and stole the letter and the money."

"You know Bob, it could get quite expensive trying to track those people down. This is a business and an investigation like the one needed would cost a lot."

"Oh hell Mr. Carter, my sister and I don't expect you to do this for free. How much do you usually charge to track someone like this down?"

"Well Bob, my daily rate is two hundred plus expenses."

"What do the expenses usually run?"

"Sometimes twenty or thirty dollars a day, but it could be more if I have to hire some extra help. So you see it could get up there real quick."

Bob rubbed his chin, smiled, and then removed a folded check from his shirt pocket and handed it to Carter and said, "Will this do as a deposit?"

Carter unfolded the check and saw that the amount was ten thousand dollars and it was a cashier's check payable to the bearer. Handing the check to Annie, Carter said, "Sweetheart, would you please give Mr. Stearns a receipt for this retainer and have him sign a standard contract for our services?"

"My sister Emily asked me to thank you in advance, Mr. Carter, for helping us, and to let you know if there is anything you need from her to just let her know, including more money."

Bob please let your sister know that I will do everything in my power to find her husband's killer, if I find out it was not an accident that killed him."

"And don't forget the guy that bopped me, I want a piece of that bastard myself."

"I won't forget Bob. Now, what I need from you is all your contact information and your sister's. I'll need your brother-in-law's full name and all the information you can give me on the company he worked for. I'm going to need a signed document allowing me to act as your representative in all dealings with the police. Annie will type up everything and then she'll drive you to a Notary so he can witness your signature."

"Whatever you need Mr. Carter."

"Bob, what was your brother-in-law's full name?"

"Teddy Houser, I never knew his middle name."

"Annie, would you take care of all the forms please?"

Once Annie had all the documents typed, and all the other information Carter required, Bob and Carter shook hands and Carter said, "I will call you just as soon as I have some information for you Bob."

"Mr. Carter, there's one other thing. I think someone's been following me. I may just be paranoid, but I keep seeing a light gray pick-up wherever I go. I wouldn't be surprised if it's parked down the street somewhere waiting for me to leave here."

Carter walked to his window and looked up and down the street but didn't see a gray pick-up truck anywhere. Walking back over to Bob, Carter said, "I don't see it out there now, but if you happen to notice it again, try to get the license plate info and call me so I can track it down."

"Okay Mr. Carter, thank you again, I'll be waiting for your call."

As Bob and Annie headed for the door, Carter said, "Annie, I need to talk with you before you leave?"

Annie said, "Bob, my car is the blue Chevy Impala parked by the fence, I'll be down in a minute."

Carter could hear Bob as he descended the noisy metal steps and said, "That man just saved our bacon, Annie.

I'm going to do everything I can to help him."

"He just helped this office a lot Mr. Carter, now we can pay bills and rent."

"After you finish up with Mr. Stearns, stop at the bank and deposit that check in the account, but hold out a thousand in cash, they'll let you do it."

"You know Mr. Carter, I could use a few bucks myself, it's been a while since I drew a pay check."

"I'm sorry Annie, I wasn't thinking clearly; write yourself a check for five-hundred. Will that do?"

With a chuckle in her voice, Annie said, "That will do just fine Mr. Carter."

"Annie, when you get back, would you see what you can find out about that Burnhart Construction Co."

"Are you going to need some help on this one Mr. Carter?"

"Yeah Annie, I just hope Mick is still talking to me, its' been awhile."

"Oh you know he always comes through for you. Okay, bye Mr. C. I should be back in an hour or two."

2

Michael "Mick" Terratello and Donald Carter first met while both men were returning from active duty in Vietnam while serving in the Army. Both men had been reassigned to Fort Hood, Texas. Although they had been assigned to different units, they had become fast friends during their flight back to the States. Over their last year of service at Fort Hood, they shared an off-base rental house until their discharge in 1975.

Mick had returned to his home state of New Jersey while Carter traveled back to his hometown of Los Angeles, where he flopped around for over a year until he joined the LAPD. Eight years later, Carter said goodbye to police work and started his own private investigation company.

Always trying to break away from his family's involvement in mob activities, Mick worked in the security and alarm business for five years in and around New Jersey until his decision to move west to California.

Working for his old friend Carter occasionally when his expertise was needed, Mick watched painfully as the many years of heavy drinking and bad decisions by Carter drove a wedge between their friendships. Over the past few years the two men kept in touch but only worked together when Carter controlled his drinking.

It took four rings before Mick finally answered by saying, "It's your dime, so get to it."

"Hey Mick, it's Carter."

"Hey Donny boy, whatcha been up to?"

"I got some work for you Mick. Are you working on anything you can get away from?"

"No, I'm free. I just finished doing some alarm shit for some big wig in Beverly Hills. She was having trouble with her high-class piece-of-shit alarm system that some moron installed."

"Good. The first thing I need you to do is get a hold of Jimmy Hudson, you got his number don't you?"

"Yeah, I got Jimbo's number. He's going to ask me about the job, so what do I tell him?"

"Tell him he asks too many fucking questions. Look, call me after you talk to him and let me know if he's free for a couple of week's work."

"Okay Donny boy, you at the office?"

"Yeah Mick, call me here. If you get a busy signal it's because I'm on the line with Croft at LAPD."

"Croft, what the hell do you have to call that asshole for?"

"Well believe it or not, he's part of the case, and I have to drag some information out of him. Okay, enough said, call Hudson and get back to me."

Hanging up Carter took a few deep breaths and then called Det. Croft at the Van Nuys Homicide Division.

Two rings and the call was answered, "Homicide, Sergeant Booker, can I help you?"

"Hey Charley, it's Don Carter, how the hell are you?"

"Hey Carter, what have you been up to, you still chasing those cheating husbands for those rich wives?"

Carter laughed and said, "Only if she pays good Charley. So tell me, is Croft around?"

"Yeah, actually he's on the phone with his house painter, you know Croft, he's trying to get the work done for next to nothing. He hired some cheap-ass painter and now he's complaining about what they want to give him for his money."

"Would you let him know that I'm on the line and I need to talk with him?"

"Hold on Carter, I think he's getting off. Yeah, here he is, take care guy."

Next voice Carter heard, "Det. Croft, can I help you?"

"Hello Croft, it's Carter."

"That's *Detective* Croft, Carter. What's on your mind, you got some speeding tickets you need fixed?"

"I didn't think you did that kind of stuff anymore Croft."

"What the hell is it that you want Carter, I'm very busy?"

"I need to get some information to help in a case I'm involved in."

"Since when have I become your supplier of information Carter?"

"Since my client came to you and reported an attempt on his life."

"And who's your client Carter?"

"Robert Stearns, you remember him don't you? He came to you after getting out of the hospital and you gave him a story that you would check things out and get back to him later. Well it's later, whatcha got?"

"First off Carter, without the written consent by Mr. Stearns, I ain't got nothing for you. Second, there ain't nothing to be got. Look Carter, don't waste the poor man's money, he has no proof of anything he was saying. And about the fairy tale death of Nathan Fishman, its all bull, the old man died of a heart attack in his bed in his own house. On top of all of this, he's trying to lay the blame on a respected member of the community, Carson Burnhart; a man who donates to charity and helps feed the homeless. Enough Carter, as far as I'm concerned, it's case closed. End of story."

"What about the attack on Stearns? Are you calling that a fairy tale also, Croft?"

"Who's to say how that happened Carter?"

Carter yelled back, "You horse's ass, do your job and investigate the man's claim."

Before hanging up the phone, Det. Croft said, "You investigate it Carter and waste your time. Oh wait, that's right, you're going to bleed the poor man of his money."

Carter sat at his desk and slammed the phone receiver down and said, "Fucking asshole."

Just as Carter got up from his desk to use the bathroom the phone rang. Picking it up on the second ring he answered, "Carter Security can I help you?"

"It's Mick, Donny boy."

"Yeah Mick, did you get a hold of Hudson?"

"Jimbo's set to go. He's staying at his sister's place in Tarzana. What's the job?"

"How about you and Hudson meeting me at Rusty's around eight tonight, and then I'll fill you both in on the case and what your parts will entail."

"Sounds good boss, eight it is."

Hanging up the phone, Carter made a quick turn and headed for the bathroom and took care of business he'd been putting off.

Once back at his desk, Carter removed the phone book from his desk drawer and looked up the Carson Wendell Burnhart Construction Corporation. After writing down the address he next wrote a note for Annie, letting her know that he might not be back before she went home, and to leave the cash and signed papers in his desk drawer.

The CWBCC was located in Beverly Hills and Carter knew his unexpected visit would most probably be met with resentment, especially when he started asking questions about an ex-employee who happened to be dead. To Carter's surprise, Mr. Burnhart made time to meet with him and was very cordial at first, as he invited him into his office to answer a few questions about the late Teddy Houser.

The first thing Carter noticed about the man was the very close resemblance to the actor John Huston, in the movie "Chinatown." His private office was exactly what one would expect a millionaire to have. Carter thought it was something right out of a movie set.

As Carter looked around possibly getting ideas for his own office of the future, Mr. Burnhart asked, "So what can I do for you? Mr. Carter is it?"

"First sir, I would like to thank you for seeing me, Mr. Burnhard."

Sitting behind his desk, smiling, the man said, "That's Burnhart with a T."

"Sorry sir." Then he asked, "How well did you know your employee Teddy Houser?"

"Oh, Teddy had been with us for only two years, but he was a valued employee. He had a good work record and was the kind of employee any boss would be proud of."

"How did Mr. Houser get along with other employees?"

"He was a team player."

"So you mean he always did what was asked of him?"

"From monthly reports I received from my foreman, Teddy was an excellent worker who performed his duties to the letter."

"You mean he never questioned what he was asked to do."

"What are you getting at Mr. Carter?"

"Well sir, even the best baseball players sometimes balk when they're told to bunt in a game, especially when they feel like hitting away. Did Teddy Houser always follow instructions and cooperate completely no matter what was asked of him?"

"Just whom are you working for Mr. Carter?"

"My client prefers to remain anonymous at the present time sir."

"And why exactly do you feel these types of questions need *my* answers?"

Carter thought a few seconds and asked, "In your mind sir, do you think there might be any reason to suspect that Mr. Houser's death was not an accident?"

Mr. Burnhart stood up and said, "I don't like where this questioning is going Mr. Carter. I feel at this time any additional questions you might have should go to my attorney. My secretary will provide you with the name of the law firm and I think it's time for you to be on your way sir."

Carter also stood up and asked, "So is that a yes?"

"Do I have to call security to get you to leave?"

"No, I think you've answered my question sir. You have a good day Mr. Burnhart."

3

Rusty's Hacienda on Lankershim Blvd. in North Hollywood has been at the same location longer than anyone can remember. The food served is authentic and excellent, with music and surroundings that make you feel like you're somewhere in the middle of Mexico. They're known throughout the Valley for the giant sized margaritas served up by a couple of bartenders who know their way around a bottle of tequila.

The bar has always been one of Carter's favorites on his list of places to sit all night and drink until finally being asked to leave at closing time. Occasionally Carter would have meetings with clients at Rusty's so he could write it off on his taxes.

Carter walked in and saw Mick and Jimmy Hudson sitting at the bar talking with one of the bartenders. Both men were clean shaven, dressed in very nice clothes, wearing sports jackets looking like GQ models. Carter was in shock since he was wearing jeans and a pull-over shirt and looking very casual.

Jimmy Hudson, a one time fine police officer with the LAPD, had ten years on the job when he had a forced retirement. While off duty one night as he entered a 7/11 store, he happened on a hold-up in progress. As he pulled out his badge with one hand and his gun with the other, he identified himself as a police officer and was immediately fired upon by a man robbing the store. Kneeling down and returning fire at the suspect in front of the counter, Hudson was shot by a second suspect who came out from behind a section of shelves in the rear of the store.

The first suspect died of his wounds before the paramedics arrived on the scene. The second suspect fled the scene and was never caught. Officer Hudson, suffered massive damage to his right shoulder from the large caliber weapon used by the shooter and had to leave the police force with an early retirement.

Walking up to the bar, Carter said, "What's with the fine duds guys, you looking for dates?"

Jimmy Hudson looked at Mick first and then said to Carter, "You know boss man, we black folks has nice clothes too."

Carter started laughing and said, "Fuck you Jimmy," then he held out his hand and the two men shook before Carter sat down in the empty seat next to Mick.

Carter ordered a double shot of Dewars on the rocks, and then quickly changed his order to a club soda. He looked around for a nice quiet table in the corner and once he got his drink the three men moved to the corner table so they could talk in private.

Carter laid out everything he had about the investigation to both Mick and Jimmy, including his trip to the construction company to meet Carson Burnhart. Then he explained what he needed from each of them, if they decided to take the jobs.

Mick's job was going to be really involved, as he was going to find all the information he could on Nathan Fishman and his young wife of only two years. Also, he had to gather information on the nurse who took care of Mr.

Fishman before his death, and the facility she worked for at the time of her death.

Jimmy was going to hang out around the construction site and see what information he could pick up about Teddy Houser and Chris Doyle. Doyle was the last guy to see and talk with Houser before his fall from the fourteenth floor.

Carter handed both men envelopes with information and cash for expenses.

Mick asked, "And what are you going to be doing boss while we're out having fun?"

Carter said, "I got a few things I have to take care of over the next couple of days, but I want you guys to stay in touch with me. Look, these people are killers, so don't take any chances, and keep looking over your shoulder."

Just as he finished talking, someone tapped Carter on his shoulder. When he turned around to see who it was he heard, "I was just thinking about you and here you are."

Cindy Prentis was an old flame of Carter's, and when it came to rolling around under the sheets, she was the best he had ever met.

Looking up at her beautiful full red lips and her heavily made-up face, Carter said, "Hello sweetheart is your husband still working nights?"

As she stroked the side of Carter's face, she said, "No hon, he's back in prison. The fool violated his parole one too many times and they sent him back to finish his sentence. With good behavior he should be out in eighteen months. How about buying this lonely girl a drink?"

With that, Mick and Jimmy got up and Mick said, "We'll stay in touch boss, you two have a nice night."

Carter said, "Remember what I told you, be careful."

Mick, while looking at the lady with the mini skirt and the tight low cut revealing sweater, said "Yeah, you too boss."

Switching to scotch, Carter and the sexy lady had a couple more drinks in the bar, and then he and the sweet Cindy walked back to her place down the street from Rusty's. Four hours later, Carter walked out of Cindy's house with a limp in his step and an ache in his groin, from just a little bit too much love making. With all he had to drink at her place, he decided he was too drunk to drive and decided to walk the few blocks to his office and then sack out on the couch once again.

It was around 7am when the phone started ringing, and whoever it was would just not quit. Finally rolling off the couch onto the floor, Carter stood on his unsteady legs, walked to the desk and picked up the receiver, "Yeah, who is it?"

"Carter, it's Detective Croft. Is this too early for you sweetheart, you sound a little out of it?"

"What do you want Croft?"

"You almost lost your client last night Carter. I need you to get the hell down here so we can have a little talk this morning."

"Hey Croft, I'm not thinking straight yet, I just woke up, which client?"

"Robert Stearns, he's in critical condition in Valley Pres Hospital. He is your client isn't he Carter?"

"Bob Stearns, oh yeah, the fairy tale guy, how did it happen Croft?"

"It was a hit-and-run smartass. Carter we have one witness who saw the vehicle. Just get down here now."

"Okay Croft, give me a couple hours and I'll be there."

"I said now Carter, you know how it works, we need to jump on this fast."

"Hey, screw you Croft! I need to take a shit, shower, shave and put on some clean clothes, take it or leave it."

"Okay Carter, two hours and if you're not here I send out a few Patrol Cars looking for you. Are we clear, Carter?"

"Hey Croft, that's not a bad idea. How about you send a limo to my house in two hours? Tell them to just come to the door and I'll have coffee and donuts waiting for them in the kitchen."

Det. Croft was not amused, and said, "Very funny wise ass. Two hours Carter, I'll be waiting for you." Then he hung up.

Two hours and forty-five minutes later Carter walked into Det. Croft's office, sat down across from him and asked, "Okay Croft, I'm here. Now what the hell have you got on the hit and run?"

"You're not here to ask the questions Carter, you're here to answer them."

"Croft, you give a little and I give a little."

"That's not how it works Carter."

"And just how does it work *Detective* Croft? I'm here voluntarily to help in any way I can. Are there any charges against me detective? No, I didn't think so. I'm going back to my office. If you decide you want my help you know where to find me."

As Carter started to get up from his chair, the detective said, "Sit down Carter and let's talk."

4

After forty-five minutes of exchanging information on Bob Stearns, with what Croft had on the hit and run, Carter walked out of the police station with only a little more than he had when he walked in. Croft revealed that he had found one of Carter's cards in Stearns wallet along with a receipt for a cashier's check made out to Carter. There was only one witness to the hit-and-run who saw a light-colored pick-up truck leaving the scene, but because of a security camera in the area on a bank building across the street, they were digging deeper, with hope of additional information.

On the way back to his office, Carter stopped to use his cell phone to call Mick. After six rings, Mick's answering machine said, "You got me, leave it after the beep."

Carter said, "Yeah, yeah, beep this. Call me at my office. Don't forget we got tickets for the Lakers game tonight."

A little over an hour later, Carter was seated at his desk when Annie called out, "Mr. Carter, Mick is on line one."

Picking up the receiver Carter said, "Hey Mick, you got anything for me?"

"Not yet boss. But I got some feelers out. The only feedback I got so far is that I'm asking some questions about some dangerous people. Hey, so what time you wanna leave for the game tonight?"

"How about we meet here at the office around five thirty, that way we have plenty of time to eat and get settled in before the game starts? Look Mick, I don't know where this case is going to take us, especially now that the guy who hired me is in critical condition in the hospital."

"What happened to him Donny Boy?"

He was almost killed last night in a questionable hit and run. We'll talk about it more tonight on the way to the game."

"You got it Donny Boy. I'll give Jimmy a call and give him a heads up on what's going on. Hey, how about a ten spot on the game, I take my Knicks and you get the pretty boys?"

"Only ten Mick? No confidence in your guys?"

"Hey you got home court advantage, you giving any points?"

"Ten bucks is fine Mick, I'll see you at five-thirty."

Once off the phone, Carter decided he was going to do a little snooping around the construction company since he had a few hours to kill.

Driving to the field office of Carson Burnhart out in the West Valley, Carter stopped on the way and picked up a sandwich and a cup of coffee so he could enjoy an early lunch while he watched the building.

Carter had just un-wrapped his sandwich and opened his coffee, when he spotted Burnhart exiting through the front door of the building accompanied by a short Hispanic man. Quickly, Carter picked up his camera with its zoom lens and started clicking off pictures of the men as they walked through the parking lot.

Standing next to a white Mercedes, the two men were talking when a gray Ford pick-up with front-end damage truck pulled up and stopped next to them. Carter watched as the third man got out of the truck, approached Burnhart and appeared to be yelling at him. The pointing and shouting was escalating as Carter kept clicking away, getting close-up pictures of the group with his zoom lens.

As things appeared to get out of hand, the short Hispanic guy had to get between Burnhart and the much taller pick-up truck driver. Carter knew he had to get a picture of the license plate on the pick-up truck, but the angle and distance made it impossible.

The pick-up driver after being escorted back to his truck by the Hispanic man, got into his truck, backed away from the Mercedes then put his transmission in drive and burned rubber as he left the lot.

Wanting to find out more about the truck driver's identity, Carter started his car and headed in the same direction as the truck. What Carter didn't know was that he was also being followed and photographed by someone in an old Ford Mustang.

Once away from the area, the pick-up truck slowed down to normal driving speeds and Carter was able at one point to get close enough to get the plate number. Dropping back to a safe distance, he continued following the truck to a more rural area of the Valley and watched as the driver entered a dirt road. Passing the road entrance, Carter read the large sign posted to its right that read, "Runyon Chicken Ranch."

Turning into the next crossroad to make a U-turn, Carter spotted the blue Ford Mustang in his rear-view mirror that looked a little too familiar. As the Mustang went by, its two occupants appeared to look at Carter's car, but kept going straight.

Deciding it was time to head back to his office, Carter took a slow ride back to North Hollywood on Victory Boulevard which runs the full length of the San Fernando Valley, East and West. At one stop light as he was bending slightly taking a bite of his sandwich, Carter spotted the Mustang in the side mirror four cars back.

When the light changed to green, Carter made a quick right turn from the center lane and accelerated rapidly.

Watching in the mirror, the Mustang, although far back, also made the turn and he knew he was being followed. Now it was time for a little cat and mouse game and he wanted to reverse the roles.

Carter decided he would use the parking garage at the Sherman Oaks Galleria to pull the switch on his follower. Slowing down to the legal speed limit, he paid no additional attention to the Mustang until he arrived at the Galleria.

Pulling up to the entrance of the parking garage on the side street, Carter stopped at the ticket dispensing machine and watched as the bar lifted allowing him to drive in. The Mustang did not enter the garage but instead parked farther down the street where its occupants could watch the exit.

The construction of the parking garage, to patrons who were familiar with it, gave access to parking areas not intended for use by customers, so it was possible to travel from one area to another. Driving through these restricted openings allowed vehicles to exit onto either Sepulveda Blvd. or into a service alley both out of sight of the parked Mustang.

Carter circled around onto Sepulveda Blvd. and parked just out of sight of the men in the Mustang, but where he could see them. After watching the exit for about thirty minutes, one of the men got out of the car and walked into the garage. Twenty more minutes went by, when the man came running back to the car and appeared to be shouting at the driver. Once back into the car, the Mustang quickly made a U-turn and sped back onto Sepulveda

Blvd. and headed for the freeway entrance east.

Carter took up his position now as the cat following the mouse, as they headed east towards North Hollywood. Keeping far back out of view of the Mustang, Carter watched as the vehicle exited the freeway onto Tujunga Ave. and drove to Chandler Blvd.

Driving by Carter's office several times, the men finally seemed to give up and headed back to the freeway entrance going west.

Letting the Mustang just go on its way, Carter drove back to his office, parked in the lot, grabbed his sandwich and cold coffee and headed for the comfort of his desk.

Walking into his front office he noticed Annie waving at him while holding the phone receiver to her ear and said, "Never mind Det. Croft, he just walked in, thank you." Hanging up the receiver Annie then said, "I've been trying to locate you Mr. Carter."

Looking to his left, Carter saw a woman dressed in black sitting in the chair next to the copy machine.

Annie said, "Mr. Carter, this is Mrs. Emily Houser, Teddy Houser's widow and Bob Stearns' sister."

Carter walked to the woman held out his hand and said, "I'm sorry for your loss Mrs. Houser."

Standing up Mrs. Houser said, "I came here straight from the airport in Burbank Mr. Carter. I wanted to meet you before going to the police station and the hospital. I'm sure my brother's accident was caused by the same people who killed Teddy."

"Mrs. Houser….."

"Please call me Emily."

"Emily, let's go to my office where we can talk and be a little more comfortable." Looking at Annie, Carter asked, "Annie, would you please bring us in some coffee?"

Carter pulled the cushioned chair up next to the desk and said, "Won't you have a seat Emily and let me know what you have on your mind."

"Well first Mr. Carter, I want you to know that I appreciate anything that you have done so far. After talking with the police late last night, I felt like they weren't going to do anything about Teddy's death, and that Det. Croft, called it a tragic accident and they had nothing additional on the driver. He said they were still investigating Bob's hit and run but had nothing he could tell me at this time."

"Well first off Emily, I'm very familiar with Det. Croft, and though my personal feelings for him are not exactly on a higher standard, he is very professional, not tactful, warm or caring, but professional."

"I just had the feeling talking with him was a waste of my time, asking him questions about Bob's so-called accident was just like it was with Teddy's so-called accident. I want to be sure Mr. Carter that you will stick with your investigation until you find the truth."

"Emily, I will keep up with my investigation, and the facts I find will be turned over to you alone. There is something I do need from you to keep me out of hot water with the police."

"Whatever you need Mr. Carter."

Carter called out, "Annie please bring in a power of attorney form for information found in our investigation?"

While Annie was typing in the information she already had on Mrs. Houser, Carter asked, "Where will you be staying while you're here in town Emily?"

"Since Bob had no one else living with him, I've decided to stay at his place until he gets out of the hospital. I'm thinking positive about Bob's recovery Mr. Carter."

"Emily, I would like to go through some of Bob's things to see if there was anything that could help me in my investigation."

"That would be fine Mr. Carter. I'm going tomorrow to see him in the hospital. Would you by any chance have some time in the morning to accompany me?"

"Emily, I would be happy to go with you, just let me know the time you wish to go and I'll pick you up."

Standing up, Mrs. Houser said, "Bob spoke highly of you Mr. Carter, now I can see why. I'm sorry I didn't ask earlier. Do you need additional funds?"

"Not at this time Emily, and maybe not at all if we can wrap all of this up and find the guilty party, and please, call me Donald."

Her eyes and face seemed to tighten as Emily Houser said, Donald, I want you to get these bastards for what they did."

5

Annie Dugan had already left the office for the day, and Carter was sitting in his desk chair with his feet propped up on the desk. Mick walked in wearing a New York Knicks jersey and a Knicks cap. He looked at Carter and said, "Are you ready to lose tonight Donny Boy?"

Carter placed his Lakers cap on his head and stood up showing off his bright purple and gold Lakers jersey and said, "I'll expect payment on our bet at the end of the game, cash only please. No checks accepted."

Locking the outer office door and the outside metal door, they walked down the steps to Mick's 1960 Cadillac Convertible.

Fighting rush hour traffic, they were looking at a minimum one hour drive to the Los Angeles Forum in Inglewood, CA.

Carter told Mick about his visit from Emily Houser and her support that she expressed and her willingness to see their investigation through to the end. He also told him about being tailed earlier that day and warned him again about being very careful not to be followed.

Sitting in the stop-and-go traffic just as predicted, Carter asked, "Did you find out anything new today?"

"Do you remember a guy named Jutty Wilson?"

"Yeah, If I remember right he was a snitch who was always trying to sell crappy information to anyone he could con, what about him?"

"Well, old Jutty has gone the straight and narrow route these days. He has a steady job running a newsstand downtown across the street from the Hall of Records. Hudson called me and told me to check out if Jutty might have something we could use. Turns out that Jutty picks up a lot of info on what's going on in the building across the street from his stand."

"Does this story have a point to it Mick, or are we just going down memory lane?"

"Hey, it's all in the set up boss, hear me out. So, Jutty gets wind of lots of property changing owners out in the west San Fernando Valley, and guess who the new owners are in this land buying frenzy?"

"Well my first guess would be the Burnhart Corp."

"Hey boss, you must have a crystal ball, because you hit it right on the head. And there was some other information the nosey snitch found that he was willing to part with for a few bucks. It seems that most of the previous owners of the properties died of questionable causes. He added that a little bird whispered in his ear that there are a lot of politicians and high ranking police officers also drawing a steady income in cash from Mr. Burnhart."

"How the hell did he get that information?"

"Well at first he was adamant about not revealing how he acquired his information. Then I reminded him about that time three years ago when he was holding something back from me when I was doing some work for Sammy Doyle Security. I had the little bastard cuffed behind his back out in Acton, and in my right hand I held a pair of large channel-lock pliers. I un-buckled his belt and his drawers fell to the ground. That little fucker told me things that went back to his childhood. With that little reminder he opened up, at no big cost to us might I add, but I threw him a twenty anyway, just for his time."

"Make a note of the twenty bucks for the files Mick and Annie will be sure you get it back. So you think his information is good?"

"Believe me boss, when I told him that if I found out he was lying to me, he could kiss his balls goodbye, he swore on his mother's grave that it was the truth."

After battling with irritated angry drivers on the I-405 Freeway, and a quick drive on Manchester Blvd., Mick pulled his old classic Cadillac into the Forum parking lot. Still having time to spare before the game started, they headed for the packed concession stands to grab a couple hot dogs and beers to bring to their seats.

The sellout crowd filled the seats of the Forum and the game started on time for a change. Two and a half hours went by of an extremely physical game that ended with the score, 'Lakers 97, Knicks 96.'

The Knicks held the lead through three quarters of the game but the Lakers tied them in the fourth quarter, with the lead changing many times before the final buzzer. As Mick handed Carter a ten dollar bill he said, "They was robbed, I want a rematch."

Laughing it up as they left the building heading for the parking lot, they passed the area where many busses were parked with the fumes and smoke from the running diesel engines filling the night air.

Neither man heard the first gunshot that shattered a nearby bus window behind them, but when the second shot from an unknown location struck Mick in the back, both men dropped to the pavement. Falling backwards, Mick hit his head on the pavement and lost consciousness. Several more shots struck the bus next to them and one hit Carter in the leg before he was able to roll Mick under the bus for better protection from the gunshots.

A small group of people who were nearby ran for cover, but by then the sounds of the rifle fire had ended. The bus the men were lying under became silent as the driver shutdown the engine and exited through the open doors.

Within minutes of the shooting, lot security was on the scene. After assessing the situation, they called 911 and asked for the paramedics. Although he was in severe pain himself, Carter was worried about Mick who had slipped into unconsciousness and was not responding to shaking or calling his name. Holding his hat tightly against the wound in Mick's back, Carter was yelling out, "Where the hell are those paramedics?"

With the heavy traffic leaving the parking lots, it took a while for the paramedics to get to the shooting scene. Working frantically the paramedics stabilized Mick and tended to Carter's leg wound. After a few minutes the ambulance arrived, loaded Mick and Carter in the back and sped away to the hospital.

The emergency surgery on Mick to repair some of the damage to his body went on for many hours and he was now in the ICU hooked up to a couple machines monitoring his life support functions.

Carter's surgery, although not life threatening, was successful but would most probably leave him with limited use of his right leg for some time.

Lying in his hospital room, not fully awake after his hectic night which included an hour on the operating table, Carter could hear the orderly and the clanking of the food cart in the hallway outside his open door and realized it was morning and he had slept a few hours.

Walking in carrying a tray, the smiling orderly asked, "How you feeling this morning Mr. Carter?" as he placed the tray on the table next to the bed.

Restricted a little by his bandaged leg, Carter said, "I feel like an elephant stepped on my leg and a bird crapped on my tongue. What have you got for me that will get rid of this nasty taste in my mouth?"

Lifting the lid covering the plate the orderly said, "Well you got some scrambled eggs, some bacon, oat meal and toast. I brought you apple juice and orange juice so maybe you want to try one of them first?"

"How about some coffee, any of that on your magic cart?"

"Give me a minute and I'll bring you some coffee."

"Thanks buddy and could you send in one of the nurses too, I need to get some information on my friend I came in with last night."

A few minutes later a cute red headed nurse came in asking, "How you feeling this morning Mr. Carter?"

"Not too bad considering. How's my friend Michael Terratello doing, he was brought in with me last night with a gun shot wound to his back?"

"Mr. Terratello is in the ICU, he is still sedated from what I've heard. I'll try and get an update for you in a little while."

"Thank you nurse, what's your name hon?"

"Elaine."

"Thank you Elaine."

"Mr. Carter, there's a detective here from the LAPD who wishes to talk with you."

"Go ahead and send him in, I might as well get this over with now."

As the nurse left the room Det. Croft stood in the doorway and said, "You ready for some questions, Carter?"

"Yeah come on in Croft, let's do it."

While the detective pulled up a chair closer to the bed, Carter saw the orderly coming in with a large cup of coffee and said, "Oh thanks buddy you're a life saver."

"If you need a refill, just hit the button and I'll fill her up again."

Croft asked the orderly, "That smells good. You think you can rustle up a cup for me?"

The orderly looked at Croft and his badge hanging on his jacket pocket and said, "Sure Detective, be back in a few minutes."

Croft unbuttoned his jacket, took out a small notebook, crossed his legs, and asked, "Okay Carter, what the hell is this all about?"

"Damned if I know Croft. Mick and I came out of the Forum after the game and were walking through the parking lot to his car. Next thing I know, someone is shooting at us. Your guys got any leads yet?"

"What the hell do you think we are Carter, magicians? That's why I'm here so damn early. So, you can start by telling me who you think it might be?"

"Look Croft, the only case I'm working on now is checking out the mysterious hit and run of Bob Stearns, and the unfortunate accident of Teddy Houser."

"That's police business, Carter."

"Yeah, that's why Houser's death was swept away and not a damn thing is being done about Stearns, right? Something stinks in your department Croft. I would hate to find out that you had anything to do with it."

"Carter, you have no idea what the hell you're talking about. What proof do you have, or is just your bullshit way of thinking?"

"Stearns came to you and told you his story and you just shined him on. Now the man's in the hospital again. Houser's accident was pushed through your department and the case was closed quickly. Why? I'll tell you why. Because some guy named Carson Burnhart whispered to, or paid off someone in a high position, and you were told to close the case. Isn't that what happened Croft?"

"You better watch out with your accusations Carter, you could get your license pulled for saying things like that without proof."

"You want some proof Croft, go to the ICU and check out Mick, all he did was to ask a few questions about some property sales in the West Valley. You want more proof. I had a couple of Carson Burnhart's goons follow me around the Valley after they spotted me checking out their boss yesterday afternoon."

"And you think Carson Burnhart, a multi-millionaire, large scale property developer, ordered a hit on you?"

"I not only think it Croft, but when I get my ass out of here I'm going to prove it. If you're clean you have nothing to worry about, but if you're dirty, you're going down with the rest of that scum."

Standing up Croft said, "Watch your ass Carter, because if you start pointing a finger and screwing around with those high society people, and the Commissioner gets a call, don't look to me for help."

"Just remember what I told you Croft."

Croft headed for the door, stopped and turned around and said, "I hope Terratello pulls through okay. He's a tough guy and I'm sure he'll be just fine. If you get anything solid Carter, call me, but don't talk about it on the phone. I would rather meet with you in private."

"So, you do think something stinks in all of this?"

Not answering, Croft just turned and walked out the door almost bumping into the orderly holding his coffee and said, "I think Mr. Carter needs a refill, just give him mine."

Carter asked, "Any chance on getting a hot breakfast buddy? That blow-hard detective talked so damn long I never had a chance to eat."

"I got a couple on the hot cart out there, I'll be right back. By the way, my name is Steve, just so you know."

"Thanks Steve, I should have asked you earlier."

"No problem Mr. Carter. Let me get that breakfast for you."

6

Carter just got the last of his eggs and bacon down and was ready to turn the TV on when a doctor accompanied by the nurse came in and asked, "How you feeling this morning Mr. Carter? My name is Dr. Wharton."

"Actually not too bad Doc, I may feel different once the drugs wear off though. Can you tell me how my friend Michael Terratello is doing?"

"Mr. Terratello is still in the ICU and he's stabilized. Other than that, I have nothing for you at this time. I was on duty when you and your friend arrived at the hospital last night. I performed the surgery on your injured leg and I'm happy to tell you that you should not suffer any permanent damage. You will, however, require physical therapy."

"So you didn't work on my friend?"

"Dr. Cisco was called in for the emergency surgery on Mr. Terratello to repair extensive muscle damage to his shoulder. From what I heard, two inches either way and Mr. Terratello would be in a lot worst condition. Now what I need you to do for me is a little toe movement and I want to check for any numbness. That bullet went through your calf muscle and slightly nicked the bone."

Carter's exam took only a few minutes and he was told he would be able to leave the hospital the next day. So with the way his brain worked, Carter had to ask, "Can't you cut me loose this afternoon Doc?"

"I suppose that could be arranged Mr. Carter, but you will need someone to drive you home. You did hear me. I said home, not work. If you don't stay off that leg you could tear open the stitches and ruin some of my best needle work."

"You got it Doc, wheelchair and crutches and no running or dancing."

Carter waited until 9AM and called Annie at the office to let her know what had happened the night before and ask her to pick him up at the hospital around 1pm.

Around noon, Carter was dressed and sitting in a wheelchair with the help of Steve the orderly, and was on his way to the ICU to check on Mick before he went to the lobby to wait for Annie.

With a little persuading and a bunch of smiles, Carter was allowed to wheel his way to Mick's bedside. Surprised to see Mick sitting up with his eyes open, Carter asked as he touched Mick's arm, "Hey Mick, double or nothing on the next Lakers / Knicks game?"

The faint smile on his friend's face told Carter that Mick was going to be okay in time. With the tube still down his throat, and lines hooked up to him with the monitors blinking different readings, Carter lightly squeezed Mick's arm and said, "You rest Mick and I'll be back to see you tomorrow."

Mick nodded his head slightly and Carter rolled away in his wheelchair meeting up with Steve in the hallway. Finding a quiet corner to park the chair in the lobby, the orderly asked, "Will your ride take long to get here?"

"Maybe twenty minutes to half an hour."

"How about I get you a cup of coffee for the wait?"

"Thanks Steve that would be great."

As he waited for Steve to return with his coffee, and Annie to pick him up, Carter thought about the past few days and where he was going next in his investigation. He planned on recuperating until he regained his strength and the use of his leg, but he knew he could make some phone calls and get a little help.

Since Mick had no family out here on the west coast, Carter knew he had to call Mick's favorite uncle back in New York, Vito Terratello, a known retired crime boss.

7

Annie Dugan arrived on time to pick Carter up at the hospital and parked right at the front door. Steve the orderly rolled Carter out in the wheelchair and helped buckle him into the front seat of her Chevy Impala. Shaking hands with Carter, Steve found a ten dollar bill folded up tucked in his hand. Carter said, "Thank you Steve. Keep an eye on my friend Mick Terratello if you can?"

"I will Mr. Carter. Remember, you're supposed to go straight home, no work for you until your leg heals, doctor's orders!"

"Thanks again Steve, I may see you tomorrow when I come back to visit my friend in the ICU."

"Annie said, "Okay Mr. Carter, visiting hours are over. It's time for you to go home now."

As they drove away Carter told Annie, "We need to make one quick stop at the office sweetheart. While I'm making a few phone calls, maybe you can pick up a few things for me at the pharmacy and some food for the house."

"I heard him tell you no work, Mr. Carter."

"A few calls and it's home for me after that Annie, I promise."

During the ride to the office, Annie asked Carter about the shooting and if he had any idea who might be behind it. Carter told her he was sure that Burnhart had something to do with it, but he needed proof before he could actually accuse him and get the police involved. Carter asked, "Annie, when you drove Bob Stearns to the notary, did he tell you anything other than he had in his statement?"

"He told me he was trying to remember everything that was in his brother-in-law's note and was writing it down so he could give it to you."

"Has Mrs. Houser called the office?"

"Yes, she told me you had agreed to go to the hospital with her to see her brother, but when she heard what happened to you and Mick, she went alone. She also asked me to call her and let her know how you were doing."

Once back sitting at his own desk, Carter made the arrangements to have Mick's car picked up at the Forum and brought to the office parking lot. His second call was to Jimmy Hudson, but all he could do was leave a message for him to call him at his home. The third call was to Vito Terratello in New York on his private line. Carter just left a short message and asked Vito to please call him back, because it was very important.

Fifteen minutes later, Carter's phone rang and when he picked it up and answered, "Carter Security," he heard, "Donald my boy, how are you, what do I owe the pleasure of your call to?"

"Hello Mr. Terratello."

"Please Donald, just call me Vito."

"Vito this is not a pleasure call, I'm sorry to say. Mick has been shot and is in serious condition. He's in the ICU at Saint John's Hospital in Santa Monica."

"How is Michael, is he stable?"

"First Vito, he is stable, but he had extensive

muscle damage to his shoulder. His surgery went well and he is awake. We had been working on a homicide investigation the past few days, but last night we were at the Lakers and Knicks game. Walking back to the parking lot someone started shooting at us."

"Are you okay Donald?"

"I was shot in the leg but they turned me loose this afternoon, after they stitched me up and kept me overnight. The bullet passed through my calf muscle and the injury is more of an inconvenience than anything, and I'll be fine with a little rest."

"Do you have any idea who did the shooting Donald?"

"I do Vito, but I have to prove it myself, since the police don't seem to buy into my theory of whom the guilty person is."

"What's his name Donald? I'll see what I can find out about him."

"I believe the person behind it is a man named Carson Burnhart."

"I'm familiar with Mr. Burnhart, Donald. He is a big land developer in your area."

"Why doesn't that surprise me that you know him, Vito?"

"Mr. Burnhart and I had some dealings a few years back, I didn't like him then and now with this happening to you and my nephew, I dislike him even more. What do you believe he's involved in?"

"Murder, plain and simple. He's been buying up property out here and in most cases the previous owners have died from strange coincidences."

"I'll see what kind of arrangements I can make and do some checking, Donald, and I'll be back in touch with you."

"Thank you Vito. It's a comfort knowing that you're in our corner."

"Always my friend. You just rest up, and I'll let you know what I come up with. When you see Michael, please let him know that I will be there to see you both soon. Goodbye Donald."

"Goodbye Vito, I look forward to seeing you again."

Placing the receiver back in the cradle, Carter thought about Vito Terratello getting involved, and was sure things would take a different kind of turn than he might like.

When Annie returned to the office she said, "Okay Mr. Carter, I have some medication, food and drinks for your recovery at home. So now it's time to follow the doctor's orders, and go home and rest."

"Annie I need you to stay here and answer the phone. I'll call a cab and have them drive me to my house. The calls I'm expecting are very important, so when they come in give them my home number and have them call me there. Vito Terratello and Jimmy Hudson are the only callers I want you to give my number to, understand?"

"Yes Mr. Carter. What if the police should call asking for you?"

"Take a message from the caller and *you* call me, I'll take it from there."

The phone rang and Annie picked up saying, "Carter Security. May I help you?"

The caller said, "Ah yeah sweetheart, this is Jimmy Hudson, I got a call from Carter that he wanted me to call him."

"Hold on Mr. Hudson." Handing the receiver to Carter, Annie said, "I'll go down and get the stuff from my car."

"Jimmy, glad you called back so quickly. Last night Mick and I were shot at as we were leaving the Lakers game. Mick is still in the hospital in pretty bad condition. I got shot in the leg, and spent the night there after they patched me up. Mick's injuries are much worse."

"Do you know who the shooter was?"

"I have no idea who actually did the shooting, but I'm pretty sure who hired him.

"Wouldn't happen to be the guy building those tall buildings in the West Valley would it?"

"One and the same Jimmy, so watch your ass. That guy is no fool and he seems to know everything that's going on around him and his projects. Mick had a talk with Jutty Wilson yesterday and then this shit happens."

"Yeah, he's a known snitch. A lot of the guys on the force know him and use him."

"Well after Mick talked with him, and I checked out Burnhart's place of business, a couple of goons started following me until I lost them. That night Mick and I go to the ballgame and afterwards someone starts taking shots at us as we walked to our car in the parking lot."

"How's Mick doing, Carter?"

"He's in the ICU at St. John's Hospital in Santa Monica. What's happening with you, have you been able to get anything at the construction site?"

"Well, I managed to get myself a couple hours work on that job site where that Houser guy took a sky dive. I did some clean-up around the job site and the foreman, a guy named Mark, paid me twenty bucks and told me to come back in a few days and he might have more work for me."

"That's good Jimmy. Like I said, watch your ass. If they figure out that you're working for me, your life will be in danger. Lie low for two or three days and then drop in to see that guy again. You know what I'm trying to find out, so work your magic. Look Jimmy, I'm about to take off for my home; I'm going to see Mick tomorrow at the hospital. I'll be working out of the house for a few days, so if you get anything give me a call there. Don't carry my number on you Jimmy. Either memorize it or call Annie here at the office, and she can give it to you when you need to talk with me."

"I can hear it in your voice Carter, you're in pain, so get the hell out of there, go home. I'll call you when I get something. Oh, give Mick a message for me. Tell him, "Duck next time Dago." Bye Carter."

Jimmy Hudson was correct in his assumption, Carter was in severe pain and he needed to take a couple of the pain pills Annie had just picked up for him at the pharmacy. As soon as she walked in the door he asked, "Annie would you please open up that bottle of pain meds and get me a cup of water. Then if you would, call me a cab, I'm going home."

8

Carter's cab ride home took him less than a half hour and another fifteen minutes to get his clothes off and get into bed. Once in the comfort of his own surroundings, Carter dozed off and didn't wake up for twelve straight hours. With his phone ringing continuously, he reached over and picked it up. Fumbling it a little, he answered, "Yeah who is it?"

In a gravelly voice Mick said, "Fine boss, I take a bullet for you and you go home to sleep."

Laughing a little, Carter asked, "Mick, how you feeling buddy?"

Still trying to clear his throat Mick said, "Like shit Donny Boy, like shit. How about you, how's your leg?"

"Right now there's no pain, but before I took a few of those horse pills the doctor prescribed for me, it hurt like hell.

"Hey Donny Boy, how did my uncle Vito find out about me getting shot?"

"I called him when I didn't know if you were going to make it or not. Did he call you?"

"He not only called, but he sent me the biggest pile of flowers you ever saw. He also told me he would be here in a few days along with my cousin Danny and a friend of his to keep an eye on me until I'm all healed. What the hell did you tell him anyway?"

"I just told him what the doctor told me. That the bullet went through your back and tore up some muscle before it came out of your chest and you had some extensive surgery. Listen, I'm going to fix myself something to eat and get right down there."

"I think you should wait a few more hours Donny Boy."

What the hell time is it anyway?" Answering his own question Carter looked at the clock and said, "Shit Mick it's two in the morning. I'll see you around seven or eight."

"Hey Donny Boy do me a favor, stop by my house and feed my fish because I don't know how long those guys can go without their food flakes. Oh, one more thing, what about my car boss, is it still at the Forum?"

"I had it picked up and brought to my office lot."

"Thanks boss, I think I'm going to try and get a few hours sleep before you get here. The doc told me if I heal fast and my body doesn't reject the medication I could be out of here in a week. Time for sleep now, I'll see you later boss."

"One last thing Mick, I'm going to call the client, Mrs. Houser, and let her know we're dropping the case and turning everything over to the LAPD."

"If it's all the same to you boss, I'm not dropping it. I want the bastard who shot us and the man who put him up to it."

"Tell you what Mick, we'll talk about it when I get there, get some sleep and I'll see you in a few hours. Is there anything you need?"

"Yeah, but I don't think Annie wants to spend the night here."

"Go to sleep Mick, and I'll see you in a little while."

9

Carter called the cab company at 6:30 AM and the cab was sitting in front of his house twenty minutes later. He was going to have the driver take him straight to the hospital to see Mick, but changed his mind and had him drive to the office where his own car was parked. It just seemed so much easier being able to drive himself around as long as he didn't take anymore of those damn pills.

Knowing that the freeway was always backed up at that time in the morning, Carter instructed the cab driver to take surface streets for the fifteen mile drive across the valley to his office. The drive should have taken only twenty or thirty minutes, but even the surface streets were backed up because of an accident on the freeway heading east. By the time Carter finally arrived at the hospital and parked in the lot down the street and hobbled slowly on his crutches, he was running an hour late from the time he told Mick he would be there.

Mick had been moved from the ICU to a private room and once Carter located the room it was around 8:15.

Walking into the room, Carter saw Mick sitting up in bed talking with a woman seated next to him with her back turned to the door.

Carter stopped in his tracks and said, "Oh, I'm sorry I'll come back a little later."

The woman turned to face Carter and said, "Please stay Carter."

Carter was surprised to see an old friend and lover, and said, "Well I'll be damned, Regina Volasko, how did you find out about Mick?"

"For the past week I've been up in San Francisco, Carter. I was taking care of some business for Mr. Terratello. He called me yesterday and asked me to meet with him in Los Angeles the day after tomorrow. When he told me about Mick, I let him know I was going to drop in and see how he was doing.

"And I suppose you were going to leave without even a phone call to me, right?"

"Carter, I didn't want to stir up old embers and give you the wrong idea. It's taken the past few years to get you out of my mind, so just let it be."

Four years had past since Regina Volasko and Don Carter pulled off a scam, and recovered some priceless jeweled eggs. In the process they found the killer of Reggie's sister and an old friend of Carter's and Mick's.

Although there had been much lying on the part of Miss Volasko in the beginning, Carter let his emotions and feelings cloud his good thinking and fell in love with the woman.

After three months of playing house and a promise of settling down, Reggie disappeared leaving only a note that said, "I can't stay or change my ways, I tried but it won't work. Please just let me go Carter and don't try to follow me, Reggie."

Seeing Reggie again quickly brought back certain feelings, but Carter kept them in check and asked, "How long you staying this time Reggie?"

Reggie smiled and said, "Only as long as Mr. Terratello wants me to Carter. I work exclusively for him these days."

Carter looked at Mick and said, "After she leaves, have the nurse come and get me, I'll be waiting down in the cafeteria."

Mick said, "Come on Donny Boy, let the past go, we can all still be friends, can't we?"

"I'll be downstairs Mick. Goodbye Miss Volasko."

Once Carter left the room, Reggie said, "I'm sorry Mick, I didn't want to rehash this crap all over again."

"You know you hurt him bad when you left, Reggie. It took him a long time to get over you, and I'm not sure he's got you completely out of his head even now. He's been doing a lot of heavy drinking, from what Annie told me."

"You think it was easy for me Mick? So many times I wanted to call him and tell him how much I still loved him and wanted to start all over again. I had to stay away and just keep my mind on work. Your uncle promised me a job working for him acquiring property in different parts of the country. I asked only one thing from him, and that was not to reveal where I was or that I was working for him to Carter."

"Well Reggie, you know how his head works, he'll have you on his mind and he ain't going to be worth shit to anybody until you're long gone."

"Well Mick, that's going to be a while, because your uncle has plans for me to stick around and check out some people he may be doing business with in the Napa Valley."

Leaning over and kissing Mick on the cheek, Reggie said, "Don't worry about calling the nurse. Carter and I are going to sit and talk this out over some coffee downstairs. Then I'll send him back up to see you."

"Are you sure you know what you're doing Reggie?"

"No, but I'm going to do it anyway. I'll probably see you sometime later today."

"Bye Reggie, go easy on him."

Walking into the cafeteria, Reggie spotted Carter sitting at a table along the back wall. When Carter saw her he just shook his head slowly side to side and took a deep breath.

Reggie walked over to the table and sat down saying, "We need to clear the air Carter."

"You and I have nothing to clear the air about Reggie. That time came and went four years ago."

"Obviously there's something still going on in that head of yours, if we can't even be in the same room visiting an injured friend."

Carter took a sip of his coffee, a slow easy breath and said, "You walked out Reggie, you ran away only leaving a goddamn note. You couldn't tell me in person that it was over between us, how am I supposed to feel?"

"I couldn't do it in person Carter, I knew if I tried, I would never leave, can't you understand that?"

"No I can't. I thought we had more than just a short relationship going for us, but obviously you didn't."

"You have no idea, Carter, how hard it was on me then, or even how hard it is now sitting here talking with you, it still deeply hurts me just seeing you, please try to understand."

"Reggie please, just go away and leave me be. It's been nice seeing you, have a good life, goodbye."

After saying what he had to say, Carter got up from the table and left the cafeteria and headed for Mick's room. Carter was hurting real bad inside, but he refused to show any more emotions.

Walking into Mick's room, Carter once again had to stop in his tracks when he saw the curtain pulled around the bed. He heard the doctor talking with Mick about removing the catheter in his penis.

Sitting down in a chair by the door, Carter waited for the doctor to finish his business and open the curtain before he said, "Hey Mick, how yah doing?"

Mick smiled when he saw Carter, then said, I feel like someone just pulled a straw out of my dick, how you feeling?"

"I'm feeling much better now that I see you still have your sense of humor."

"How did it go with Reggie down in the cafeteria Donny Boy?"

"Everything is fine Mick, all settled."

From behind him, Carter heard Reggie say, "You only think its settled Carter."

Carter said, "Shit, are you still here?"

"Yes I'm still here, and I'm going to be here, until the bastard who's behind both you guys getting shot is either in jail or dead."

Mick smiled, but Carter said, "We don't need your help Reggie, like I asked you before, just go away."

"Mr. Terratello is calling the shots on this one Carter. I'll leave when he tells me to, not before."

Carter looked at Mick who had a big smile on his face and asked, "Did you know about this Mick?"

After a small laugh, Mick said, "I didn't before, but now I think it's a great idea."

Not looking too happy, Carter asked, "Okay, when is Vito supposed to be here?"

Reggie spoke up, "He moved up his plans one day, his plane gets in at LAX around 2 pm tomorrow and I'll be there to pick him up."

Carter said, "You mean we'll be there to pick him up?"

Now Reggie smiled and said, "Yes sir, Mr. Carter sir."

Taking a deep breath, Carter said, "Come on Reggie; let's go get something to eat. I guess we have more talking to do, I'll be damned if I'm going to put up with you all day on an empty stomach."

Looking at Mick, Carter said, "We'll talk later Mick, maybe by then you'll be able to wipe that smile off your face."

"I was just thinking about what a cute couple you two make Donny Boy."

"Keep it up Mick, and I may come back and pinch off that tube that's feeding you those drugs you're getting, and shove that other tube back in your pecker again."

Mick laughed and asked, "Hey Donny Boy, have you heard anything from Jimbo?"

"Yeah, he's hanging around the construction site trying to get the foreman to give him some work cleaning up the area."

"Tell him to watch his ass Carter."

"Already did Mick, already did. See you later."

Walking out of the hospital on his crutches, Carter asked, "Where would you like to go for lunch Reggie?"

"Some place quiet Carter, nothing fancy though."

"Do you have a rental car here or did you just take a cab from the airport?"

"I have a rental car, but I can leave it here and pick it up later."

"Where will you be staying while you're here?"

"The Beverly Hilton. Vito already made the reservations for the whole crew from New York."

"I'll meet you there in an hour and maybe we can find a nice quiet table in the coffee shop and see if we can work out a truce."

Reggie laughed and said, "Why an hour Carter?"

"Tell you the truth Reggie, I didn't bring any pain pills with me and my leg is throbbing to beat the band. I can make it home and back to the Hilton in an hour."

"Okay Carter, just ask for me at the desk and I'll meet you in the coffee shop."

Watching Carter slowly making his way to the parking lot, Reggie ran after him and said, "Hold it Carter, there's no sense in you driving all the way home and then back to the Hilton. I have another idea."

Carter turned slowly and said, "What's on your mind Reggie?"

"How about I follow you back to your house and pick up some lunch on the way. You know, soup and sandwiches or something like that?"

"You know what Reggie. I think that's a great idea. I still live in the same house in the West Valley, how about I meet you there?"

Taking out his wallet, Carter handed Reggie a couple of twenties and said, "Lunch is on me."

Carter was home about half an hour sitting in the living room when he heard a car pull up in his driveway. Using one of his crutches, he hobbled to the front door and opened it for Reggie when he saw her coming up the walk carrying two bags.

Making her way into the kitchen, Reggie asked, "What do you have around here to drink Carter?"

"Well there's beer in the fridge, some vodka and rum in the cabinet in the corner, and I think there's some kind of wine in the china cabinet in the living room."

As they ate their sandwiches and soup, Carter explained about Bob Stearns and Teddy Houser and a few of the suspicions he had about Carson Burnhart. Reggie had mixed a couple of drinks and as she sipped on hers, she noticed how Carter drank his down quite quickly and was pouring another for himself. By the time Reggie had finished her first drink Carter had finished three, and was asking her if she wanted a refill. Reggie said, "I don't know what kind of pain pills you took Carter, but I would be careful mixing too much booze with the pills."

That was all it took to set Carter off. After pouring a healthy amount of Vodka in his glass and topping it off with a dash of orange juice, Carter said, "You know Reggie, that was one of your problems. You always thought you knew what was best for us, and I never had a say without an argument from you."

"You know what Carter; this was a mistake coming here. I thought we could talk out some of our problems with each other, but I can see that's not going to happen."

Watching as Carter took a long swig from his glass, Reggie said, "And that's one of *your* biggest problems Carter, you can't put the cork back in the bottle once you start and then you make a fool out of your self."

Carter stood up, finished his drink and tossed the glass in the sink, hearing it shatter with glass shards flying upward. Making an attempt to turn and walk away from the table, Carter's eyes seemed to haze over as he passed out and fell to the floor."

When Carter awoke, he realized he was lying on his couch in the living room. Trying to focus his eyes in the totally dark room, his blurred vision could only make out a little bit of a street light through the window from down the street. Lying there trying to recall the last thing before he passed out, Carter mumbled, "You horses ass, what the fuck did you do you fool."

Out of the dark, Carter heard, "You made an ass out of yourself, some things never change Carter."

The pole lamp across the room suddenly came on and Carter covered his eyes until they got used to the light. Looking at Reggie sitting in a recliner with a blanket pulled up to her neck, Carter said, "I'm surprised you're still here Reggie."

Pulling the blanket off, Reggie stood and said, "I wanted to make sure you didn't die you damn fool. Now that I know you're okay I can leave."

"How long have I been out Reggie?"

Looking at her watch, Reggie said, "About six hours. You had a nice long sleep. I'll see you tomorrow after Vito gets in."

"Don't go Reggie, please stay. I'm sorry about how I acted. I don't know what came over me."

"I do. How many of those pills did you take?"

"I'm supposed to take one every eight hours, but I was in so much pain I took two I think, maybe three."

"Real smart Carter, and then you poured in the booze, you damn fool."

"I think I could use some coffee Reggie, how about you?"

"Carter, I don't know if you and I are ever going to work out the problems between us, but I do know you have some problems you need to work out on your own with your drinking. I realize that taking the drugs for the pain was necessary, but watching you pour that alcohol down your throat like it was water, I can't deal with that."

"Is that a no on the coffee?"

Walking for the door, Reggie said, "That's it, make a joke out of it Carter, it's what you do best."

"And you walking out is what you do best Reggie. When you left me it took me months just to stop looking for you each morning and realizing that you weren't coming home. It took me over a year before I had one day I didn't think of you at least once and wonder how you were. The big strong man who never let anything get to him cried like a baby many nights just wishing we could try again. And now you're ready to walk out again. Go Reggie; just go please, I'll be fine."

Standing with her hand on the door knob staring at Carter, Reggie walked slowly towards the kitchen and asked, "Coffee black Carter, or do you want some shit in it?"

Sitting at the kitchen table talking out some of the past problems they had with each other, the hours went by and two pots of coffee were consumed. As the reflection of the rising sun shone through the window in the living room,

Reggie said, "Christ Carter, look at the time. I need to get back to the hotel to shower and change clothes."

"You could shower here you know?"

"That's not going to happen. Vito's plane is due to land in a few hours and I would like to be presentable when I meet him."

"I'd like to go with you Reggie?"

Appearing as she was thinking it over, Reggie said, "Okay, put together what you intend to wear and let's get going. You can shower and change at the hotel."

As Carter smiled slightly, Reggie said, "I can tell where your thinking is going Carter, forget it. Don't read anything more into this offer than it just being a time saver for both of us. And get this straight, our talking is not over, we have a lot more to settle before we work together. This whole arrangement was Vito's idea not mine, so let's be professional and do what needs to be done."

Carter stood and said, "Yes ma'am."

Driving away from the house Reggie and Carter were so involved in their exchange of what one expected from the other, that they never noticed an old black Mercedes pull out of a side street and take up a position following them.

10

After they both showered separately at the hotel, and dressed, Reggie called the airport and found out that Vito's flight would be arriving earlier than expected. She then called the limo service and gave them the time they wanted to be picked up at the hotel for the ride to the airport. Because of a nice tail wind, Vito's flight would arrive around 10:10am instead of the planned 10:30. It was only ten minutes later when the phone rang and Reggie was informed that the limo had arrived. Carter grabbed his crutches and they headed for the door.

With a little help from a baggage handler at the airport, who found Carter a wheelchair, Reggie rolled him along at a fast pace until they found the proper gate. They sat in silence for awhile and just watched the planes landing and taxiing to different gates. When the plane finally pulled into the area in front of them, she stood near the door waiting for the first class passengers to deplane.

Vito was the fourth person off the plane followed by two well dressed men. Reggie greeted Vito with a hug and when Carter stood and put out his hand to shake hands, Vito said, "We're closer than that Donald," followed by a manly hug.

Vito pointed to his two companions and said, "Donald, I would like you to meet my son Daniel and my legal advisor Paul Conti."

Vito asked, "How's Michael doing, Donald?"

"You know him Vito. He's got the constitution of a bull. We had to tie him into the bed to keep him from coming with us to meet you here."

Vito laughed and said, "Just like his mother, my sister-in-law, she has always been a tough one to keep down. My brother,

God rest his soul, would have been very proud of the man Michael has become."

Carter asked, "How long are you staying Vito?"

Vito looked at Reggie and asked, "All is set with the reservation at the Beverly Hills Hotel Miss Volasko?"

"Yes sir. I reserved a bungalow for you, a poolside suite for Danny and Paul, and an inside room for myself."

Vito asked, "I guess we'll be here for a week or two, we'll see. How far is the hospital from the hotel Donald?"

"Actually Vito, we're only a couple miles from the hospital now, we almost have to drive right past it to get to Beverly Hills."

"Fine Donald, lets make a quick stop there on the way, I would like to see Michael before going to the hotel."

"Vito, may I suggest that you and I go to the hospital in the limo and possibly Miss Volasko could take a cab to the hotel and get Danny and Paul settled in?"

"You know Donald, I think that is a good idea. Looking at Reggie, Vito said, "We'll see you at the hotel Miss Volasko, Donald and I have some catching up to do."

A small protest came from Reggie, but Vito held up his hand and said, "All will be fine Miss Volasko, trust me."

As Reggie looked at Carter she saw the smile on his face and knew there was nothing she could do to change the plan he orchestrated.

Taking only a leather brief case with him and giving Reggie the claim checks for the baggage, Vito asked, "Is there anything else we need to know Miss Volasko?"

"For now there is nothing else, Mr. Terratello. I can fill you in later on my trip to San Francisco. Give Michael my best and tell him I will come to visit him tomorrow possibly."

Vito said, "Fine, I will see you later at the hotel," then he and Carter headed for the limo."

On the way to the hospital Carter filled Vito in on everything that had been going on with his investigation. When he was finished Vito asked, "And what are your plans now Donald?"

"Vito, I'm sorry to say, this investigation has been one problem after another. Since this latest turn of events with Mick and me getting shot, I'm prepared to turn everything over to the LAPD and just get the hell out of it."

"What about your clients, how do they feel about you giving up on your investigation?"

"I will be contacting them later today and letting them know of my decision."

"And what does Michael think about that?"

"You know how head-strong he is Vito. Mick wants to go on until Burnhart is either in jail or the morgue."

"And you're sure Carson Burnhart is behind it?"

"I know he is, but I don't want to see anyone else risking their life because of my desire to get the bastard."

Vito smiled slightly and asked, "So Donald, it's not that you personally want to give up, it is more that you are worried about your friends risking their lives. Is that correct?"

"That is correct, I almost cost Mick his life and I don't want that to happen again."

"Donald, maybe you just need to go about it in a different way, a set-up maybe, and then elimination."

"Vito, you know I respect you but I can't do anything like you're proposing. Killing is out of the question unless it's in self defense."

Smiling again slightly, Vito said, "There are other ways to eliminate a problem without physical violence, although that is sometimes the last option. Making a rich man into a poor man is another. Destroying a man's reputation is also another way of elimination. Please Donald, give me some time to work on your problem before you throw in the towel so to speak. For now let's concentrate on getting you and Michael back on your feet and I'll convince my headstrong nephew to hold back his anger until the proper time."

"Thank you. Vito, there is one other matter that we must discuss: Miss Volasko."

"Ah Miss Volasko, Donald do you still carry strong feelings for her or do you resent her for leaving you when she did?"

"Vito, some women can get under your skin and into your heart and no matter what they do to you, you just can't shake yourself free. Miss Volasko in my eyes is one of those women."

"Are you still in love with her Donald?"

"To be honest, my heart says one thing and my brain another, I don't know. I loved being around her, her personality, her sense of humor, waking up next to her in the morning. There is so much I loved about her, but spending the rest of our lives together? I don't know, we needed more time together to answer that question."

Reaching over to Carter and putting his hand on his arm Vito said, "Donald, I'm sorry,

sorry for deceiving you and not informing you about Miss Volasko coming to work for me in New York. The one and only condition she put on her return to my employ was that her whereabouts be kept confidential. While working for me these past few years she used the alias Christina Hamilton and her real identity was kept secret from all of my other employees. Miss Volasko has a complete set of identification that has been tested and run through the FBI and came up clean."

Carter thought for a few seconds and said, "I can see where that might come in very handy. Will you be staying this time for a long visit?"

"Actually Donald, I have some business I have to attend to in San Francisco and Las Vegas, but while I'm out here on the west coast, I'll make Beverly Hills my home base and stay close to your situation."

As the limo pulled into the hospital parking lot Carter told the driver, "Please drop us off at the front door, driver. We should be back out in less than an hour."

Vito asked, "Will you need a wheelchair Donald?"

Smiling Carter said, "As long as you don't walk too fast I can use the exercise."

Getting out of the car Vito said, "All will be fine Donald, trust me."

11

Vito spent a good part of an hour visiting with his nephew before he finally said, "Michael I will see you in a few days; hopefully by then we will know when you will be discharged. When that time comes I would like you to join me as my guest at the hotel where you will have a private nurse to see to your needs." Looking at Carter, Vito said, "If you're ready Donald, it's time for this old man to check out the comforts of the hotel bungalow?"

On the ride to the hotel Vito said, "Tell me what you know about Carson Burnhart and the people in high places you think he has in his pocket."

For the next thirty minutes, Carter told Vito everything he knew and some of what he suspected of Burnhart's connections to government officials and the police.

Arriving at the hotel the valet parking attendant came over to the limo and Vito waved him away saying, "Give us a few minutes please."

Putting his hand on Carter's shoulder Vito said, "Donald, I will be taking a trip to San Francisco tomorrow accompanied by my son Danny and Miss Volasko. Paul will remain and will assist you in any way you need him. If you do not need his help he will be spending his time keeping Michael company and providing security."

"Thank you Vito."

"One other thing, Donald, that I must ask you about. Over the years I feel that we have become very close and I think of you as part of my family. It has come to my attention that your dependence on alcohol has become a problem. I need to know from you whether or not you have this problem fully under control. A yes or a no will do."

"Yes Vito."

"Fine my boy, we will not speak of this again."

"Vito, I appreciate the offer of Paul's services, but for myself, I intend to just rest up and enjoy the time away from the office. I think Michael would enjoy Paul's company though."

As Vito and Carter exited the limo, Vito called the driver over and handed him a cash tip and asked, "Your name please?"

"My name is Rico sir, and thank you," the driver answered.

Vito shook the man's hand and said, "I will be contacting your employer and I will let him know what a fine service you provided. I will also request you the next time I am in need of a limo service."

With a smile, the driver said, "Thank you sir."

Carter and Vito shook hands and Vito said, "Would you like to come in Donald, or would you rather wait here for Miss Volasko. She will be driving you home?"

"I think I would rather wait here and avoid the extra walking."

After the two men embraced, Vito walked through the front doors of the hotel as Carter watched. Five minutes passed and Carter was joined by Reggie who walked up to him and said, "The valet is getting my car; it will be here in a minute. We need to get a few things straight between us Carter, where it concerns Mr. Terratello."

The valet drove the car up and got out and opened both front doors.

Once they drove off, Reggie tried several times to engage Carter in a conversation but he wasn't buying into it. Finally she yelled out, "Goddamnit Carter, enough of this shit. What was all of that about with you and him?"

Pulling off the Ventura Freeway at Topanga Canyon Blvd., Reggie found the first place she could to park. Slamming the shift lever in park, she said, "Okay, let's get all the shit out now."

Carter was steaming because he knew he didn't have the upper hand so he carefully chose his words, "Look Reggie, I needed some time alone with Vito, just the two of us. There were things that had to be taken care of before the business at hand. You and Vito will have plenty of time for discussions during your trip together to San Francisco."

"Bullshit Carter, I know there's more going on in that mind of yours. Now what is it! We don't move until you start talking."

"You were out of my life Reggie, and I was moving on. I didn't hate you, I just didn't think of you anymore. And now here you are, and I'm asked by a man I know and respect to put all my feeling aside and work with you again."

"It will be strictly business Carter, nothing more."

"I don't know if I can do that Reggie. I think the best thing would be for me to cut my losses and return the retainer to my client and back away from everything. This way Mick and I can heal with no pressure and Vito, you, Danny and Paul can go on with your work, and in time it will be just water under the bridge."

"Oh bullshit Carter, who the hell do you think you're talking to? I know you and I know Mick. I know you're not going to let this thing go away. So Mr. Donald Carter, forget all that crap and give Vito a chance to figure out a way to help. Put your pride aside."

Putting the car in drive and pulling away, Reggie headed for Carter's house. As she turned left off Topanga Canyon Blvd., Reggie notice a pair of headlights making the same turn and got a little suspicious so she pulled over to the side of the road and turned off the ignition.

Carter asked, "What the hell are you doing Reggie?"

"I think we're being followed, there's a dark colored sedan back there that was behind us ever since I first pulled off the freeway, and now he's pulled over behind us back a few hundred yards."

"Do you have a gun with you Reggie?"

"Hell no!" she said.

"Well neither do I. Try driving off slowly and we'll see what he does."

"I think he suspects something Carter, he just made a U-turn and took off."

"Okay then, head for my house."

Pulling into the driveway, Reggie put the shift lever in park and said, "See you in a few days. Keep your eyes open for any intruders tonight."

Carter just stood on his porch and watched her drive away.

12

The few days had turned into a full week. During that time, Carter had time to heal both physically and mentally. At the beginning of the week Carter met with Emily Houser before she returned to Texas. With her brother Bob home from the hospital and mending quickly, Mrs. Houser decided it was time for her to return home. She asked Carter to please continue with the investigation after he told her he wanted to back off and turn everything over to the LAPD. She was very persuasive as she handed him a second check for five thousand dollars and simply said, "Please Mr. Carter."

To Carter's surprise, when he visited Bob Stearns at his home, Bob had reconstructed a copy from memory of the note his brother-in-law had left with the found money.

After reading the copy of the note, Carter asked, "How accurate do you feel this is Bob?"

"I think it's pretty damn close Mr. Carter, if not word for word."

Stopping at his office, Carter dropped off the note and checked with Annie telling her he was going to visit Mick at the hospital. While Carter was looking through some of his incoming mail, Annie said, "I spoke with Mickey this morning. He told me the doctor would be signing him out tomorrow."

"Mickey?" Carter said smiling.

"Yes Mickey, when he's well enough we're going out on a date."

"I think that's great Annie."

"Mr. Carter, you don't think Mickey is too old for me, do you?"

"Not at all Annie, I think you and *Mickey* could be a perfect fit."

With the use of an Ace bandage wrap, Carter was getting around without his crutches and had also put aside the medication for the pain. And since he quit drinking, his sense of humor that had been long gone was returning.

Leaving the office, Carter called out to Annie, "Sweetheart, I'll give Mickey a big wet kiss for you and tell him you'll be there later to stroke his weary brow."

"Thank you, but you can forget the kiss. I'll take care of that when I see him tonight."

Heading for the freeway, Carter thought he noticed a dirty old black Mercedes following him, but when he pulled over for a few minutes to watch in his mirrors, he decided he was just being paranoid. Little did he know he was correct in his suspicion, it's just that the person following him had become a little more cautious.

Walking into Mick's room, Carter found his bed empty, but a few seconds later Mick rolled in sitting in a wheelchair and said, "Hey Donny Boy, they're cutting me loose from this place tomorrow, how about picking me up around noon?"

"That's great news. Sure I'll pick you up."

"Would you do me one other favor and stop by my house and feed my fish?"

"Sure, who do I feed them too?"

"Oh you're mean, boss. I'd be surprised if my neighbor's cat isn't stalking my front door waiting to charge in as soon as you open the place up."

"Okay, now for the serious stuff Mick. Mrs. Houser went back home to Texas, and though I've been seriously considering calling this whole investigation off, I knew how you felt about that. So, as soon as you're ready to resume, we're going to nail the bastard."

"Have you talked with Jimbo, boss?"

"No, have you?"

"Yeah, I talked to him last night. With everything that's been happening he's worried that your office phone might be bugged so he called me. He left a message on your office answer machine and gave the name Larry Parks, and was going to leave his home number, but changed his mind."

"So what's he been up to?"

"He's been working around the construction site and keeping his ears open. Without pushing it too much, he has heard stories about the accident of Teddy Houser. I told him if he's worried about calling you at the office he could call me at home and I would get the messages to you."

"There's something else that's going on. I'm pretty sure I'm being followed and the guy is becoming a little harder to spot. Once you're out of here we're going to have to team up and expose the snoop and find out whom he's working for."

"Do you think it's Burnhart's guy?"

"I'm pretty sure he is. Oh, I got something else for you. Annie wanted me to let her sweet Mickey know that she would be here to see you tonight. And if she asks, no I didn't give you a big wet one for her."

"She's a sweet kid boss. You know, I really enjoy her company. She's been here every night since I arrived at this place."

"Hey Mick, you know I'm not the best person to give advice on matters of the heart, but I hope you know what you're doing. She is a sweet kid, and you are a great guy, just go slow okay?"

"Slow and easy, you got my word."

"Okay Mick, I'll see you at noon tomorrow unless things change. I'm going to head back to the office and make a few phone calls and sign a few checks so Annie can pay some bills. Try not to offend the nurses by chasing them down the hall with your wheelchair."

Leaving the hospital, Carter walked to the parking lot keeping his eyes open for the black Mercedes, but the car was nowhere in sight.

Back at the office, Carter asked Annie to make a phone call to Mrs. Houser in Texas and to please let him know when she was on the phone. After fifteen minutes of trying to phone the woman, Annie came into Carter's office and said, "Mr. Carter, something strange is going on. When I tried calling the number Emily Houser gave us for our files, all I get is a message that the line is no longer in service."

"Did you try the phone company?"

"Yes sir and they told me that there is no other number for the address and that the old number had been disconnected at the homeowner's request."

"Annie, try calling Bob Stearns at home and see if he knows what's going on with his sister's phone."

About twenty minutes passed and Annie called to Carter, "Mr. Carter, I have Bob Stearns on the line and he wishes to speak with you."

Picking up the receiver, he said, "Hello Bob, it's Donald Carter, how you feeling?"

"Actually I'm feeling pretty good Mr. Carter, at least I was until your secretary called and told me she couldn't get hold of my sister. I tried also but no dice. I called the operator and she confirmed that my sister cancelled her phone service. I tried calling our mother also but there was no answer. Do you have any suggestions Mr. Carter?"

"I'm going to have Annie send a Western Union telegram and ask her to call us both as soon as she gets it. If you hear from her before I do, please call me Bob and let me or Annie know what's going on."

Once off the phone, Carter called Annie into his office and said, "Annie, I need you to send a telegram to Emily Houser. Let her know that we are unable to contact her by phone because her phone has been disconnected. Tell her to call here and also contact her brother."

"Do you want that sent out and dated today Mr. Carter?"

"Is there any reason why it shouldn't be dated today Annie?"

"Well the Western Union office is near my apartment building and I could send it first thing in the morning on my way into work."

"What's today's date Annie?"

"Friday, March sixth."

"You know Annie its' been over a week since the shooting and four days since Emily Houser left for Texas. Yeah date and send it today, you can close up the office when I leave and stop by Western Union on your way home. Oh, and give Mickey a kiss for me when you see him tonight."

At noon the next day, Carter arrived at the hospital and took the elevator up to Mick's floor. Walking into the room Carter found Mick dressed and sitting on his bed talking on the phone. When Carter motioned as to who it was, Mick wrote on a notepad "Croft". It was only a few more minutes and Mick was off and said to Carter, "Croft would like me to come in as soon as possible and talk about the shooting. He wants me to give him a complete detailed statement of what had happened."

"I thought you gave him a statement already?"

"I did, but he said there were some discrepancies that he would like to discuss."

"Yeah I bet. The man is such an ass."

"Donny Boy, Jimbo called me late last night. He said to look for him at your house Sunday morning. I told him your house might be under surveillance by someone so he needs to keep his eyes open."

"I'll watch for him. Maybe he'll disguise himself as the milkman. So you ready to go Mick? I parked out front so they can wheel your ass straight to the car."

"Yeah, I just need to let the orderly know I'm ready."

"I'll go get him, which guy is it?"

"He's the tall Hispanic guy named Castro, just ask one of the nurses and they'll tell him."

The ride to Mick's apartment took less than a half hour and as they rode and talked, they both casually looked around to see if they were being followed, but the black Mercedes was nowhere in sight. Mick told Carter that he had given Annie a key to his apartment so she could pick up a few things for the house.

Carter said, "Oh shit, I forgot to go and feed your damn fish last night."

Mick laughed and said, "Its okay boss, Annie told me she fed them. Hey, she told me about not being able to contact the old lady, and that she had to send a telegram. So what do you think that's all about?"

"Got me, I hope she contacts me once she gets the telegram, then we'll see."

When Carter pulled up in front of Mick's apartment building they were greeted by Annie who had been waiting for them. Carter said, "Annie can take it from here."

13

Sunday morning a little after sun up, Carter awoke hearing his dog barking down stairs in the kitchen. When he walked down the stairs with his gun in his hand, he slowly made his way to the kitchen and saw Jimmy Hudson standing at the back patio doors smoking a cigarette.

Sliding the door open, Carter said, "A little later would have been better Jimmy. Come on in and I'll make some coffee."

Petting Carter's dog, Jimmy said, "They hired me as a casual laborer at the construction site, feels good to be employed again. So anyway, the stories going around between the workers is that Teddy Houser was a fink, you know, unstable. I guess he was doing a lot of private shit for the old man but he was drinking and doing drugs and couldn't stop talking. Some of the stuff he was talking about to try and come off like a big shot was filtering back to Burnhart and the old man didn't like what he was hearing. It seems that Teddy was doing a little too much drinking and snorting of the white shit up his nose. The talk around was that he needed to be silenced."

Jimmy Hudson had Carter's full attention. "Jimmy, do you think any of these people would come forward as witnesses?"

"Not a chance boss, but I got another lead for you. The stories going around were that Teddy Houser was screwing one of the nurses who was taking care of some old timer named Fishman. It seems that Fishman owned a big farm in the west valley and he died kind of unexpectedly. A short time later the widow sold the property to the Burnhart Corporation and moved away to some nursing home in the Napa valley, about four hundred miles north of Los Angeles."

"Look Jimmy, don't stretch yourself out there too much. They might start to suspect you as a plant, watch your ass, these people are dangerous."

"Yeah I know boss, I just wish there was another black man working at that site. I look around at all those white faces and I feel like a black golf ball in a bag full of white balls."

Pouring coffee into a couple of mugs, Carter said, "Black or white, just watch out for your balls and your ass."

A half hour went by and Jimmy said, "Okay boss I'm out of here. If I need to get in touch with you I'll leave a message with Annie. If you need me just let Mick know, he'll know how to get word to me. You watch your ass too Carter."

Carter was heading back up stairs to get dressed when the phone rang. On the fourth ring he picked it up and said, "Hello."

The caller said, "Carter, it's Reggie."

"Reggie, and what did I do to deserve this early morning call?"

"I got back to LA late last night Carter. Vito and Danny will be back in a few more days. Maybe we can meet for breakfast at the hotel and I can fill you in on a few new bits of information that we gathered up north."

"Okay, what time Reggie?"

"How about ten, I can reserve a table here for us in the coffee shop?"

"Sounds good, I'll see you at ten."

When Carter walked into the coffee shop in the hotel, Reggie's smile from across the room seemed to light up the place. Not giving in to the urge to return the smile, Carter walked to the table and sat down. Reggie waved the waitress over and asked for a cup of coffee for her guest.

"Good morning Carter, how's your leg feeling?"

"Feeling pretty good, so what's the new news?"

"Right to it huh Carter? Okay, I thought we could be a little cordial with each other but I guess I was asking too much."

Carter shook his head a little and said, "Sorry Reggie, I'm just trying to work out of a confused state."

"What are you confused about Carter?"

"Us damn-it, I don't know where we really stand."

Pausing a few seconds, Carter said, "Okay, let's not go there again. I had a visit first thing this morning from an old friend who's working the case for me. Mick and I have known him for many years and he and I worked together on the force until we both split to check out other ways of making a living. His name is Jimmy Hudson. He's been working undercover at one of Burnhart's construction sites. He gave me a rundown this morning on some of the shit he's come up with and it looks like this Burnhart character is in it up to his eyeballs. I'm worried about Jimmy, he's a pro but he's surrounded by some people who would just cut his throat and not think anything of it."

"Maybe it would be a good idea to pull him out and let Vito tell you what he has in mind?"

"For now Reggie, Jimmy Hudson stays in place. The information he's gathering is extremely valuable and I'll only pull him out if it looks like his life is in danger, or he wants out. So what's going on up north that you wanted to talk to me about?"

"Well Carter, Vito has been scouting the possible purchase of a vineyard in the Napa Valley. He already owns a small vineyard but is looking to expand and start producing some quality wines to introduce to the upper echelon of the wine drinkers worldwide."

"So why should that interest me Reggie?"

"It seems that Burnhart is involved in the wine trade also, and Vito is trying to find out just how involved."

14

At 9am Monday morning while he drove to the office, Carter hoped there was some news from Emily Houser, because It had been three days since the telegram had been sent. When he arrived, Annie let him know that they had an answer. The telegram from Emily Houser read, *"Mr. Carter, sorry about the phone. Stop. End the investigation at once. Stop. Do not worry about returning retainer. Stop. Our business together is finalized. Stop. Thank you. Stop. Emily Houser. End."*

The telegram was notarized and dated March 9th by a notary named Martin W.

Larson and along with it was a copy of their original contract.

After reading the telegram, Carter told Annie, "Well that's that sweetheart. At least we made some money for the pain we had to suffer."

"Are you really going to give up Mr. Carter?"

"Annie we don't have a client any longer, so as far as I'm concerned the case is closed. What I would like to do is type up a report and hand it over to the LAPD."

That afternoon when Carter paid Mick a visit and told him about the news and his decision to end the investigation, Mick said, "Bullshit buddy, I ain't giving up on getting that bastard. You can't just walk away from it Donny Boy, it would eat at you like a shark on raw meat. Before you do anything else talk to Uncle Vito and see what he says. When he called me last night he told me he has an idea on how to chop Burnhart off at the knees and send him crawling into poverty. You don't want to miss that do you?"

"When's he due back Mick?"

"Day after tomorrow on the thirteenth, he's flying into Burbank Airport. Let's see what he's got to say."

Carter said, "Okay Mick, how you feeling anyway?"

"I'm feeling fine, a little tight in my chest but the doc says if everything looks okay I'll be up and running in a couple more days."

Carter asked, where's Paul, I thought he was going to act as your gun slinger bodyguard?"

"He's working on becoming an attorney Donny Boy, no gun needed."

"Well just the same. The mobster cuts up his victims with a knife or shoots them with a gun. The lawyer can make or destroy a person with words."

"Donny Boy, Uncle Vito is very careful about the people he hires or associates with, and for Paul to be going to law school, you know he has to be a person with a clean record."

"I don't know Mick. Without a client, I have to watch how the expenses go. I still have a nice chunk of the money from Mrs. Houser, but that won't last forever."

"What about the brother boss, have you talked with him yet?"

"No, but I'll stop by and see Bob after I leave here. He's not the one with the money though. His sister was the one financing the whole investigation. Maybe with any luck he got to talk with her and she changed her mind."

"Well call me and let me know what's happening. What about the guy following you, have you spotted him again?"

"No, he seems to have disappeared. Listen Mick, you take care of yourself and I'll see you in a couple of days, rest alright."

Bob Stearns lived in a modest two bedroom home just off of Sepulveda Blvd in Van Nuys. The house next door to his was for sale and vacant, and the neighbors on the other side almost never spoke with him. Carter pulled up in the driveway and could see the front of the old Ford through the two partially opened garage doors directly in front of him. Getting out of his car, Carter walked to the front porch steps and then up to the front door. Looking for a doorbell he only saw an old fashioned door knocker. Carter knocked several times and waited. After a minute he knocked again with the same results.

First looking through a small window in the door and then through the front windows of the living room, Carter then tapped on the window looking for some movement from inside. With no response Carter tried the front door but found it locked. Walking back down the steps Carter walked down the driveway towards the rear of the house looking for a back door. As he rounded the corner of the house he noticed the back screen door wide open and the glass in the back door broken and the door ajar. Pushing the door open with his foot, Carter called out, "Bob, it's Carter. Hello, Bob."

Stepping into the kitchen, Carter could smell natural gas from the stove but when he checked everything was turned off. Continuing to call out for Bob, he walked to the base of the stairs leading to the second floor. Moving slowly up the stairs, Carter said, "Bob if you're here please say something."

After checking both bedrooms and the bathroom, Carter went back down to the first floor and back into the kitchen where the gas smell was strongest. Looking around the kitchen Carter saw a door he believed went to the pantry, but when he opened it he saw that it was to a stairway to the basement. The gas smell had gotten extremely stronger. Looking for a light switch, he decided that would not be a good idea because it could trigger the gas. Finding a flashlight in one of the kitchen drawers, he next soaked a towel from the counter by the sink with water so he could hold it over his nose like a filter.

As Carter slowly descended the basement steps he started to get a little light headed, and as he reached the bottom step, he felt the gas was way too much to handle. Shinning the flashlight briefly around he thought his mind was playing tricks seeing a body hanging from a rafter with a rope around its neck. Starting to lose visual focus he decided to turn around and return up the stairs and get out of the house as quickly as possible. Dropping the flashlight, Carter crawled step by step reaching the floor of the kitchen. Closing the basement door behind him he made his way to the sink and splashed cold water on his face.

Once outside he walked around to the other side of the house looking for the gas meter and shut-off valve. Trying to turn the valve off he realized he would need a wrench or a pair of pliers to turn the frozen valve.

Trying to move a little faster, Carter made his way into the garage and headed for the work bench in the rear corner. Before he could find either tool, there was a huge explosion that knocked him to the floor and shattered the garage door windows, followed by a burst of heat off the flames that engulfed the house. Crawling along the floor next to the old Ford, Carter reached one of the garage doors pushing it back open, stood and carefully stepped over the broken glass. With no way to go towards the street out the driveway, Carter climbed over the fence between the two yards and moved quickly through the property to the street. When he reached his car, Carter got in, started it and backed out to the street to get it away from the burning bushes next to it. As he got out and stood there watching the blaze, the sounds of the sirens from the fire trucks got louder as they came down the street.

It took the firemen about thirty minutes to knock down the flames to a smoldering pile of burnt and charred lumber. The police had arrived on the scene and started asking question of the twenty or thirty people from the neighborhood who had gathered to watch the firemen at work. When one of the officers questioned Carter about why he was in the neighborhood, he told him that the man who lived in the house was a client along with his sister who resided in Texas. As they talked, the second officer came over and informed his partner that one of the firemen told him that the charred remains of a body was found in the basement.

After further questioning, Carter told the officer to contact Det. Croft of the Homicide Division and let him know what they had found at the home of Robert Stearns.

As they waited at the scene, Carter's thoughts weren't on Bob Stearns or Det. Croft or any kind of investigation. His only thought was about something to calm his nerves as he noticed for the first time that his hands were shaking uncontrollably.

It was a half hour later when Det. Croft arrived at the scene and Carter filled him in on everything leading up to the explosion. His shaking had subsided but the detective's way of questioning him was starting to get him annoyed. At the point where he felt that he had given the detective all he had, Carter said, "Look Croft, I'm not feeling too good, so if you have any more questions for me you can call me at my office."

Det. Croft studied Carter for a few seconds and said, "That's it for now Carter, go do what you have to do. If I need anything else, I know where to find you."

Leaving the scene, Carter headed for the freeway but passed up the on ramp and instead pulled into the parking lot of a corner bar a block away.

15

Vito Terratello's plane landed at Burbank Airport around 9am the next morning. As Danny arranged for the baggage to be loaded into the limo, Vito called Mick to let him know that he and Danny were back from San Francisco. Once he found out that Mick was on the mend, and feeling much better, Vito asked if he would like to join them for a late lunch at the hotel. Although Vito had wanted Mick to stay at the hotel after leaving the hospital, where a room had already been reserved for him, Mick explained to his uncle that he wanted the comfort of his own home. Vito told Mick, "Michael my boy, I will send the limo to pick you up around two o'clock, and if by chance you can get hold of Donald, I would like him to join us also so I can tell him of my decision to retain his agency's services."

Mick called Carter catching him at home and told him about Vito's return to L A and his request for him to join them for lunch. Carter's response, after a few coughs and a gravelly sounding voice, was, "What time Mick?"

"Hey Donny Boy, you're not sounding so good?"

"I'm fine Mick, I just woke up, I'll fill you in later, so what time?"

"Probably around two, I'll have to let you know."

Carter asked, "So how you feeling Mick?"

"Not a hundred percent yet boss but I'm getting there."

Considering what Mick had been through, he was in great shape and couldn't wait to get back to work on the investigation. When he told Carter that he would be ready in a couple days for work, Carter said, "Didn't you hear me when I told you that we don't have a client any longer? Mrs. Houser called it off, and now her brother is dead. What the hell do I have to do to make that clear Mick, no client no pay check"

"The brother's dead?"

"I'll tell you all about it later."

"Donny Boy, "I think that's one of the things Uncle Vito wants to talk to you about."

"What are you talking about Mick?"

"I think he wants to hire you."

"And what exactly is the case? I don't want charity."

Sitting propped up in his bed, Mick said, "It's not charity boss, all the bullshit from before, plus the attempted murder of you and me. I talked with him early yesterday and he told me of his decision to hire you, but let that be his surprise."

"Don't get me wrong Mick, I'm happy about it, but I just have to wonder what he has in mind."

"That he didn't tell me, but whatever it is, be sure he researched it to death."

"Okay, how about I pick you up later and we go to the hotel together?"

"My uncle's sending the limo to pick me up at one-thirty, so why don't you come here around one and we'll ride in luxury to the hotel?"

"I'll tell you what, I'm going to stop by the office first and see if Annie needs anything from me. Now with Bob Stearns dead and his sister turning off the funds for the investigation, I guess my next move is to find out what Vito has on his mind."

"Okay boss, tell Annie that after we leave the hotel we'll stop by your office, and if it's okay with you, pick her up and give her the thrill of riding in a limo with us two big shots."

After a few cups of coffee, a half dozen aspirins, and a hot shower, Carter left his house a little before noon and got on the freeway quickly making it to his office. What Carter didn't know was that the black Mercedes was back in the picture and following him once again.

Other than having to sign a few checks, Annie told Carter that everything was under control and she couldn't wait for her ride in the limo later on that day. While standing by the window looking west on Chandler Blvd., Carter spotted a black Mercedes parked with the driver still seated behind the wheel. Removing a pair of binoculars from his desk drawer, he returned to the window and focused in on the driver. The man who appeared to be in his sixties did not look familiar at all to Carter. Reading off the license plate number to Annie so she could write it down, he said, "I'll be right back, I'm going to see if I can sneak up on that guy and find out who he is."

Carter went down the steps on the side of the building and walked around the block approaching the Mercedes from behind. About a hundred feet away, the Mercedes that had been idling quickly sped away from the curb leaving Carter standing there still not having a clue who the person was.

Leaving his car parked at the office in clear view of the crew of the repair shop, Carter decided to have Annie drive him to Mick's apartment and surprise him.

While Annie and Mick sat in his living room talking, Carter, figuring to give the couple a few minutes of privacy, went into the kitchen to fix himself a cup of coffee and check out the sports section of the newspaper. When Mick's phone rang, he called out to Carter, "Hey boss, would you get that please, it should be my uncle calling to let me know the limo's on the way?"

Carter picked it up the receiver saying, "Hello can I help you?"

"Donald, is that you?"

"Yes Vito, welcome back how was your trip?"

"Longer than first expected Donald, how is Michael doing?"

"He's doing fine Vito and we're both looking forward to joining you for lunch. Mick told me you have something you wanted to talk with about, an investigation. I assume Mick told you that my original client ended our contract?"

"Yes Donald, I'm aware of that, but we can talk about that later this afternoon. My call is to inform you that the limo driver is on his way and he should be there shortly, I look forward to seeing you both."

"Okay Vito, I'll let Mick know, and we'll see you shortly."

After hanging up the phone, Carter called out to Mick, "Okay lover-boy, the limo will be here in a few minutes."

Annie called back, "Mr. Carter!!!"

Mick laughed "Ah he's just a little jealous sweetheart. You know how those old guys get."

Walking down stairs, Carter said, "Annie, after our meeting with Vito, Mick and I will come back to the office and pick you up. We should be there before five but I'll give you a call and let you know that we're on our way."

Holding hands with Mick, Annie gave him a kiss on the cheek and said, "See you later Mickey, have fun."

Watching Annie drive away, Carter said, "She's a sweet kid Mick, you're very lucky."

"Speaking of luck and romance Donny Boy, how are things going with you and Reggie. Is the old spark still there?"

"I don't know Mick. We've had some deep conversations rehashing all the crap I've had stored up in the back of my mind. To be honest, I don't know if we'll ever get back together again. I guess it's possible, but I have no clue on what's going on in that pretty head of hers. I know this: I will not let her screw with my head again."

"Donny Boy, can I tell you something without you getting too pissed off at me?"

"Sure Mick, go for it."

"You're so full of shit. You know you're still in love with her, but you have some big issues you need to work out. You've been like my brother ever since we met, and I'll tell you brother, you have a problem with true commitment, a problem with authority, and a problem with drinking. You may be able to bullshit other people about your drinking, but don't try it on me."

"Hey Mick, I've been sober all week, I haven't touched a drink the whole time."

"Big deal, so you're dry drunk. You act like you're sitting on a fence and one big problem comes your way and you're off to the races. By the way Mr. Sober, you forgot to put some eye drops in to clear up those red road maps you have under your eye lids. Check out my medicine cabinet. There should be some Visine in there. Use it to at least clear up your bloodshot eyes before you see my uncle."

"Okay, you busted me. I had a real rough time yesterday and I needed something to calm me down."

"Like I said Donny Boy, you have a drinking problem and you need help. And please, don't try to bullshit me about it."

16

Vito had arranged for a private dining room for the lunch meeting. Mick and Carter were led to the room by one of the hotel staff and when they entered they were greeted by Danny, Paul and Reggie. When Carter asked about Vito, Reggie said, "Mr. Terratello is in a meeting with the hotel manager and will be joining us in just a few minutes."

Reggie was correct. After a few minutes, Vito entered the room followed by an older gray-haired gentleman meticulously dressed wearing a very expensive looking suit that was tailored perfectly to his person. Vito introduced the man as an old friend and manager of the hotel who spoke softly and said, "My name is Wallace Boyantano and I would like to welcome you all and let you know that anything I or the staff of the hotel can do to make your visit here a pleasant one, we are at your disposal."

Vito shook hands with the man and said, "Wallace my dear friend, your hospitality and generosity as always is greatly appreciated and I am in your debt."

The manager said, "If all your guests have arrived, I'll send someone in to take your order my friend?"

Vito looked at everyone and said, "For now Wallace, maybe just our drink order and we'll place our food order later."

Once everyone was seated at the large round table, Vito said, "It is nice to be seated here with friends and family. As you are all aware, I have just returned from the Napa Valley. I am trying to initiate negotiations to purchase some property that is adjacent to my existing vineyards for the purpose of expanding my production into the fine wine market. To my surprise, with the help of Paul Conti, it has been discovered that the property I have been pursuing is secretly owned by The Carson Burnhart Corporation."

Carter sat speechless and just stared at Vito.

Mick asked, "Uncle, how long have you known this Burnhart person?"

"An old friend of mine from back east in Bronx, New York, Gino Vochelli and myself had the misfortune of doing business with a man who had Mr. Burnhart as a silent partner. When the business arrangement came to a sudden end because of the unforeseen passing of the gentleman, his silent partner, Carson Burnhart showed up with signed documents claiming ownership to property located in New Jersey, and several other businesses owned by both men. Gino and I knew that the documents were forged, but they stood up in eyes of the court and we had to yield to Mr. Burnhart costing us a very large sum of money. Once Burnhart established legal ownership, he liquidated several businesses and left the state, taking up new residence in California. Now Donald, with Mr. Burnhart sticking his head up out of the hole he had been hiding in, this coincidence is too much to pass up. I have already contacted Gino Vochelli and informed him and he is looking forward to evening up an old score with Mr. Burnhart."

A knock came on the door and a few seconds later a waiter in a white jacket was allowed to enter the room and took everyone's beverage order and said to Vito, "Sir, when you are ready to place the food orders, you may have someone call on the phone on the table in the corner and ask for Ricardo. At that time I will inform you of the luncheon specials and provide you all with special menus if you wish."

Once the waiter left the room, Carter said, "Vito, I know you must have given this a lot of thought before your decision to go after Burnhart, but legally I'm not sure it's a wise thing to do. My personal feeling about this man from my one encounter with him is that I don't like him. I will do whatever you wish if you're sure you want to follow this path and take him down at the knees. My worry is that this man has connections with the police and politicians out here. These connections could cause lots of trouble for you and Mr. Vochelli."

"For now Donald, let's enjoy a fine meal and if it's convenient, we can meet at your office tomorrow afternoon and discuss this further, say around four. Everything I have revealed to you about Burnhart was just to give you background of my past dealings with him. My new interest with this man is the attempt on my nephew's life and his best friend. For this I wish to hire you and to sign a contract and make it official?"

"That would be fine Vito. I'll have the papers ready for your signature and maybe we can talk more about it then."

Mick asked, "Uncle, How long ago was it that you and Mr. Vochelli had your run in with Burnhart?"

"It's funny you should ask Michael. Gino and I talked about this only yesterday. It has been thirty-four years, but it feels like only yesterday. Back in those days it would have been so easy to end Mr. Burnhart's future, and he knew it. The problem was that back then we would have been the number one suspects because of the recorded court actions against him. Gino and I decided to let the anger settle and pick a better time because of all the problems at the time with the infighting of the major families on the east coast. Enough for now, no more business talk today."

The lunch was wonderful, followed by a terrific choice of desserts and after dinner drinks. Paul and Danny had talked about going out that night to a couple of clubs and asked Mick and Carter for suggestions and to join them. Mick was the first to decline saying that he had a date and was looking forward to spending some quality time with the young lady.

Carter also thanked them for the invitation but declined saying that he had a date with his TV set and the recliner in his living room to rest up his leg that had been acting up. Vito had made up his mind to sit out by the pool and catch up on some reading that he had been putting off.

When Reggie was asked about her plans, she said, "I may join Carter in front of his TV, if he promises to make some popped corn."

It was obvious that Carter was surprised at Reggie's answer and sat there with his mouth slightly open. As everyone stood and exchanged hugs, Vito said, "Donald, I'll see you tomorrow at four. Paul, before you and Danny go out, I need to talk with you for a few minutes. Have a pleasant day everyone."

As everyone headed for the door, Carter said, "Reggie, if you have a minute please?"

Mick said, "I'll be out front Donny Boy."

Once it was just the two of them left in the room, Carter asked, "What was that about Reggie?"

"Don't read too much into it Carter, I just thought it would be nice to spend a little time together, but I need your word that you're not going to pressure me about my decision to leave when I did years ago. I would prefer to let that be the past."

Carter said softly, "Butter?"

"What?"

"Do you like butter on your popped corn?"

"Yeah Carter, but easy on the salt."

"Reggie, Mick and I promised Annie a ride in the limo after the meeting, so I won't be home until probably five or six. If I'm not home when you get there, the spare key is under the third flower pot on the right."

"That's okay Carter. I need to talk with Mr. Terratello and then go out and do a little shopping, so you won't see me until seven or eight. Another thing, don't expect me to be spending the night, that's not where I'm coming from with this offer to spend some time with you. Are we clear on that?"

Carter smiled and said, "Heavy on the butter, light on the salt, and no nookie, got it. Did I miss anything?"

"Yeah, make some iced tea also Carter."

At 4PM exactly the next day, Vito entered Carter's outer office followed by Reggie, Danny and Paul. Annie greeted them and before she could tell Carter, he was already walking towards them with his hand extended. After shaking hands Vito informed the others, "Please wait out here while Donald and I have a short conversation in his office."

Once the door was closed and both men were seated, Carter said, "You're looking fine Vito. Your time at the pool gave you a little color. I believe this west coast climate agrees with you."

"The pace out here Donald is so much more suitable to a man of my age than the fast pace of the east coast. The weather north of here is much cooler this time of year, but I believe it would be a nice place for me once I purchase some additional land and increase the size of my vineyard."

"Have you given the investigation more thought Vito?"

"I have, and I still wish to retain your services. The one thing I will ask of you is that before any reports are filed or turned over to the police, I would like to check them out to make sure there are no incriminating circumstances."

"Vito, while I am in your employ, everything I uncover will be divulged to you. I understand that Paul Conti is a law student. May I ask how much longer it will be before he takes the Bar Exam?'

Vito smiled and said, "Paul passed the bar three weeks ago. He is now retained by me for my real estate dealings. On my return trip to the San Francisco area, Paul will be accompanying me to handle the possible purchase of the vineyard I have been inquiring about."

"Vito, Mick told me that you might have a plan for Mr. Carson Burnhart, are you ready to discuss it at this time?"

"Michael jumped the gun a little Donald. I do have an idea but the details need a little more work. I have a few more pieces to put together before we can discuss it fully."

Taking a check out of his pocket, Vito handed it to Carter and said, "This should cover your expenses for a while, but if more is required please let me know Donald."

Looking at the check, Carter saw the figure $25,000 and said, "Vito, I believe this is more than adequate. Let me call Annie in here with the paperwork."

Once the contract agreement was signed Vito asked, "What are your plans for dinner tonight Donald?"

"Actually Vito, I told Mick I would pick up some Cheese steak sandwiches a six-pack of beer for him, some iced tea for me and we were going to watch a basketball game on TV."

"I think that's a fine idea. I myself intend to have an early supper, turn in and hopefully get a good night's sleep."

As they both stood up, Carter said, "I want to thank you for your faith in me."

Once again shaking hands followed by a hug, both men walked to the outer office and Vito said, "Our business here is completed Miss Volasko, it's time to head back to the hotel."

Reggie said, "Sir, I would like to talk with Carter for a couple of minutes if that's alright with you?"

Smiling, Vito said, "We'll be down stairs Miss Volasko, take your time."

Walking back into his office with Reggie following, Carter said, "Yes Reggie?"

"Carter, I just wanted to tell you, I had a great time last night and I would like to do it again sometime soon." Walking over to Carter, Reggie kissed him on the cheek and said, "Soon Carter, maybe in a few days, if our plan doesn't start by then."

Reggie ran out and caught up with the others as they all walked slowly down the steps.

When everyone had left the office and there were no more footsteps that could be heard going down those noisy metal steps,

Annie walked into Carter's office and said, "Mr. Carter, I know this might sound strange, but I think I love that man," holding up the check and smiling.

Over the next two days, Carter didn't hear from Vito, but Reggie had called and asked about going out for dinner and he decided to be an ass and play hard to get. Mick knew what was going on and decided to stick his two cents in and said, "Give the girl a break Donny Boy. I'll tell you what, I need to get out of this house again and maybe Annie would like to go out also, so maybe we can go out on a double date, if that don't get your shorts in a knot."

"Hey Mick, do the letters FO bring anything to mind?"

Mick smiled and said, "Field Operative?"

"No but close. Alright I'll call her."

17

Rather than picking some fancy expensive restaurant, Mick told Carter he just wanted to go to a deli if that was okay with everyone. Carter checked with Reggie and Mick checked with Annie, and the decision was made to visit one of the best, Jerry's Deli in Studio City.

When Carter, Mick and Annie arrived at the famous eatery of the Valley deli circuit, Reggie was already seated in a booth far from the foot traffic of the other patrons.

The first half-hour of the late dinner meeting, Reggie and Annie got a little better acquainted while Carter and Mick talked sports.

As Reggie and Mick started to talk of old times when they were tracking some jeweled eggs that belonged to a museum in Russia, Carter sat quietly. Annie sat and listened in amazement at the stories that were told and asked, "Are you feeling okay Mr. Carter, you're being so quiet?"

Finally Mick got up, throwing his napkin down on the table and said, "You know what, I'm tired of this crap. I'm heading for the john. If you two aren't talking by the time I get back, Annie and I are walking out and taking a cab home."

Carter said, "Stay out of it Mick and sit down."

"And what - piss in the booth? I got to go. Talk to Reggie, Donny Boy. And you Reggie, talk to him and work things out or we're gone."

Mick walked away leaving the table in silence.

"You know he's right Carter. We have to act like professionals and put our private feelings aside."

"I don't think I can do that Reggie. Since you've been back in town I just can't seem to get you out of my head. The anger that I have been experiencing is not like me at all. Knowing that you're going to disappear again as soon as all this bullshit with Burnhart is over has been bothering the shit out of me. Telling you my feelings and hearing nothing in return is tearing me apart."

Reaching over and putting her hand on Carter's, Reggie said, "Carter you damn fool, can't you see it wouldn't work.

Annie said, "I think I'll go visit the ladies room, I'll be right back."

Watching Annie walk away, Reggie said, "This isn't the right time to get into this Carter."

"It seems like it's never the right time Reggie."

"You want feelings Carter, okay. When I was with you years ago, the time we spent together was some of the best time of my life. I was falling in love with you and I knew it was all wrong. We would be so bad for each other, in time we would just be tolerating each other."

"Reggie, somehow we need to work this out, because if we work together again, I know I'll be trying my damnedest to keep you around."

Walking back to the table, Mick asked, "Where's Annie?"

Reggie said, "Ladies room."

Sitting down, Mick asked, "You two work things out any?"

Carter smiled and said, "Did you make it to the john or did you pee in your pants?"

Mick gave him the finger and smiled."

Carter said, "Sit down Mick, we have a lot to talk about."

When Annie returned to the table, Reggie ordered coffee and cake all around, then Carter took a telegram out of his pocket and said, "As Annie knows, I got this delivered to me this morning, it's from a friend of Mrs. Emily Houser in Texas. Mrs. Houser was the widow of Teddy Houser and the sister of Bob Stearns our former client."

Mick asked, "Was?"

"Yeah was. Mrs. Houser and another man from their town were killed in a fiery collision out on the interstate on March 8th not far from their homes. The telegram is from Mrs. June Larson, the widow of the dead man. She had been told by her husband that his life and Mrs. Houser's were in danger but she didn't believe him."

Carter next took out the notarized letter he had received two days earlier from Mrs. Houser and said to Reggie and Mick, "Look at the date of the telegram and the Notary stamp."

Reggie was the first to spot the name of the Notary, "Martin W. Larson" and the date, March 10th two days after both their deaths.

Mick asked, "Do you think it's possible they just got dates mixed up or do you think it stinks from a Burnhart connection?"

Reggie said, "Hell of a coincidence."

"As much as I hated calling that ass Croft, I knew he would be able to contact the authorities in Texas and follow up on the information. Oh Mick, I got a call from Hudson and he told me about a ton of crap he uncovered hanging out with a couple guys from that construction site."

Mick asked, "How's Jimbo doing?"

"He feels bad about not coming to see you Mick, but he doesn't want to take the chance that he might be followed. It seems that Teddy Houser was screwing around with a woman who was a private nurse for some old rich guy who owned a large ranch in the west San Fernando Valley. The old guy, Nathan Ira Fishman, had been bed ridden with a bad heart for six months before he died. A rushed autopsy and a cremation followed and just last month the property was sold by the widow. Care to guess who bought the property for a bargain twelve and a half million, with two mill cash down?"

Mick said, "My wild guess would be Carson Burnhart?"

"Give that man a cigar. The sale has not been finalized yet because of a search for liens or loans on the property, but it's a sure bet Burnhart will get it. The widow, Bella Fishman, who has changed her name to Fisher, moved to the Napa Valley up north and invested in a vineyard. The old man's nurse, Barbara Williams, aged twenty nine, was found dead in her apartment out in Simi Valley of an apparent drug overdose."

Reggie sat back and said, "Very tight package, all neatly tied up with no loose ends."

Annie put her hand to her mouth and said, "Oh My God Mr. Carter."

Carter asked, "Mick how you feeling? I mean no bullshit now, really how you feeling?"

"Well now that you two are working things out, I'm feeling better than ever, whatcha got in mind?"

"Are you up for a road trip to the Napa Valley?"

"Wine country, it's been a long time since I've done some wine tasting. How about you Reggie, you like the juice from the grapes?"

Carter said, "Whoa, the trip is just you and me Mick."

"Donny Boy, I may need some nursing along the way and Annie needs to take care of your office. Reggie needs to come along with us boss. Think about it. We're going up there to talk with some old woman. Reggie can be a big help. I'm not going unless she goes."

Reggie asked, "Anyone care what I think?"

"Okay, what do you think, yes or no?"

"Yes, I needed to go up there anyway for your uncle with Paul and take a look at that property he wants to buy."

Carter said, "Reggie, its one thing bringing you along, but for what I have in mind it wouldn't be a good idea to expose Paul to the trouble we may cause."

Reggie said, "I'll talk with Vito tonight and tell him of your plans. He may not want me to go either."

Early the next morning everyone met at Carter's office and Reggie informed him, "I talked with Vito last night and told him what your plans were for today."

"And what did he have to say?" Carter asked.

"His main concern was that we be very careful. Vito also asked me about your leg injury and Mick's injury and wants assurance that you are both up to it."

"My leg is fine and so is Mick. So are we on for the trip?"

Reggie asked, "When do we leave Carter?"

Carter looked at Mick, "You ready?"

"Let's do it Donny Boy."

With the sun shining brightly and the temperature expected to be in the high seventies or low eighties, they decided to take Mick's 1960 Cadillac convertible for the drive up north. After gassing up the car, all three of them sat in the front seat and Mick put down the roof and the road trip was on.

Heading north away from the Valley, the traffic was light at 7AM. They had talked about taking the coast road but it would have added extra hours to their already long drive ahead. After about an hour on the road Reggie took out a note from her jeans pocket and handed it to Carter.

Unfolding it he read aloud, "Donald, I'm sorry I couldn't be with you on this trip, but I have arranged accommodations for all of you at the Hyatt Hotel in Sacramento. Miss Volasko has all of the information. Please forgive me for being so presumptuous. Enjoy your trip and please call me if I can be of any assistance. I'm looking forward to your report when you return. Stay safe--Vito."

Carter asked, "Mick, did you know about this?"

Reggie spoke up, "Vito sent the night manager with the note at 5am this morning. Mick knew nothing about it."

"Well it wasn't exactly where I had planned on spending the night, but who's to argue with Vito's good taste in hotels."

Since Mick's Caddy only got about twelve to fourteen miles to a gallon of gas, they stopped a couple of times to gas up before arriving in Sacramento.

The Hyatt Hotel was beautiful and the rooms Vito booked could not be beat. After a great dinner in the main restaurant it was time to check out the other amenities of the hotel. The indoor swimming pool and hot tub were just the things the three weary travelers needed, and after they rested even Carter loosened up and talked with Reggie like all had been forgiven.

The main bar had a piano player who covered a range of music. After about twenty minutes of listening to Carter and Reggie talk about old times, Mick said, "I'm going up to the room Carter. You two have a lot to talk about, so I'll see you later."

Once Mick left, Reggie said, "He's right you know? We do have a lot to talk about. What are you thinking about Carter? Tell me some of your feelings. Not things, but feelings."

"Reggie, my feelings are that I want to be with you, not just working with you, but as a couple. Do you understand that?"

"That's just not enough Carter. If you put all the time we have actually spent together as a couple, we're talking maybe what, sixty days at tops?"

"That's because you ran out on me Reggie."

"Don't go there Carter, that was the result of spending those sixty days together. What you wanted me to become I could not be."

They sat silent for about five minutes when Carter got up from the table and walked over to the piano player, made a song request and put some money in his tip cup. Once Carter sat down, the piano player started playing an old Nat King Cole tune, "Unforgettable."

After the song was over, Reggie leaned over and kissed Carter on the cheek and said, "Thank you Carter."

As they left the bar, and walked to the elevator, Carter said, "I won't rush you anymore Reggie, I promise. Just let me know if I'm pushing to hard."

Carter walked Reggie to her room, and after opening the door she turned and gave Carter a full warm kiss on the mouth and said, "See you in the morning hon."

When Carter walked into his room, Mick said, "What happened, I thought you and Reggie might have patched things up?"

"This is new territory for me Mick. Reggie and I need some time to heal and work things out."

As Carter sat on the bed, Mick walked over to the courtesy bar and took out two small bottles of Jack Daniels and tossed one over to Carter. Mick said, "What the hell, one won't kill you."

Carter unscrewed the cap, looked at the bottle, and put the cap back on.

Tossing the bottle back over to Mick "To be honest, this won't help.

The plan was to meet in the coffee shop at 7am for breakfast before driving to the vineyard in Napa Valley. The name of the vineyard they would be searching for was the recently renamed, "Fisher/Holtz Vineyard."

At 6:50am Carter and Mick were already seated at a table in the coffee shop when

Reggie walked in, smiled and said, "Good morning gentlemen. Did you order coffee yet?"

"Mick said, "We just beat you by a couple minutes Reggie. See if you can get the waitress's attention."

Carter was busy studying a map of the area that listed the vineyards with details on wine tasting availability when the waitress came over. Everyone ordered their meals and the coffee came a couple minutes later. The map that Carter was studying had the Holtz Vineyard listed and he figured it to be around seventy miles from the hotel. He figured the driving time would most likely be around ninety minutes hitting some traffic.

It was a beautiful drive with lush green plants and trees on both sides of the road, compared to the Los Angeles area of mostly sun burnt vegetation. One would think they were in a different state.

Carter was close with his estimation of travel time, but he didn't mind the trip at all. Several times during the trip, Reggie, with the wind blowing through her hair, placed her hand either on Carter's arm or his leg giving a little squeeze and smiling. It was a warm feeling that Carter enjoyed and gave him a little hope for the future.

With three sets of eyes looking for the posted road leading to several vineyards, Mick slowed the car down and made the turn on to a long dirt road off the main highway. The sign at the turn-off was bright yellow with large black letters that listed about a half dozen vineyards with number six being "The Holtz Vineyards.

They drove approximately two miles before finding the newly painted sign that read, "Fisher/Holtz Vineyards," with an arrow pointing to a nicely graded road.

Driving an additional half mile, the road led to a bright red large building that sat nestled between many large trees. More signs pointing the way to the parking area were in plain view and easy to follow.

There were a dozen or more cars and pickup trucks parked in the parking lot and Mick parked the Caddy at the end several spaces away from the last vehicle.

Following the signs to the tasting room, the trio studied their surroundings as they walked.

Mick asked, "So Donny Boy, I suppose you have some kind of plan?"

Carter said, "Mick, for right now we're just going to wing it."

"Mick, you should know by now, that's usually what Carter's plans are. Wing it and hope for the best."

"Okay you two, you just watch the master at work, and don't drink too much wine."

The building they were being led to by the signs looked newly constructed, and above the massive double doors there was a large sign that read, "Welcome to the Fisher/Holtz Vineyards tasting room."

The inside of the building resembled a large hall or recreation room, the kind used for social gatherings or parties, with a long bar along the entire left wall. Seated at the bar were ten or twelve visitors listening to a man standing behind the bar giving a history on wine making.

Finding three empty bar stools, they sat down to join the other visitors.

After about five minutes the man was joined by a woman who appeared to be in her early sixties, but was trying to look much younger by the way she was dressed. The man smiled and held out his hand saying, "Well ladies and gentlemen, I would like to at this time present Ms. Bella Fisher, one of the owners of Fisher/Holtz Vineyards."

Many at the bar stood and applauded, but Carter just stood and studied the woman for a brief while. As everyone sat back down Ms. Fisher said, "Thank you, how about a hand folks for my long time friend and General Manager Will Gruber?"

After a slight hand of applause, Ms. Fisher said, "I would like to thank you all for coming today to visit my home and my life's passion, where we try to bottle some of the best wine in the country. My family has owned this land and produced wine here for over forty years.

Carter said, "Excuse me Mrs. Fishman, but I was under the impression that you recently purchased this property?"

The woman looked at Carter and said, "That's Fisher young man, and no, this property has been in my family since the late forties."

Once again Carter spoke up, "But aren't you the widow of the recently deceased Ira Fishman from the San Fernando Valley in Los Angeles?"

Seeming to be at a loss for words, Ms. Fisher looked at her manager.

The manager said, "I realize that you all may be interested in the history of the Fisher/Holtz Vineyards, but at this time could we keep all questions only about wine producing and marketing?"

As if scripted, a man at the other end of the bar asked, "How many kinds of wine do you bottle here and do you ship your wine to other countries?"

As Ms. Fisher answered the man's question, the manager kept his eyes on Carter. Once she completed her answer, Reggie spoke and asked, "Have you always lived in these beautiful surroundings Mrs. Fishman?"

Smiling, the woman said, "That's Fisher dear. I have spent ninety percent of my time here, and the other ten percent traveling around the world studying how other countries produce their wines."

Carter couldn't let it go so he said, "What about the time you spent living in the west San Fernando Valley, Mrs. Fishman?"

Will Gruber said, "Thank you all once again for coming today. There will be a guided tour of the vineyards and bottling plant in about a half hour, it will be leaving from the front of this building. Thank you again for coming.

Taking a walk outside, the threesome decided to take their own unguided tour of the grounds, and walked towards the tall red building. Parked next to the building were several pickup trucks with freshly painted signs on their doors that read, "Fisher/Holtz Vineyards."

As they walked around the building they could look out at the many acres of grape vines that grew in straight lines away from the buildings. Parked near the rear of the building was an old flat bed truck that looked like it hadn't moved in twenty or more years by the weeds growing around and through the bed.

Wiping away the dust and dirt on the driver's door, Carter read, "Braumholtz Farms."

Continuing to walk around the building they started back towards the wine tasting room when they saw Will Gruber and another guy who was a cross between a giant oak tree and a 1958 Buick, walking towards them. Will Gruber was no little slouch himself, and the look he had on his face was far from friendly.

Before Gruber could say anything Carter said, "Nice speech in there Will."

But it didn't seem to go over too well with him, as Gruber asked, "What is it that you are looking for, it's certainly not wine?"

Carter said, "Actually Will, I was hoping to talk with Mrs. Fishman about her dear departed husband."

Gruber said, "That won't be happening today or any other day, I think it's time for you three to leave."

Mick spoke up and said, "But we haven't had our tour yet, big guy."

The big guy behind Gruber said, "Like the boss says, it's time for you to leave."

Gruber spoke and made a slip when he said, "You're not welcome here Mr. Carter, I suggest that you leave now, so there won't be any trouble."

Carter said, "Just one more question Will. How do you know my name? I never mentioned who I was."

Gruber smiled and said, "Otto here will help you to your car, or if need be, he will carry you there. Choice is yours!"

Walking away Gruber signaled for two other men to assist Otto if needed, but Carter put his hands up and said, "We're going. No need for help. Oh Will, nice place you have here, tell Mrs. Fishman goodbye for us, we had a great time."

As Otto stepped closer, Mick said, "Back off big boy, we can do this without your help."

18

Sitting in the Caddy in the parking lot, Mick said, "Donny Boy, there's a whole lot more going on here than just squeezing grapes and making wine.

Reggie chimed in, "Did you see the size of that guy Otto? He needs his own zip code. He has got to be at least six eight or six nine and weigh what, three seventy-five?"

As Mick started the car, Carter said, "Looks like Mrs. Fishman has something in her past she is trying to keep out of the public's eye."

Pulling out of the parking lot slowly, Carter noticed that they were being watched by the small group of people standing in front of the wine tasting building. Bella Fishman was also standing in the doorway watching with her arms folded on her chest. So just to jab the spike in a little further, Carter said, "Let's smile nice for the people as we leave and give them a little wave."

Driving back down the nicely graded dirt road kicking up a small cloud of road dust, Reggie asked, "So is that it, are we done here, or are we going back to Sacramento and try again for that interview with Fishman tomorrow?"

Carter said, "No, that's it Reggie. When we get back home I'll try to do some digging into the past of Mrs. Fishman and Braumholtz?"

"Hey Donny Boy, how about we take the coast road back home, you know, through Big Sur and maybe see a beautiful sunset and stop for a nice seafood dinner along the way?"

"Nah, all it's going to do is make the trip home longer and we'll be getting in so late."

Reggie put her hand on Carter's leg and said, "Come on Carter, live life a little more, it'll make the trip home so much nicer, a little longer, but nicer."

"Sounds like a conspiracy to me by you two. Okay Mick head for the coast."

Avoiding the heavy traffic of San Francisco, Mick took the straighter route driving through Berkeley, Oakland and then across the San Mateo-Hayward Bridge out to the coast at Half Moon Bay. Driving south along Highway 1 with the beautiful coastline on their right, the trio would have hours of viewing the dark blue-green Pacific.

With many miles of the highway being cut into the high cliffs along the coastline, there were times when the speed limit was reduced to 25 miles per hour to avoid driving off into the heavy brush or a cliff to the beach below.

During one of the slowdown areas of the road, Mick noticed a fast moving pickup truck that had quickly come up behind them and he started looking for a turn-off to let the driver pass. Instead of trying to pass though, the driver of the truck came right up on the rear of the Caddy and tapped the bumper repeatedly.

Mick sped up a little but the driver of the truck slammed the bumper again, this time accelerating as he made contact, pushing the Caddy up to a dangerous speed.

Trying to ride the brake and control his speed, Mick yelled out to Carter, "That son of a bitch is trying to kill us."

Looking back at the truck Carter said, "He's that big fucker, Otto from the vineyard. Try to get away from him Mick."

With speeds up to a very dangerous 50MPH, Mick was taking up both lanes of the two lane road. There were many hair-pin turns twisting up and down around the mountainside. Each time a vehicle approached in the opposite direction, the Caddy swerved barely staying on the road avoiding a collision. As the truck continued to try and push the Caddy off the road, Carter asked, "Either one of you have a gun?"

Mick said, "Didn't think I would need one on this trip boss. I should have known going on a trip with you that I needed to be armed, especially after our last trip to the ballgame."

Once again the truck came up hard, ramming the Caddy's bumper, this time pushing the car slightly sideways. Mick floored the gas and got away briefly. Looking over the cliff, Carter said, "The drop down to the beach below is about a hundred feet Mick, we got to get away from that idiot."

Mick trying hard to keep the car on the road said, "Hey boss, you know I'm no coward, but this is starting to worry me a little."

"Hey Mick, just pretend you're at Disneyland on the wild toad ride."

Hanging on to the steering wheel with both hands, Mick said, "I'm open for suggestions boss, but you better make it quick, because here he comes again."

Slamming into the Caddy bumper and accelerating, the pick up pushed Mick across the road slamming him hard until the rear left fender scraped the rock mountainside, kicking up dirt and pebbles that landed on the hood of the truck, and then Mick floored it again pulling ahead.

As the truck seemed to drop back with a sharp double hairpin turn coming up, appearing to wait as several cars passed in the opposite direction, it once again started a rapid acceleration. The sound of the truck engine could be heard echoing off the rock mountainside as it sped towards the rear of the Caddy.

With the sweat beading up on his forehead, just before the truck could slam into the rear of his car again, Mick jerked the steering wheel hard hugging the opposite side of the road next to the mountainside while jamming on his brake with both feet.

With the truck now next to the car, Mick jerked the steering wheel hard to the right smashing the right side of his beautiful Caddy into the left side of the truck. The driver of the truck held tight and pushed to his left moving the heavy Caddy only slightly away. Mick once again rammed his right side into the truck as the roadway made a sharp curve to the left. Before the driver of the truck could respond, he was heading over the cliff and a 100 foot drop to the beach below.

Pulling over onto a narrow dirt shoulder of the road, Carter, Mick and Reggie got out of the car on Mick's side and watched as the truck burst into flames as it lay upside down on the rocky beach below. Mick, careful not fall off the steep cliff, looked at both sides of his precious 60 Caddy and said, "I think it's going to take a little more than paint to fix this one Donny Boy."

Pointing to the truck below, Carter said, "Hey it could have been a lot worse Mick."

"Yeah Donny Boy, you may be right, but that's not what the woman who does my laundry is going to say when she sees my shorts."

19

About four hundred miles to the south, sitting in a bar in the West Valley, Jimmy Hudson was sipping on a beer accompanied by two construction workers from the Carson Burnhart Construction Corporation. After one week of showing up each morning at the construction site and asking for any job that he might make a few bucks, the foreman finally decided to give Hudson a small clean-up job that no one else cared to do.

Now in his third week of work at the site, Hudson had been put on the books and hired as casual labor so he didn't have to join a union and the foreman didn't have to pay him out of his own pocket.

Always smiling and having a joking personality, Hudson soon wormed his way into a small click of men who sat and drank at a neighborhood bar near the construction site each night after work.

Not trying to dig too hard into everyone's background, Hudson picked up certain things after many nights of drinking with the group that were not for everyone to know.

Much of the gossip was about who was screwing whom in the company, where they might be working next, who might be stealing supplies from the site, or how old man Burnhart always screwed someone out of their land to build his high-rise buildings.

Not trying to be too obvious, Hudson said with a laugh, "I read in the paper a few months ago about one of the crew falling off the fourteenth floor, somebody catch him screwing the old man's secretary or something?"

At first there was silence by everyone then one of the older guys in the group said, "Nah, he just knew too many secrets about the family background."

The foreman Mark Warren said, "I think you had too much to drink Charlie, so shut the hell up because you don't know what you're talking about. The wrong person hears you, and you could wind up taking a dive off some tall building."

Hudson said, "Sorry guys, I didn't mean to start any trouble, how about a game of pool. I can't play worth a shit, but at least from the pool table I can get a better look at those two good looking bimbos at the end of the bar.

While Hudson and a guy named Chester played pool, the foreman stayed seated at the bar with Charlie and even with the music playing on the jukebox, the words, "Keep your damn mouth shut" could be heard from the foreman.

Hudson knew he had heard something that was not talked about with strangers, but it was something he needed to find out. The slip by Charlie Waters would be passed on to Carter and in time Hudson hoped to pry a few more facts out of the man.

20

While Mick surveyed the damage to his classic Caddy, several vehicles had stopped to observe the burning wreckage of the pickup truck on the rocky coast below. One of the drivers told Mick, "I can't imagine what possessed that madman to keep on ramming into the back of your car like that."

Carter asked the man, "You witnessed the whole thing?"

"You bet we did, my wife and I were in the Chevy Suburban behind him. He almost ran us off the road as he flew past us trying to get behind you."

As Carter was getting something for the man to write his name and address on, a highway patrol cruiser was pulling up with lights flashing behind them. The officer quickly got out of his vehicle, opened his trunk and started removing red cones and reflector triangles and started placing them on the roadway. Returning to his vehicle he got on his radio and called in his location to his dispatcher for additional assistance.

Approaching the group, the officer asked, "Could somebody tell me what happened here?"

Mick was the first to speak, "Yeah, the crazy son-of-a -bitch tried to run us off the road."

Taking out his notebook the officer asked, "And you are?"

"My name is Michael Terratello and the banged up Caddy here is mine. My friends and I were heading home from visiting a vineyard in Napa when that crazy bastard came up behind us and started ramming the back of my car."

The old man who witnessed the whole thing said, "My wife and I saw the whole thing Officer."

The officer said, "I'll get to you in a few minutes Sir."

"So Mr. Terratello, you had been drinking at the vineyard is that what you're saying?"

Carter stepped in and said, "No officer, that's not what he was saying."

The officer looked Carter up and down and asked, "And you are?"

"My name is Donald Carter and I was a passenger in Mr. Terratello's vehicle, along with Miss Volasko who is standing over by the car there. The older gentleman, who just tried to get your attention standing next to her, witnessed the atrocious assault by the man at the bottom of the cliff."

Standing silent for a few seconds the officer said, "I'm going to need a statement from you Mr. Carter. Walking over to Reggie and the older couple, the officer asked, "Folks. Are you all witnesses to what happened here?"

The old man spoke up, "That madman tried to run these people off the road."

The officer asked, "Could anyone see if the driver happened to get out of the vehicle before it went over the cliff?"

Reggie said, "No Officer, he was in the truck when it went over the edge."

Studying the damaged right and left sides of Mick's car, the officer said, "From the looks of this, it appears he had a little help going over the edge."

Carter who was walking alongside the officer said, "Before you pass judgment officer, might I suggest you take a look at the rear of the car. We were rammed several times by that driver as he tried to push us off the road to *our* certain death. The actions by Mr. Terratello were in self defense that saved our lives."

"Thank you Mr. Carter, if you would be so kind as to put that in your written statement, it will no doubt help to determine the outcome of the investigation."

While the officer was getting a statement from the older couple, a second patrol car pulled up followed by a paramedic unit. A helicopter soon followed that landed on the beach below to look for survivors, but the fire had been very intense and consumed the vehicle's interior and driver.

The second patrol car that arrived contained the first officer's superior. After a brief conversation between the lieutenant and the sergeant, a field sobriety test was given to Mick who agreed because he hadn't had any alcohol that day at all.

Looking at the officer's name tag, Carter sarcastically said, "Are you sure you don't want to test everyone here Lieutenant Douglas?"

The lieutenant said, "Thank you sir, but your statements will be all that I require. One thing though. Would you have any idea why he was trying to run you off the road? By some chance did you know that man?"

"Well Lieutenant, I can tell you that he worked at the Fisher/Holtz Vineyard in Napa. We were there earlier asking some questions about an investigation we're involved in and were rudely asked to leave. The man in that vehicle at the bottom of the cliff was the one who made some serious threats towards us before we left the vineyard, under instructions from his boss."

Looking a little puzzled, the lieutenant asked, "Questions about an investigation? Are you in law enforcement?"

Handing the lieutenant one of his cards, Carter said, "The questions involved a case I'm working on and our visit was not taken in a very favorable light. I believe I ruffled some feathers, so we were asked to leave."

"May I ask Mr. Carter, whom you are working for?"

"Sorry Lieutenant, but that part is confidential."

"May I assume that you and your friends are returning to the Los Angeles area?"

"Yes Lieutenant, that is correct."

"What I will require from you and the others is proper identification along with phone numbers where you can all be reached."

"No problem Lieutenant. As for Miss Volasko, you will be able to reach her through my office. If it will help you in your investigation, you might call the LAPD at the Van Nuys Police Department, Homicide Division and ask for Det. Stanley Croft. Although we don't see eye to eye most of the time, he can vouch for my identification Lieutenant."

"Thank you Mr. Carter, I may just do that. You and your party will be free to go after you've provided the information I requested."

"Lieutenant, you might want to prepare yourself for a bit of double talk at the vineyards. Our presence there was not appreciated."

"I'll be in touch with you Mr. Carter, once I've conducted *my* investigation."

An hour later, Carter, Mick and Reggie were on their way again but this time they had more suspicions about the Fisher/Holtz Vineyard than before.

21

The remainder of the drive heading south on the Pacific Coast Highway was a slow go on the winding road. With a twenty-five or thirty-five mile per hour speed limit, even the clear road ahead took an hour after the incident. After that it was open sailing. There was a problem though; the Caddy had developed a horrendous shimmy in the front end that limited their speed well under the speed limit. Stopping in Ventura to check the car's front suspension and get something to eat, the threesome sat in a booth at a diner and had burgers and fries along with coffee as they discussed the events of the day.

The only thing Mick had found wrong with the steering, when he inspected it, was a bent wheel and a damaged front tire. Once the front wheel was replaced with the spare, they were back on the road again, and able to make better time.

Cleaned up and a little rested, Mick and Reggie sat on one side of the booth while Carter sat by himself facing them. The eye contact between Carter and Reggie was getting kind of steady along with the slight smiles and occasional hand touching across the table. Mick made several remarks like, "So it looks like you two have mended the riff? Does this mean all is forgiven? Would you feel more comfortable if I found myself another table?"

Both Reggie and Carter slipped Mick the bird and smiled, and then Carter said, "Reggie and I have a lot more to work out between us Mick."

"Hey Donny Boy, whatever you and Reggie want between you two is your business, wink, wink."

Once again both Carter and Reggie wiggled their middle finger at Mick, and then Cater said, "Time to get back on the road."

A little more than an hour later, Mick drove his beat up, banged up Caddy up to the front door of the Beverly Hills Hotel, and Carter said, "Reggie and I are going to continue working out our problems Mick. I'll catch a cab later. Take the car over to Jack's Auto Body tomorrow and see Mark for an estimate on the repairs. Meanwhile I'll get you a rental to help you get around."

Mick smiled at the two of them and said, "Thanks boss, now you two behave yourselves tonight."

Reggie smiled, took Carter's hand in hers and said, "That's one thing we're not going to do tonight, Mick."

Carter couldn't help but smile and said, "Get the hell out of here Mick, sorry about the car."

"Yeah, me too boss. Good night you two."

It was around 9pm when Reggie and Carter stepped up to the concierge's desk and Reggie asked, "Any messages for me Armando?"

A short balding man dressed in a black suit said, "Welcome back Miss Volasko. No messages ma'am, but Mr. Terratello asked me to inform him when you returned."

"Is Mr. Terratello in his bungalow Armando?"

"Actually Miss Volasko he's in the cocktail lounge with his two associates."

"Thank you Armando, we'll find him."

172

Seated along a back wall with a clear view of anyone entering the lounge, Vito, Danny and Paul were talking when Vito spotted Carter and Reggie walking in. Waving them over, Vito then got the attention of one of the waiters and asked him to please set up a second table adjoining his.

Reggie reached Vito first and gave him a kiss on the cheek and then Carter extended his hand for a handshake. Vito asked, "How was your trip? Successful I hope?"

Carter said, "Many strange things happened on our trip Vito. It will take much time to properly explain all that happened."

Vito smiled and asked, "How did Michael fare during your long trip Donald?"

"Michael did fine Vito, and I want to thank you for the wonderful accommodations you set up for us in Sacramento."

"It was my pleasure Donald, and did you by chance visit many vineyards on your trip?"

"Only one Vito and we were abruptly asked to leave when I started asking too many questions. If I could explain more of our trip tomorrow, I would greatly appreciate it, I'm sure you will understand once you've heard of our troubles. We've had a long day. Reggie and I still have some matters to discuss before I leave."

Looking at Reggie, Vito said, "Perhaps you and Miss. Volasko will join me for breakfast in the morning at say, 10am in the main restaurant?"

Carter stood along with Reggie and said, "I look forward to it."

Reggie who had been quiet said, "Good night Vito, Paul, Danny. Until tomorrow gentlemen."

Walking to the elevator Carter asked, "Am I staying the night or calling a cab?"

"Push the damn button Carter, and stop trying to pretend we're on a first date."

Stepping into the elevator and waiting for the door to close, Reggie pushed the button for her floor and then threw her arms around Carter and planted a kiss on him that he returned with great pleasure. When the door to the elevator opened Reggie took Carter by the hand and led him quickly down the hall to her room.

Once inside the room the passion heightened, as both of them started removing their clothing while walking to the bedroom. By the time Reggie fell backwards onto the bed, all she was wearing was a bra and panties. Carter, bare-chested fell softly on top of her. Between heavy kissing and groping they managed to remove the rest of their clothing. With no talking, Carter reached down between Reggie's thighs and tenderly rubbed her moist vagina, inserting a finger momentarily as they kissed with tongues darting in and out.

With Reggie pushing her pelvis up, Carter began kissing her breasts and slowly moved his lips down her flat stomach removing his finger from her now extremely wet vagina, replacing it with his darting tongue.

As Carter gently spread her tender lips and licked and kissed the hottest spot on her entire body, the two of them maneuvered themselves around on the bed so that Reggie could grasp Carter's very hard and erect penis and place her lips around it and take it slowly deep into her mouth.

As Reggie's back stiffened she moaned as she climaxed and was soon followed by Carter's moans of pure pleasure.

Continuing to caress each other they soon rotated around so they were face to face looking into each other's eyes, when Carter said, "I love you Reggie and I want you in my life more than just for short periods of time."

"Carter you know I love you too, but it would never work on a full time basis, because of the kind of work we do and the traveling I have to do. In time we would grow to hate each other and I couldn't let that happen. Your life is here, mine is wherever I need to be to accomplish what needs to be done. Please let's enjoy each-other's company while we can, and not look too far into the future."

"I don't know if I can do that Reggie."

"Carter please, one day at a time for now. If for some reason my life style changes, you are the only man I would want to spend the rest of my life with."

With the long hours of the day behind them, and their passionate love making pleasantly exhausting their bodies, they drifted off into a comfortable sleep. Through the night they both awoke several times and snuggled closer together feeling the comfort and warmth of each other's love.

As the room grew lighter from the rising sun shining through the slightly opened drapes, Carter slowly rolled over and opened his eyes and could hear the shower, and noticed that he was alone in bed. Getting up, he walked to the bathroom door and opened it and saw Reggie through the clear glass shower doors soaping up and asked, "May I join you sweetheart, or do you want your privacy?"

Opening the door Reggie said, "You're just in time to scrub my back."

Closing the door after stepping into the shower, Carter said, "It's not your back I'm interested in pretty lady, but I'm yours for as long as you want me."

Lathering up Reggie's back, Carter slowly moved his hands around her hips and upward cupping her breasts in his hands. Lifting her head up looking at the ceiling Reggie said, "Don't start something you're not ready to finish."

Carter was ready okay, and when Reggie reached around she could tell by the firm erection she felt in her hand.

Twenty minutes later when they stepped out of the shower Reggie tenderly held Carter's face in her hands, kissed him and said, "I guess you were readier than I thought."

Carter standing tall said, "We better hurry or we'll be late for breakfast with Vito."

While they were getting dressed Reggie told him, "Carter, please try not to be too surprised by what Vito's plan is for me."

"What kind of plan?"

"It's something Vito has been working on ever since you and Mick were shot, and it is better that he explain it to you. I'll tell you

177

this much, it involves Burnhart and that vineyard up in the Napa Valley. It will however require me to be out of town for a few days."

"And you just decided to tell me this now?"

"Carter, this is exactly what I was trying to tell you when I said I didn't think we should get involved again, no matter how much we cared for each other. I still work for Vito. He has a job for me to do and if you have a problem with that, we have a problem."

"What kind of job Reggie?"

"That I don't know yet, but if we move our asses a little faster we might just make it downstairs in time to find out and enjoy a good breakfast while we're at it. Come on Carter, we're both professionals at what we do, I know we can get through this and then get back to enjoying each other's company."

Walking up behind her as she removed a sweater from a hanger in the closet, Carter kissed the back of her neck and said, "I love you Reggie. Although it's hard for me to accept or understand the things you have to do, I know we'll work it out. Please try to understand that, will you?"

Turning around Reggie placed her hands on Carter's cheeks, kissed him on the lips and said, "I think there may be hope for you yet Carter. Now let's finish getting dressed and get downstairs before Vito sends someone up here to get us."

22

The phone rang as Reggie was brushing her hair, "Hello."

"Miss Volasko, it's Vito. Are you and Donald ready to join me for breakfast?"

"I'm sorry for the tardiness sir. Donald and I will be joining you in just a few minutes."

"As you know we need to work out the final details for this assignment."

"Sir, I'm just going to run a brush through my hair and we'll be right there."

As Reggie placed the receiver down,

Carter asked sarcastically, "Did you just tell Vito that you just needed to run a brush through your hair?"

"Smart ass, it's your fault we're late, are you ready?"

Reggie looked in the mirror, ran the brush through her hair a few strokes and said, "Let's go."

Walking into the restaurant it took a few seconds for Carter to spot Vito who was seated with Danny and Paul in a back corner at a large round table. As Reggie and Carter approached the table, all three men stood up and Vito said, "Good morning, I hope you both slept well?"

After the exchange of greetings Reggie and Carter sat down as did the others. Danny signaled the waitress over and they all ordered breakfast, a pot of coffee and a carafe of orange juice for the table.

Vito nodded to Paul Conti and said, "Paul if you would please?"

Reaching down at his side to his briefcase, Paul removed a folder and placed it on the table in front of Reggie and said, "The folder before you, Miss Volasko, contains a promissory note signed by Nathan Fishman for $7,500,000.00. Mr. Fishman had put up his forty-nine acre property as collateral for the loan. The year old note, held by The Bronx Holding and Loan Corp., was never paid off by Mr. Fishman.

The Burnhart Corp. which has entered into a purchase agreement with the grieving widow, Mrs. Bella Fishman, transferred a substantial deposit amount to her private account. Although the final transfer of ownership has not been completed, Carson Burnhart has decided to go ahead with his plans to raise and develop the property.

Carson Burnhart has recently been notified by his attorney's of the existing loan on the property. Also that The Bronx Holding and Loan in Bronx, New York, has filed a demand for payment in full on the loan.

The property being worth twice that amount looked like a steal to Burnhart, so it appeared he quickly jumped on it, but looks are deceiving."

Carter asked, "Excuse me Paul, but wasn't that property sold to Burnhart by the widow after her husband's death--what, in the past couple months?"

Paul answered, "Same property Mr. Carter."

Carter asked, "How then could such a big company like Burnhart Corp. make the purchase without their legal eagles doing a complete search on the property ownership for any liens or mortgages?"

"Simple, they did, Mr. Carter. At the time of their search they found no liens on the property, but their search had not been completed. The original search of the records showed a clean ownership by Fishman, but then they had some surprises coming. There is also an adjacent property of five and a half acres that Mrs. Fishman included in the sale, but for some reason was not mentioned as a separate property. We also have in our possession, a signed affidavit from Mr. Fishman, stating that in case of his death, the forty-nine acres of property would be donated to the state, and his surviving spouse would have only the five and a half acres to do with as she pleases."

Carter said, "Seven million sounds like a hell of a big mistake for a big outfit like Burnhart. How can that all be explained?"

Vito spoke up, "It was no mistake Donald. Let us just call it a big favor that I called in that required some help from people in high places. We will let Mr. Burnhart's people try to figure it out as pressure is put on him to make a deal that is being presented to him."

Reggie asked, "So what will my part be in this operation sir?"

Vito looked at Paul.

"Miss Volasko, you will once again be Christina Hamilton, and you will be an executive officer with the Bronx Holding and Loan, and I will be accompanying you as your legal representation. We will be joined tomorrow by a friend of Mr. Terratello's whose name is Bradford Gilman. Mr. Gilman represents Gino Vochelli, the major stock holder in Bronx Holding and Loan. Burnhart has conducted business with Mr. Vochelli and Mr. Terratello in the past and his actions were not handled in a favorable manner."

Everyone looked at Vito and he did not have a pleasant look on his face as he waved his hand for Paul to continue.

Carter asked, "Vito?"

"I have told you a little of my memories of Mr. Burnhart, Donald, and they are not some that I care to remember. But there are things that will be rectified if everything planned falls into place."

Carter said, "So you have some information that can bring the bastard down from his high horse?"

Vito said, "Through some extensive investigating, Donald, we found out some very interesting information about Mr.

Carson Burnhart. Besides mine and my dear friend Gino's personal vendettas for him, he has a history he has tried very hard to keep from the public eye. Paul, would you care to elaborate?"

Removing another folder from his briefcase, Paul opened it and passed out copies of a report to Reggie and Carter, then read. "Carson Werner Burnhart, real name Kraus Wilhelm Braumholtz, born March 13, 1920. At seventeen he joined the German Army after a several year involvement in the Hitler youth movement. By the age of twenty-four, he became a captain and was assigned to a death camp in Poland where his duties were to oversee, torture and exterminate captured prisoners of war, mostly Polish Jews. In 1945 to avoid capture he fled as the allies closed in. His path took him to Austria where he lived with forged papers for several years before entering the United States illegally. With the aid of gold, money and valuable art that he had stashed away by the time he entered this country, he was a very rich man. He was able to purchase property in the Napa Valley region and start growing grapes and other fruits and formed the Braumholtz Farm with the aid of a hungry property seller who was tired of farming."

Danny said, "Maybe we can just kill the son-of-a-bitch and bury his ass in a hole out in the desert."

Vito smiled a little and said, "Please continue Paul."

"At the time of his disappearance in 1945 from Poland, Braumholt's mother and sister were living in Berlin. His sister Bella Braumholtz was only thirteen when their mother died in 1950. Bella came to America illegally to live with her big brother and continued the lies that they were born and raised in Austria. When the word started spreading around the country that the hunt was on for Nazi war criminals, the Braumholtz name was quickly changed to Burnhart and the small vineyard was called, "The Holtz Farms." With the money and power that he possessed, there was nothing that Burnhart couldn't buy or order including an occasional death or disappearance of anyone who disagreed with him as he accumulated more property adjacent to his."

Carter said, "I'm a little confused. Mrs. Fishman, or Fisher, supposedly purchased the vineyard with money from her late husband's ranch in the West Valley."

Paul continued, "In 1959, fearing that their true identity would be discovered, the farm was sold in a phony sale to one of Burnhart's employees. One year later it was sold again to a London millionaire in name only. Two years later the property was sold again and became part of The Holtz Corp. in Modesto, CA, which was secretly owned by Burnhart. He tried very hard to cover up his ownership with a phony paper trail but through diligent investigating we uncovered his deception."

Carter asked, "And what part did Mr. Vochelli play in all of this?"

Looking at Vito first, and seeing a slight wave from him, Paul said, "About twenty years ago, Mr. Terratello and Mr. Vochelli joined in a venture to purchase two vineyards adjoining the Holtz Vineyards in Napa. While the deal to purchase was almost completed, it was brought up by unknown sources at the time that the prospective buyers were involved with organized crime and the sale was vetoed by the city council. The property was eventually purchased by The Holtz Corp. and became part of the new Holtz Vineyards, Inc."

Carter sat back in his chair, smiled and said, "Looks like Burnhart has a lot to answer for?"

Paul said, "More than you know, Mr. Carter."

"There's more?"

Again looking at Vito first before he continued, Paul said, "A young investigator working for Mr. Vochelli and Mr. Terratello started asking questions around town trying to find out who put the proverbial finger on the prospective buyers. The man was not heard from again until his remains turned up two years later in a shallow grave not far from the Holtz Vineyards.

The young man, who was a family member of Mr. Vochelli's, never had a chance to pass on what he had discovered. There were rumors that he was last seen the night of his disappearance with someone working at the Holtz Vineyards, but it could not be confirmed."

Laying the report on the table, Paul asked, "Anything you wish to add Mr. Terratello?"

"Thank you Paul for your hard work. Gino Vochelli and I have not forgotten the past and we wish to confront Burnhart. The death of a young man whose birth I celebrated many years ago with my dear friend Gino is also something that must be answered for. What we have planned for Mr. Burnhart, will hopefully clear up the ghosts of the past and put an end to his empire."

Looking at Paul, Vito said, "Paul, will you please explain what we have in store for Mr. Burnhart?"

Paul looked around the table and said, "Mr. Burnhart is a womanizer, he chases after anything in a skirt. Pretty women like Miss Volasko will have him drooling and chomping at the bit. That's what we're counting on."

Carter said, "Wait a minute, you mean you're going to use Reggie for bait?"

Paul said, "In a manner of speaking, Mr. Carter, yes. Miss Volasko has been informed of what part she will have to play, and if all goes as expected, she will never be in danger,"

Carter angrily blurted out, "And if it doesn't go as expected?"

Reggie said, "We're all professionals here Carter, so knock it off."

As Carter stared at Reggie, Vito held up his hand and said, "Please Donald, hear the rest of the plan."

Removing additional papers from his briefcase and passing copies to everyone at the table, Paul said, "These statements are all copies, assembled after the death of Nathan Fishman. You will notice that all of these statements from Fishman, Teddy Houser, Mr. Gilman, and our own Christina Hamilton (Miss Volasko) are notarized. Each is a forgery, but don't be concerned with that. The single statement by Miss Barbara Steele, who was Fishman's private nurse for the six months before his death, is not a forgery however. Miss Steele, a twenty-nine year old, was having an affair with Teddy Houser at the time of his death."

Carter asked, "How the hell did you find that out?"

Vito said, "Daniel would you care to take that question?"

Danny Russo said, "Sure Pop. With the assistance of a couple of local contacts in Los Angeles, I was able to locate and question an employee of the Burnhart Corporation. Dieter Wentz, the assistant foreman for the company was very helpful after a little persuasion by my associates. He not only provided information about Mr. Fishman's death, but also the death of the nurse, Miss Steele, who died mysteriously of a drug overdose. Mr.

Wentz revealed that he had at his home certain documents that he was sure would protect him from future prosecution, if any investigation might occur from the two deaths in question."

Removing two envelopes from his jacket pocket, Danny handed them to Carter and said, "After some additional persuasion, Mr. Wentz brought us to his home, opened his safe, and provided us with the documents you have before you."

The first letter Carter looked at was a statement from Miss Steele, stating that she had been having an affair with Carson Burnhart while she was a private nurse for Nathan Fishman. Under the threat of death, she was instructed and provided with an arsenic-laced drug that she was told to add to Mr. Fishman's daily medication. During the months she was attending to Mr. Fishman, she was being watched by Teddy Houser. A relationship started between Houser and Steele, and not long after Fishman's death, Steele was found dead in her apartment in Simi Valley."

The second letter Carter recognized as the missing statement from Teddy Houser, the same one that Bob Stearns had found and spoken about before his death.

Carter said, "I knew about this letter from Houser, his brother-in-law came to see me and that's how I got involved in all of this. Did that Wentz guy admit to killing the nurse?"

Danny said, "We never got that out of him before he…, well let's just say, he took off for a better place."

Carter asked, "What do you mean, he took off for a better place, you mean he left town?"

"You could say that Mr. Carter, I'd rather not speak on that matter any further."

Carter looked at Vito and said, "Vito please, I've told you before that I can't be involved in anything illegal, especially murder."

"Donald, there's no talk of murder, only of a very bad person leaving town, for places unknown. Is that not correct Daniel?"

"Pop, I can honestly say I have no idea where Mr. Wentz has traveled to."

Vito said, "Are you okay with that Donald?"

Carter sat quiet for a few seconds, then asked, "Okay gentlemen, so where do we go from here?"

Paul said, "We have a small window of time, but we have to put everything together as quickly as possible. The longer our deception goes on, the more the possibility for failure. Mr. Carter, I understand you have a man working undercover at the Burnhart Corp.?"

"Yes Paul, but his cover may be starting to unravel. A few more days and I'll have to pull him out."

Pulling out a few more papers Paul said, "Here are copies of Fishman's loan agreement for the seven million five hundred thousand dollars. At eight percent interest, his monthly payment of interest, insurance and principle came to around fifty thousand dollars. According to the contracts that you see before you, Fishman had a plan *he* put together, it involved having his loan paid to him in two checks. The first check went directly to his bank for two point five million. The second check was issued to the Manhattan Gold Exchange for five million dollars. That money was to purchase gold bars that would be delivered to his West Valley ranch."

Carter said, "Are you serious Paul?"

"It's only on paper Mr. Carter, the transaction never took place, but the documents are all notarized. Miss Volasko, Mr. Gilman and myself will try and convince Burnhart and his attorneys, that the gold is somewhere on the Fishman property that he now has in escrow. He will find out that the escrow will never close, not without full payment of the existing lien on the property."

"What about bank records Paul, won't he be able to check that out also, and find out there was never a deposit that large?"

"That's already been handled. Am I correct Mr. Terratello?"

Vito sat back in his chair and said, "That's correct Paul. When the call is made to confirm that transaction last year, it will show up with a date that matches the loan agreement and issuing of the funds."

Carter smiled and shook his head asking, "Vito, please excuse me, but how in hell did you arrange that?"

"Some things I cannot talk about Donald, this is one. I can say that an old debt is being taken care of by an old friend, someone I helped many years ago.

Carter asked, "You never cease to amaze me Vito. So where does the gold come in? Do we supply Burnhart and his men shovels, picks and metal finders?"

Vito laughed and said, "Not quite Donald, but we will convince him that the Bronx Holding and Loan Co., and Gino Vochelli in particular, are not going digging either. We will try to convince Burnhart, with the money returned from the bank, and a fifty percent loss on the balance of the gold. They will clear the title, void out the lien, and approve the sale to the new owner. If that is not acceptable, then the property will be split up and sold by the loan holder, after excavation of the property to find the gold. Basically Donald, he is being told he can clear everything up for two and a half million dollars and he can go digging for gold himself."

Carter asked, "You think he'll buy into that Paul?"

"He's a very greedy man Mr. Carter, so yes I think he'll buy it, as long as it's presented in a sneaky under-handed proposal that fits his way of doing business."

Carter asked, "So where does Reggie fit into all of this?"

Vito said, "For now Donald, its better you don't know."

Carter said, "Vito, please, please don't leave me in the dark."

"Donald, all will be fine, trust me."

23

While Carter was hearing about plans to put a dent in Burnhart's finances, and initiate a plan to prove that he alone ordered the deaths of many people, Jimmy Hudson, using the alias Harper, was experiencing some difficulty with his position at the Burnhart Construction job site.

Jimmy Hudson was pushing a wheelbarrow loaded with scrap wood, rebar cutoffs, and trash from around the construction site, when Mark Warren, his foreman, called him over to the blueprint shack, "Jimmy, I need to talk with you."

Carefully setting down the wheelbarrow out of the way, Jimmy walked over to the shack and up the few steps and stepped through the doorway, "What's up boss?"

As Jimmy walked in, he saw that the foreman was on the phone, so he sat in a chair next to the desk and waited, but couldn't help but hear what was being said. Mark Warren yelled, "What? Why do you think I would know where the hell he is, I haven't seen him all week. Look, call me if you hear from Wentz, tell him he better get his ass back to work or he's fired. Okay, I have some other crap I have to deal with. No, no he wouldn't say anything. He knows what would happen to him. I got to go, I have someone standing here. Talk to you later."

Hanging up the phone and looking at Jimmy, the foreman said, "Harper, I got a call from the payroll department downtown, they told me the Social Security number you put on that W-2 you filled out ain't no good. Call her damn-it and give her the correct number, or I have to let you go, understand?"

"She's crazy boss. That number I gave her is mine."

"Well, you better call her and straighten it out, because I don't have time for this."

"Okay I'll take care of it; I'll stop by the office on my way into work tomorrow morning and bring a copy of my social security card."

"It's almost quitting time Harper, go take care of it now, and I'll see you tomorrow, but *only* if you straighten it out with payroll, faushstay?"

Jimmy said, "What?"

"It means, "Understand." Now get the hell out of here."

Since Hudson was on foot, not appearing to own a car, he walked a few blocks away from the building site to a gas station to use the phone. After dialing the number, he heard, "Carter Security, may I help you?"

"Sweetheart, it's Jimmy Hudson, I need to talk with Carter right away."

"I'm sorry Mr. Hudson, but Mr. Carter isn't in the office yet. I'm expecting him to call in anytime. I have no way of getting a call to him, and his cell phone seems to be turned off or on the fritz."

"Please tell him I called and let him know it's real important that we talk as soon as possible."

"How can Mr. Carter get in touch with you Mr. Hudson?"

"He can't, just tell him I'll call back at his house sometime tonight."

"Okay Mr. Hudson, I'll tell him what you said."

"How about Mick, sweetheart, has he been around?"

"I believe he's with Mr. Carter, but I'm not sure."

"Okay doll, I'll talk to you later. Bye."

24

With the meeting over, Reggie and Carter headed for the exit after paying their respects to Vito. Walking hand in hand with no words spoken out the front door of the hotel, finally Carter said, "Reggie, to be very honest with you....."

"Forget it Carter. I know what you're going to say, and I don't want to hear it. It's my job, it is what I do, and it is who I am. If you can't deal with that, then there's no hope for us at all."

"Reggie, these people are really dangerous. From what I've seen so far, they're responsible for the death of at least a half dozen people. They tried to kill us on the way back from our trip and Mick and I are still healing from being shot."

"Carter, I've dealt with these kinds of animals before I met you and I'm still standing. Look, I promise, if things get too tough, I'll walk away, but the plan that we have can't work without me in it. So please back off and let me get busy so we can get this bastard. You know Vito will do everything in his power to protect me, so you need to back off and let me do my job."

While they were standing talking, Mick pulled up with a Toyota Four-runner SUV that he had rented after dropping his Caddy at the body shop. Carter had called Mick from the room before he and Reggie had come down for the meeting to find out how his appointment went with his doctor. Mick still hadn't seen the doctor for his appointment, but he would later in the day.

Walking over to the Toyota, Reggie asked, "Hey Mick where did you get the new set of wheels?"

Smiling, Mick said, "You like it babe, I think I might just buy one of these. Carter Security is paying the rental on this one, while my Caddy is getting a facelift."

Standing next to the SUV, Carter slowly reached down and took Reggie's hand in his and said, "Okay, enough of this crap, Reggie needs to get to work and so do you and I Mick."

Reggie said, "Everything will be fine Carter. I'll see you in a few days. I may call you, but don't you try calling me."

After a warm affectionate hug and kiss, Carter said, "I know you're good at what you do, but still, watch that sweet ass of yours."

Reggie smiled and said, "Get the hell out of here Carter."

Carter got into the Toyota and he and Mick drove away, but he was not a happy guy.

Mick asked, "So what's up Donny Boy, what's next on *our* agenda?"

"Well I guess for the next few days you and I just sit on our asses and wait to hear from your uncle."

"And what the hell is everyone else going to be doing while we're sitting around doing nothing?"

"I'll tell you what Mick, let's head to the office so I can talk with Annie and check for messages. After that we'll find a nice quiet restaurant down at the beach and I'll fill you in on the master plan to take down the mighty Burnhart and all his murdering crew. So tell me. What time is your appointment for your shoulder?"

"I called him and he told me I was good to go, just no tennis or football for a while. I'm still going in to see him later."

A half hour later they pulled into the parking lot at the office and had to navigate around a yard full of trucks, all waiting for repairs at the truck shop.

When Carter and Mick walked into the office, Annie was on the phone talking with Jimmy Hudson. When she saw Carter she said, "Hold on Mr. Hudson, he just walked in."

A few seconds later Carter was on the line, "Hey Jimmy, what's up?"

"I got trouble Carter. The social security number I gave them at Burnhart's came back as no good."

"So why didn't you give them your real number?"

"Think about it Carter. If I did that, they could find out about my past, like who I worked for in the past. They could do a trace and find out I was once with the LAPD."

"Did you give them your real name?"

"Nah, I told them my name was Harper."

"Give me an hour Jimmy then call me back. I'll see what I can do."

"There's something else going on around there. I just overheard the foreman talking with someone. It appears that one of their people disappeared and has been gone for a week. From what I heard the guy knows something they don't want him talking about. If I hear anymore about him I'll let you know."

"What's his name?"

"Don't know yet."

"Okay Jimmy, call me back in an hour."

"I don't have an hour Carter. I'm supposed to be on my way to the payroll office now with the correct number, or my ass is fired."

"A half hour, call me back in a half hour. You can stall that long Jimmy. I need some time to work on this."

"Okay Carter, a half hour."

Getting on the bus in the West Valley, Hudson headed for the main office in Beverly Hills. A block away he got off the bus and found a phone booth. Before calling Carter back he went into a deli and ordered a sandwich. As he munched away on his ham and cheese he called Carter back.

As Carter was explaining things to Mick with their trip to the beach called off, the phone rang and a few seconds later Annie called out, "Mr. Carter, it's Mr. Hudson again."

"Okay Jimmy this is what you do. Check the number you gave them when you walk into the office and change one number. By the time it comes back again you'll be out of there."

"Hey, if I ain't outta here, my ass could be in some deep shit. I hope you know what you're doin boss?"

"What are you worried about Jimbo? If I have to, I'll kidnap the bookkeeper."

"Hey Carter, the way some of these guys look at me and talk, you would think they never saw a black man before. The first time I see someone wearing a white sheet, I'm truckin."

"Very funny Jimmy. Look, if things get bad around there, get the hell out."

"You got it boss."

25

It was 9AM on a Monday morning when the call was made to the Burnhart Corp. by Christina Hamilton who was requesting to set up an appointment with Carson Burnhart. Miss Hamilton told the secretary, when asked, that she along with legal counsel, Paul Conti for the Bronx Holding Company of New York, needed to speak with Mr. Burnhart about an existing loan by Nathan Fishman on the property The Burnhart Corp. was in the process of purchasing.

The secretary, Diana Moyer, said, "I'm sorry Miss Hamilton, but Mr. Burnhart is out of the office at the moment. If you will leave a number where you can be reached, I will inform him of your call."

"Yes dear and your name is?"

"Diana Moyer, I'm Mr. Burnhart's personal assistant."

"You can reach me at the Beverly Hills Hotel. You might mention that Bradford Gilman, a representative for Gino Vochelli is also staying at the hotel, and will be accompanying me and Paul Conti when we meet."

After a slight pause and a little shakiness in her voice, the secretary said, "Did you say Mr. Gilman is here on behalf of Mr. Vochelli?"

"Yes dear that is correct. Mr. Vochelli, being the primary share holder in the Bronx Holding Corp., has a personal interest in this matter. If you would Miss Moyer, please give this matter your full attention so it can be settled and we can return to New York as soon as possible."

"Yes Miss Hamilton, I will try to get hold of Mr. Burnhart immediately and call you back."

Once Reggie gave the woman her room number and was off the phone, she turned to Vito who was seated next to her and said, "Step one complete sir! She's going to get in touch with him right away. I could tell when I

207

mentioned Gino Vochelli, she was aware of who he is, so I don't suspect it will be too long before we receive a return call."

Vito smiled and said, "We'll see how long it takes for the fish to nibble at the bait Miss Volasko. He's not going to be an easy one to catch, but I'm counting on his greed to swallow the hook when he gets the idea and tastes the gold."

It took only fifteen minutes for the phone in Reggie's suite to ring. Smiling she answered, "Hello. Yes Miss Moyer. That will be fine. We will be there this afternoon at 2PM. Thank you."

Hanging up, Reggie smiled and told Vito, "The fish would like to meet with us at 2PM at his office, time to set the hook."

Vito, no longer smiling said, "Handle him very carefully Miss Volasko. Remember, he's a wise old fish who has been around this big pond for a long time avoiding capture."

After calling Paul Conti and Bradford Gilman, Reggie informed them of the meeting. Excusing herself, she told Vito, "It's time for me to put together my outfit for the meeting sir, something between a hooker and an heiress."

"Miss Volasko, although you are part of the bait, knowing of his desire to bed every beautiful woman he meets, please be very careful and don't go too far with him. Burnhart may come on like a gentleman, but he has a reputation for violence with women when he is rejected."

"Sir, I am aware of his violence toward women, and I will back away if it gets too rough."

"Okay Miss Volasko, good luck."

Once Vito left the room, Reggie called the front desk and said, "Roberto, this is Christina Hamilton in room 110."

With her registration information already changed, and Roberto taken care of financially, he answered, "Yes Miss Hamilton, how can I help you?"

"Roberto, I need a referral for a beauty shop near by where I can get in immediately without an appointment."

"That won't be necessary Miss Hamilton we have a beautician on site. I'll connect you if you like."

"Actually Roberto, it might be better if you call the beautician for me as a favor to Mr. Terratello. I need to get in immediately. It will be very rewarding to you both."

"I'll take care of it Miss Hamilton and have her call you right back."

"Thank you Roberto."

It took only five minutes before the phone rang. Reggie picked up and said, "Hello?"

"Miss Hamilton, this is Lila. I just received a call from Roberto and he told me you have an emergency, how can I help you?"

"Oh thank you Lila. I need a cut and color just as fast as you can do it."

Lila gave Reggie directions on how to get to her shop, and Reggie said, "I'm on my way, do you have coffee there?"

"Yes I do, get here quickly please. I have a full day today."

26

Through copies of records provided by Paul Conti, Carter was checking out previous owners of several large properties bought up by Carson Burnhart over the past twenty years. In most cases the previous owners were either deceased or had moved out of state which made it hard for Carter to contact them and question them about selling their properties.

Joan Unger, a sixty-seven year old firecracker, lived in the town of Acton, CA. The desert community that is mostly open land with large ranches accessible by poorly maintained dirt roads is located about forty-five miles north of the San Fernando Valley.

Mrs. Unger, who lived in a trailer on fifteen acres of dried out land five miles from the main highway, welcomed Carter after seeing the clouds of dust he kicked up with his car by standing on her makeshift wooden steps with a shotgun in her hands.

As Carter got out of his car, the woman yelled out to him, "I don't know who you are mister, but you can get back in your car and get the hell out of here."

Not moving towards the trailer, Carter yelled back, "Mrs. Unger, my name is Donald Carter and I would like to talk with you about the Burnhart Corporation. You know, the people who bought your property years ago out in Woodland Hills?"

"I got nothing to do with that property anymore mister, so just get back in your car and go away. Those people robbed me and my husband and then killed him. I can't prove it, but I know they killed him, now get out of here."

"Mrs. Unger, if you could just give me a little of your time, I think you can help me. I believe Burnhart is responsible for the deaths of many people and stealing their property. I just need a little help proving it so he can be prosecuted for it."

Now aiming her shotgun at the ground, the old woman said, "Well come on then, and let's talk, I got a whole barrel of information about that bastard."

The inside of the trailer looked more like a storage container, packed from floor to ceiling with stuff the woman must have been collecting for years. The smell of cat urine hung in the air like a heavy fog, and no matter how many pine tree branches the woman spread around, nothing could hide the stench.

Carter could see the cat litter box next to the stove, but there were no cats in sight, so he asked, "Is your cat in hiding ma'am?"

"I put Lula-Bell and Tinkle in the back room before I opened the door to see who was coming down my road. Now what is it that you want mister, tell me how I can help you get that old son-of-a-bitch."

Taking some papers out of his pocket, Carter said, "Back in the sixties, when you and Mr. Unger sold your property to Burnhart, did he pressure you in anyway?"

"Pressure mister? That bastard beat up our son, or at least he had someone else do it. When that didn't work, he had my husband followed everywhere he went. One night after my husband Walter had been playing cards with a few of his friends in Van Nuys, and of course drinking some, he got pulled over by a police car. They put him in handcuffs and took him to jail. I didn't know what happened to him for two days. I called the police but they told me they didn't know anything about him, and I should just wait for him to show up."

"They never let him make a call to let you know that he had been arrested?"

"No. On the third day, Walter was found dead in his car at the Sepulveda Basin with a bullet in his head. The police tried to convince me it was suicide, but I knew they were wrong. Walter had no reason to commit suicide. He was a happy man with a loving family. They killed him mister and it was covered up by the police, hell, the police were the ones who killed him."

"Things do change ma'am, people get depressed and do strange things."

"Mister, what you don't know is that there was a witness who saw the whole thing. He told me how they drugged my husband, drove his car to that deserted spot, and saw the killer put the gun in Walter's hand and pull the trigger."

"Didn't you go to the police and tell them what you knew?"

"Of course I did. They told me I was just a grieving widow who refused to believe the fact that he killed himself."

"What about the witness? Wouldn't he support what you were saying? Wouldn't he give his statement to the police?"

"You don't understand mister, he *was* the police."

"Are you telling me that your husband was killed by a police officer?"

"That's exactly what I'm telling you. The man was so guilt ridden he felt I had to know. Two weeks later he took his own life, but even that I question. I believe he was murdered also to keep from revealing the truth."

"Did you ever contact an attorney and tell him of your suspicions?"

"Yes I did, and I was told I had no chance of proving what I knew, but I told him I wanted to try anyway. One week later my son was beaten and left on the road leading into our farm in Woodland Hills. He was told that if I continued to pursue trying to prove that his father was murdered, the next beating would end in his death. A few days after that, someone came knocking on my door trying to buy our farm, and he told me he represented the Burnhart Corporation."

"But how can you connect the two together?"

"I got a phone call mister. I was told to sell my property to that Burnhart bastard or my son would have the same kind of accident as my poor Walter."

"Did you report *that* call to the police?"

"First I called the lawyer, and he told me that he would not represent me any longer, and that I should not contact him again for any reason. I thought about moving back to New York where my sister Gerti lives, but changed my mind."

"It sounds like they got to him too ma'am."

"Yep that's what I figured. So I sold the farm to that bastard, bought this piece of land out here, and gave my son a few thousand to put down on a place in Palmdale."

"And that was the last contact you had with Burnhart?"

"Yep, never heard from him again, and I hope it stays that way."

"Well ma'am, I hope that I can let you know some day that justice has been served."

"My poor Walter never did anything to hurt anybody, and I only hope that the people who killed him pay for it."

As Carter headed for the door he said, "If all goes right Mrs. Unger, Burnhart will pay for all that he has done."

Driving away from the trailer, Carter couldn't help feeling bad for the woman, and hoped that he could return one day and give her some news that would make her feel like her Walter got his justice.

27

At exactly 2PM Christina Hamilton, Paul Conti, Bradford Gilman and Danny Russo walked into the corporate offices of the Burnhart Corporation in Los Angeles and were met by Miss Moyer. The long beautiful flowing strawberry-blond hair of Reggie Volasko was now a very short cropped jet black French cut with matching black eye brows, set off with contrasting bright red lipstick.

Miss Moyer said, "If you will all please follow me to the conference room, I will inform Mr. Burnhart of your arrival. If you would like refreshments, there are fresh coffee and other beverages available. Mr. Burnhart will be joining you momentarily.

Approximately five minutes after they were seated, Carson Burnhart entered the room followed by two other gentlemen who were introduced as attorneys representing the Burnhart Corporation. Everyone stood and shook hands and when it came to Miss Hamilton, Burnhart took her hand in his, held it to his lips and tenderly kissed it saying, "Who may I ask is this vision of loveliness?"

With a very seductive smile Reggie said, "Christina Hamilton, Mr. Burnhart, very nice to finally meet you sir."

"Please, Miss Hamilton, I don't believe I have ever met a more beautiful woman in my life. I would be honored if you would call me Carson and may I call you Christina?"

Slowly sitting back down exposing a generous portion of her inner thighs as she crossed her legs, Reggie said, "Why Carson, I do believe you're flirting with me?"

"My dear Christina, how could I help from doing anything else when I'm exposed to such beauty?

Sitting down at the far end of the long table, Carson Burnhart said, "What do I owe the pleasure of this meeting to?"

Bradford Gilman stood and said, "First may I say thank you for taking this meeting on such short notice Mr. Burnhart. Gino Vochelli sends his regards."

Burnhart asked, "How is my dear friend Gino doing these days?"

"Actually Mr. Burnhart, Mr. Vochelli is a little concerned as to what has transpired lately. At the center of his concern is a large parcel of land that the Burnhart Corporation is in the process of purchasing in the West Valley."

First looking to his legal advisors who had no idea as to what was going on, Burnhart asked, "I'm sorry Mr. Gilman, but you'll have to be more exacting as to which property you're talking about. We are at this time involved in the purchasing of several large parcels of land in the West Valley."

"The property in question sir is the large parcel owned by the late Nathan Fishman. The Bronx Holding and Loan Corp. of New York currently holds the mortgage on that property with a substantial amount of money still due before any sale could be approved."

"Mr. Gilman, my inquisitive nature has me asking first, what concern of my purchasing this property is it to Mr. Vochelli?"

"Well sir, Mr. Vochelli, being the major stock holder in Bronx Holding, has taken a personal interest in these proceedings because of his relationship with you."

Removing copies of all the transactions involving the Fishman properties, Bradford Gilman passed them to the lawyers and Burnhart. After studying them briefly for a couple of minutes, Burnhart said, "This is ridiculous! The property in question had a clean title." Looking at one of his attorneys, Burnhart said, "Isn't that correct Stewart?"

Millburn Stewart, a long time associate and legal advisor for The Burnhart Corp., continued studying the documents and said, "These documents look to be in order, but I will need additional time to check their validity. I will need a couple of days to check them out with the County Recorder."

Gilman removed additional documents from his briefcase and placed them on the table in front him. Before he said anything further, Christina Hamilton said, "Carson, while your people are checking out the documents, I want to present you with a proposal straight from Mr. Vochelli, but if you don't mind I would like that we speak in private, before any of it is placed on the table."

Standing up, Burnhart said, "Gentlemen, while you discuss the possible ways to resolve this problem, Miss Hamilton and I will visit my office so we can speak in private. We will return shortly, please do not disturb us. Miss Hamilton, if you would please join me in my office?"

Leaving the table, Miss Hamilton picked up the papers in front of Mr. Gilman and followed Burnhart to his office. As they passed through the front office, Burnhart instructed his secretary, "Miss Moyer, no phone calls please. I do not wish to be disturbed. For any reason Miss Moyer."

With a look on her face, as if she had just finished sucking on a very tart lemon, Miss. Moyer said, "But sir, you have another appointment in a half-hour with Mark Warren."

"Please get hold of Mr. Warren and have him come in later in the day." Looking at Miss Hamilton and smiling he continued, "I think my next couple of hours will be occupied."

Miss Moyer said, "But sir."

"Later in the day Miss Moyer, thank you."

Leading the way to his office, Burnhart opened the door and said, "This way Miss Hamilton."

Burnhart pointed at a group of deep cushioned chairs in front of a large picture window as they entered his office and asked, "Would you please join me in a drink Christina?"

With a coy smile she answered, "Scotch neat would be a welcome treat."

Fixing the drinks and handing one to her, Burnhart sat in a chair across from her and asked, "Okay Christina, you have the floor, what's on your mind?"

Handing Burnhart a copy of the gold report, Christina said, "This is a copy of a transaction that Nathan Fishman worked out with The Bronx Holding and Loan Corp. several months before he became ill. As bizarre as it seems it was the sole idea of the late Mr. Fishman. The bank transaction funds have been frozen and will be returned to the holding company once the sale of the property is finalized."

Burnhart calmly said, "But my dear Christina, the sale has been finalized. My company purchased the property from Mr. Fishman's widow one month ago."

"Carson, as of 8AM this morning, that sale has been frozen and will be nullified if we cannot reach an agreement today. Your legal eagles can verify what I have just told you and I'm sure they will, once they do some additional checking."

"So Christina, what is it that Gino Vochelli proposes and in a nut shell, what has gold got to do with all of this?

"Here it is in a nutshell Carson. Five million dollars in gold was delivered to the property in question. Nathan Fishman purchased the gold but no one knows what that eccentric old fool did with it."

"Does Gino think the old man buried it on the property?"

"No one knows for sure. Putting all the cards on the table Carson, Mr. Vochelli is aware of the 5.5 acres of adjacent property that was being included in the sale of the Fishman property. As far as he is concerned, that attachment is between you and your people, and does not have to be disclosed. The gold however, is something that must be dealt with."

"Christina, please believe me, I have no knowledge of any gold or its whereabouts. This whole story sounds like a foolish tale and I'm surprised that Gino Vochelli could be hood-winked in this way."

"Mr. Vochelli thought you might have some doubt as to the reliability of the documents, but as you'll notice, they have all been notarized and recorded. I have been authorized to present you with a proposition. You may reject it if you choose, in which case the property in question along with the extra acreage will be immediately taken over by the Bronx Holding Corp., or the amount of the lien can be either paid in full, or it can be assumed by your corporation."

"Christina, you're not trying to pressure me in anyway are you?"

"I'm just the messenger Carson, with a lucrative solution to a very severe problem. Mr. Vochelli does not pressure people as you well know, he solves problems."

"Okay Christina, let me hear Gino's proposition to a solution to this glitch we seem to have."

"First Carson, as of the opening of the stock market this morning, the price of gold has gone up since Fishman's transaction by five percent. That means the five million has increased in value by two hundred and fifty thousand dollars, and by the looks of it, gold will continue to rise in value. Mr. Vochelli is making you a one time offer. You will transfer two million five hundred thousand dollars to the Bronx Holding Corp. and in exchange you will receive full title to the property in question."

"Why may I ask, Christina, would a smart businessman like Gino Vochelli, settle for half of what is owed him and not go after the whole pie?"

"That Carson is something Mr. Vochelli will discuss in private with you at your earliest convenience. I might suggest you call him after our meeting today."

"This entire proposition seems a little far fetched to me, and not something I would be interested in."

"I have been instructed to tell you, if you choose not to cooperate and decide on another direction, the Bronx Holding Corp. will assume full ownership to the property, break it up into smaller parcels, start excavation and begin the search for the gold."

Laughing, Burnhart asked, "You mean to tell me that Gino Vochelli will have his people searching for gold on my property?"

"Your property Carson? You don't own that property. It legally belongs to The Bronx Holding Corp. and they will take possession at the close of the business day tomorrow. So Carson, you have a big decision to make."

"Christina, that property has been bought and paid for and Mrs. Fishman has already received partial payment for that land."

"Please Carson, Mr. Vochelli is well aware that Mrs. Fishman is your sister, and that no money has changed hands with the sale of the property, but that is between you and your sister.

"That's ridiculous!"

Opening a note held in her hand, Miss Hamilton read, "Carson, or should I say, Crouse Wilhelm Braumholtz, I am aware that the paperwork that has recorded a change in ownership of the Holtz Farms in Napa Valley is a complete forgery. If you question my knowledge on this matter, please contact me personally and we can discuss it in depth."

Looking up Christina continued, "The note is signed by Gino Vochelli. Again Carson, I am only the messenger and I have no feelings either way about your decision. I can only recommend that you personally contact Mr. Vochelli."

With a new look of concern on his face, Burnhart asked, "When do you need my decision on this Christina?"

"May I suggest you talk things over with your legal advisors? Then I would call Mr. Vochelli."

Gazing slowly around the room with his focus finally coming to rest on a pair of beautiful crossed legs in front of him, Burnhart asked, "May I ask if you have plans for dinner tonight?"

"If you like Carson, we can possibly find time for dinner tonight, and maybe you can show me the sights, or if that is not an option, we can talk tomorrow morning."

With a smile now on his face, Burnhart said, "Why Christina, I believe you are now flirting with me?"

"There's an old saying Carson, what goes around comes around. I think it's time for us to join the others and end this wonderful meeting of the minds."

"When we go out, I will check with my secretary on my appointments for the next couple of days to see if we can spend a little more time discussing my options."

Burnhart found that his evening was free and he would be able to take Christina to dinner, but his calendar for the next two days was full.

Returning to the conference room, Burnhart asked, "Have you been able to do any checking Stewart?"

"No sir, but Mr. Gilman and I have been able to work out a time line for postponing any foreclosure on the property in question if it is satisfactory with you and Mr. Vochelli. I have pointed out that I will require at least a couple of days to research all of the new information before us."

Burnhart pushed a button on the intercom in front of him and said, "Miss Moyer, would you come in here please and bring a list of my appointments for the next few days."

Looking at the others in the room, Burnhart said, "Gentlemen, and Miss Hamilton, if possible we may be able to work everything out as soon as I speak with Gino Vochelli. For now I need to check my calendar for a time when we can meet again."

As the secretary came in, Burnhart asked, "Miss Moyer, What are my obligations for tomorrow?"

"Well sir, you have to attend a luncheon at the Bonaventure Hotel tomorrow in your honor. It is for your support and contributions to the homeless shelter. You have a dinner engagement with the Mayor and Councilman Miller tomorrow evening. You are supposed to be discussing the possible signing of the contract to build the battered women's shelter in the West Valley on your donated property."

Burnhart asked, "And the following day Miss Moyer?"

"That would be Wednesday, you have appointments through the morning and part of the afternoon, but you are free in the evening."

Looking at Christina, Burnhart said, "Christina, perhaps we could have our dinner engagement on Wednesday. I will call you personally and confirm."

"That should be fine Carson."

"Speaking to the others, Burnhart said, "Gentlemen, if you would be so kind to leave your contact information with Miss Moyer, I will contact you as soon as I speak with Gino Vochelli. I think that should do it for today?"

As Bradford Gilman stood he offered his hand and said, "Mr. Burnhart it has been a real pleasure and I look forward to our next meeting."

Burnhart looked at Milburn Stewart and said, "Stewart, if you and Mr. Howard would join me in my office we have some very important issues to deal with."

Taking Christina's hand in his and kissing it gently, Burnhart said, "Until Wednesday then?"

"Fine, I look forward to it, Carson."

Watching Burnhart and his advisors leave the room, Bradford Gilman glanced at Christina and nodded his head slightly."

Exiting the conference room and walking through the outer office past the secretary's desk, Christina paid little attention to the man seated reading a magazine and watching her as she walked by.

Mark Warren, the head foreman for the Burnhart Corporation asked as the door closed behind the visitors, "What was that all about Diana?"

Diana Moyer said, "It's none of your business Mark, but they're some people from the east coast who had a meeting with Mr. Burnhart."

Looking again at the closed door, Mark Warren scratched his head and said, "I swear I know that woman from somewhere."

"Well, I don't know how Mark, she and the others just arrived here yesterday from New York."

"I'll place her in time Diana. Is the boss ready for me yet?"

"I'll let him know you're here Mark."

28

Carter sat in his office with his feet crossed and propped up on a chair next to the desk, staring off into the corner of the room.

When Mick walked in and sat on the couch across from him, Carter asked, "So what's on your mind Mickey T.?"

"You hear anything from Reggie, Donny Boy?"

"So far nothing Mick, I hope she hasn't stuck her neck out too far, that Burnhart is dangerous."

"What about Jimmy Hudson, any word from him?"

"Not since he called me about some screw up with his social security number that was being questioned by the payroll people at the construction company."

"I'll tell you what boss. I'll give my uncle a call tonight and see if there's any news on Reggie."

"Did you find out anything more from your connections downtown Mick?"

"Yeah, but I don't think it's anything new. Burnhart is one dirty bastard. Just the mention of his name closes doors and shuts mouths real quick. Although none of it can be proved, this guy seems to leave dead bodies in his wake. He has weaved a group of high ranking people together and seems to get cooperation for anything he wants passed, like approval for building plans and financing when needed."

"That fits right in with what I learned from talking with a woman out in Acton. She told me her husband was killed because he refused to sell their property to Burnhart years ago. Her son was almost beaten to death before she gave up and sold the property. Get this. She's positive the police were behind the death of her husband and when she hired a lawyer to help her prove it, someone must have intimidated the poor bastard and he quit."

"You got some connections with the boys in blue. Maybe you need to make a few calls Donny Boy?"

"That sounds like a good idea Mick. I'm going to try getting hold of Hudson and see what he can find out if he's still working with that construction crew. Also, I'm going to call Croft at LAPD and put a bug in his ear. The guy may be an asshole, but I always thought of him as an honest cop. How about meeting me at Rusty's Hacienda tonight for a few drinks and we can talk a little more after we get more information."

"Drinks, are you going to start that shit again?

"You drink the hard shit and I'll drink club soda, okay buddy?"

"Okay Donny Boy. Oh by the way, where's that little sweet pea Annie? I didn't see her in the outer office."

"I told her to take a few days off while all this crap is going on. She'll be back next week after she visits her mother in Arizona."

"So what time do you want to meet at Rusty's, boss?"

"It's four now, how about I meet you there at eight, that'll give us a few hours to dig a little?"

Carter stayed at his office a couple hours longer making phone calls and going over notes and information he had gathered on Burnhart. The phone call to Detective Croft at LAPD was like a roadblock. When Carter questioned the death of Walter Unger he was met with attitude and denial. When asked about Burnhart's involvement with any other crimes, Carter was told, "Accusations like that could get you in a lot of hot water Carter."

"Hey Croft, I'm not accusing him of anything, I'm just asking for some information."

"Yeah, I get that Carter, but this ain't no information bureau." Just that quick, the call was over.

The hang up made Carter pull the phone away from his ear and say "Asshole!"

The phone call to Jimmy Hudson's home wasn't answered, so Carter figured he would call him later in the evening.

Carter's final call was to Vito Terratello's suite and was answered by Mick's cousin, Danny Russo. Danny told him, "Dad is having dinner with an old friend, but I'll have him give you a call if you leave me your number Mr. Carter."

Carter asked, "Danny, do you have any information about Reggie?"

"I know that she has dinner plans with that Burnhart guy for Wednesday night. I don't know where they were going but I do know that she is supposed to meet dad when she gets back to the hotel after dinner."

"Danny. It won't be possible for Vito to get in touch with me tonight. I'll call back later. I don't know why, but my cell phone crapped out on me. Let Vito know I called."

Locking up the office, Carter was down the stairs and starting his car getting ready to leave when the phone in his office rang twenty times with no one there to take the call. In his clouded state of mind, Carter forgot to turn on the answering machine.

Rather than driving home, Carter decided to take a walk around the block onto Lankershim Blvd. and try to clear his head. It had been a long time since Carter walked anywhere and though his leg had healed quite fast, there was a little soreness.

Stopping a couple times to rest, he looked through store windows of thrift shops, clothing stores and even a Japanese restaurant. Walking past the Magnolia Bar, Carter sniffed at the smell of stale beer and cigar smoke drifting out of the open door. Stopping to look in at the half-filled barstools, and hearing the music blaring in the background, he shook his head, smiled, and then continued walking.

One more block of looking into storefronts and then he turned and headed back towards the office. Getting closer to the bar, Carter slowed his pace and when he reached the bar he went in and sat on the first empty stool he came to. When the bartender came over Carter said, "Just a club soda."

Sitting there sipping on his club soda for a few minutes, Carter called the bartender over and said, "How about throwing a couple shots of Jack Daniels in there buddy."

Three hours later, after shooting many games of pool, talking with whoever would listen, and drinking five or six doubles of Jack and club soda, Carter with a slight stagger made his way back to his office. Once back in the office resting his eyes, he lay on the couch and didn't move until his phone rang and startled him awake.

Answering, Carter said, "Yeah who is it?"

"It's me Donny Boy, what happened, you forget about our meeting?"

"What time is it Mick?"

"Almost nine Donny Boy, are you okay, you don't sound so good?"

"Just tired Mick, I'll be there in about fifteen minutes."

29

Mick was sitting at the bar talking with the bartender at Rusty's Hacienda at 9PM when Carter walked in and tapped him on the shoulder. As he turned in his seat, Carter asked, "Whatcha drinking Mick?"

Pointing at a secluded table in the back corner of the room, Mick said, "We need to talk right away boss."

Without any questions, both men walked to the table and sat down. Carter asked, "What's up?"

Looking at Carter in the dim light, Mick asked, "You alright Donny Boy, because you look like shit and you weren't walking to good either?"

Trying to keep his head from shaking and bobbing, Carter said, "Never mind what I look like. What have you found out?"

"I went to visit my uncle tonight before I came here and he gave me some news. After Reggie, Brad Gilman and Paul Conti went to see Burnhart this afternoon Burnhart got on the phone and made some calls back east, which was expected. He next spoke with Gino Vochelli who went right along with the set up. He questioned all the information he had been fed, and then told Mr. Vochelli that before he laid out one nickel, he needed more proof of the existence of the gold. Mr. Vochelli told him that he would be arriving at LAX the next morning, and if necessary he would provide him with additional documents about the existence of the gold.

Uncle Vito told me he didn't like the way everything was playing out and it might be a good idea to scrap the whole plan."

"Where is Reggie now Mick?"

"Reggie's staying around the hotel playing the Christina Hamilton role and not making any contact with anyone."

"So I can't call her to find out how she's handling things?"

"No contact Donny Boy, that's Vito's orders. She'll call you when she finishes up with Burnhart in a few days."

"I heard she's going out to dinner with Burnhart tomorrow night or the next night?"

The waitress came over to the table and asked, "What can I get you gents?"

Before Mick could answer, Carter said, "Yeah hon, give me a club soda with a double shot of Jack in it."

Mick looked at Carter and said, "You sure Donny Boy?"

Carter blasted back, "What are you, my mother? Yeah I'm sure."

Mick held up his hands in front of him in a stopping motion and said, "Whoa, Carter, what's going on?"

Carter knew he crossed the line, because Mick never called him Carter, so after a few seconds he said, "Mick, I'm sorry. My mind is on Reggie, it's been on her ever since I heard about her going anywhere near Burnhart."

"So you had a couple too many today already?"

"Actually Mick, I had about a half-dozen too many today. I thought I had it under control, but I need to check on getting some help. Maybe AA isn't such a bad idea. I don't know. I just know I can't do it on my own."

"Hey Donny Boy, what ever you need from me, or what ever I can do to help, just say the word and I'm right there with you. If you decide on AA, I'll even go to meetings with you if you think it will help. As far as Reggie goes, trust her, you know she's tough and smart, give her the space she needs to do her job."

The meeting with Mick only accomplished one thing for Carter. That was the fact that his drinking was causing him a big problem and he needed to seek help.

Refusing to let Carter drive himself home, Mick said, "Let me give you a ride home Donny Boy and tomorrow morning I'll pick you up. We can go out for a good breakfast, pick up your car, and go check out one of these AA places. I've heard a lot about AA. Those people ain't no wimps."

When the waitress came back to the table with Carter's drink, he handed her a five dollar bill and said, "Dump it sweetheart, I changed my mind."

30

On Wednesday afternoon, Reggie met with Vito Terratello and Gino Vochelli. Mr. Vochelli had flown into LA the morning before so they could discuss possible situations that might come up at Reggie's dinner engagement with Burnhart. After going over every detail, it was all systems go. Christina Hamilton had received a message from Burnhart's assistant informing her that Mr. Burnhart's chauffeur would be there at 5pm to pick her up. Burnhart was in a meeting with the mayor, but by the time she arrived back at his office, his business would have been concluded and she would be able to be introduced to his honor the mayor.

At 5pm exactly, Miss Hamilton was notified that Mr. Burnhart's limo was out in front of the hotel to pick her up. When she walked outside she saw the limo with its back door open and the chauffeur said, "Good evening Miss Hamilton."

As she bent to enter the vehicle she heard from inside, "Hello Christina, at the last minute my plans were changed and I thought I would surprise you."

Smiling she said, "What a pleasant surprise, Carson."

The Palms Restaurant in Los Angeles for many years has been known for its excellent food and being regularly frequented by celebrities. When Carson Burnhart walked through the front door with Christina at his side, he was immediately greeted and escorted to one of the private tables reserved for special clientele.

After a warm welcome by the owner of the establishment and a complimentary bottle of a very expensive wine, Burnhart took it on his own to order a complete lobster and steak dinner, the specialty of the house, for both of them.

As they sat enjoying their wine, Burnhart in his own sneaky way, questioned Christina about her past, trying to find out as much as possible about his beautiful dinner companion.

With a carefully rehearsed story of her past, Christina fed her over-curious and pompous dinner host a full load of crap about her exclusive employment for Gino Vochelli, and the Bronx Holding Corp.

Approximately one hour into their dinner date, Burnhart was informed by the waiter that there was an important call for him. Like for many of the VIP's who dined at the restaurant, a phone was brought to the table and plugged into a jack in the wall.

At first, Burnhart said, "Please tell the caller I don't want to be disturbed," but then said, "Wait a minute, I'll take it."

Not even asking who was calling, Burnhart said, "This better be important."

Burnhart's responses were short and quick. "Yes! Aha! Yes! Okay! Is that so? Well, that's very interesting. And you're absolutely sure? Okay, you know what to do then. Yes. We should be leaving here within the next hour. Yes! I'll see you then. Yes. Goodbye."

Calling the waiter over to remove the phone, Burnhart then stared at Christina a few seconds and said, "I'm sorry for the interruption my dear, but I just received some very interesting news that I will have to act on after our dinner date tonight."

Christina asked, "I hope it's nothing too serious, Carson?"

"Actually my dear, I think it's something that was caught just in time to avoid a bigger problem and will be handled swiftly. Fortunately, I have good people working for me who are very proficient in what they do. It's nothing you should be worried about my dear. Let's just enjoy the rest of our evening together and let nature take its course."

As coffee and dessert were being served, Burnhart's chauffeur came into the restaurant and walked over to the table and whispered a short message in his ear. Smiling slightly, Burnhart said, "thank you Hans, we will be leaving shortly. Go ahead and pull the car around front."

Ten minutes more passed before Burnhart and Christina exited the restaurant and walked to the limo parked at the curb. Once seated and the driver back behind the wheel, Burnhart instructed him, "Hans, we'll be making one quick stop before returning Miss Hamilton to her hotel."

Turning to Christina, Burnhart said, "I hope that's okay with you my dear?"

"No problem Carson, I'm in no rush."

The driver asked, "Yes Sir, and our destination is?"

"I need to drop something off at our Pico warehouse, Hans. Someone will be waiting there to open the gate when we arrive."

"Yes Sir."

Turning to Christina, Burnhart said, "I'm sorry for the inconvenience my dear, it will only be a small detour."

Traffic being rather light at that time of the evening, it took only twenty minutes to arrive at the warehouse owned by Burnhart in the Pico Rivera area. As they approached the large fenced-in lot in front of the building, the gate was opened by a man who had been standing next to it. Once the gate was fully opened, the limo drove in and pulled up in front of a large twelve foot high metal door.

Within seconds, the door started to rise up and when it was fully opened, the limo pulled in. Hearing the door behind them close, Christina had an uneasy feeling that something was very wrong but kept her composure. Turning off the engine, Hans stepped out of the limo and opened the rear door on Burnhart's side of the vehicle.

Offering his hand to Christina, Burnhart said, "Would you please join me Miss Hamilton, or should I say, Miss Volasko?"

Getting out of the vehicle slowly, Christina said, "Carson, I have no idea what you're talking about."

"You will soon Miss Volasko. It is Regina, am I correct?"

Reggie stood in silence, knowing she was in deep trouble.

31

The sun was just coming up when Carter heard his dog Brandy barking in the backyard so he knew it was time for him to get up and see what had the pooch's attention. Moving slowly, Carter walked to the window and saw his neighbor walking past the side of the house with his shepherd on a leash. Carter whistled and Brandy ran to the doggy-door in the kitchen and then came charging up the stairs to Carter's bedroom.

After a quick stop in the bathroom, Carter made his way down to the kitchen to get some coffee brewing before he went out to the front porch and retrieve the morning newspaper.

He had just poured his coffee and was about to open the paper when the phone rang. Answering in his early morning mode, Carter said, "Yeah, hello."

"Hey Donny Boy, it's Mick, we got trouble."

Carter said, "Yeah good morning to you too. What kind of trouble?"

"Reggie's missing."

"Ah shit Mick. What do you mean she's missing?"

"The last time she was seen was when she was picked up at the hotel by Burnhart's chauffeur around five, for their dinner date and meeting."

"Do you have any idea where they went?"

"No boss only that they were going out for dinner."

"What about Vito, what's he doing about this screw up?"

"He made a couple of calls late last night and was trying to locate Burnhart and Reggie."

Carter took a sip of his coffee and just stared off to the side and said, "Son of a bitch. I was worried about something like this happening."

Trying to ease the tension, Mick said, "Uncle Vito has people watching at

Burnhart's home and office. He's called in some favors with people connected to the LAPD and they're on the lookout for the limo. He told me to tell you that he will contact you as soon as he hears something about Reggie. By the way, you forgot to turn on your answering machine at the office."

"Mick, have you heard from Jimmy Hudson?"

"Not a word. I tried calling him at home last night a few times but no answer."

Getting up from the table, Carter said, "Meet me back at the office in about an hour Mick. I'm going to make one quick stop by Hudson's house and then pick up something to eat. I'll get you something too; it's going to be a long day."

"What are you going to get?"

"I'll find something. Don't worry about it."

Sitting in his rental car parked in the driveway in front of the locked gate at Carter's office, Mick had been sitting listening to Moody Blues on the radio waiting for Carter to show up. Being Sunday morning, the repair shop was closed and the neighborhood appeared deserted, with very few cars driving by the little side street where the driveway was located. Carter flashed his headlights as he approached; pulling up behind Mick's car, then got out and opened the gate.

After Mick drove in, Carter followed and parked by the metal steps. Walking back to the gate he closed and locked it again. As he retrieved the bags of food and a small tray holding two coffees from his car, he walked to the steps where Mick was seated and said, "Anything new on Reggie?"

"Nothing new so far, I'll try calling my uncle again when we get upstairs."

"That fucking Burnhart, I knew this was risky Mick."

Mick asked, "So what are we dining on this morning boss?"

"Take a whiff Mick and you tell me."

Getting closer so he could take a good sniff and see the logo on the bags, Mick said with a laugh, "Hot dogs, since when is hot dogs a breakfast food?"

Continuing to walk up the metal stairs, Carter said, "What did you expect? Steak and eggs? I went to Wienerschnitzel. You got your choice, mustard and kraut or chili and cheese."

"I think I may take a pass on both boss. Hey, don't forget to turn on your answer machine before you forget again. No one might think of calling here on a Sunday, but at least after we leave there will be a way of someone leaving a message. What happened to that new cell phone you got?"

"It's a piece of shit. The damn thing has a problem with reception, so I put it in my desk drawer."

"Well turn on the machine before we leave."

"Leave, whose leaving? I'm staying here until we find out Reggie's safe."

Sitting down at the desk, Carter tore open one of the bags with hot dogs and asked, "Sure you don't want any Mick?"

"Oh what the hell, give me a chili dog, I hope that's coffee you got for drinks?"

"Yeah its coffee, here, take two dogs. They're small."

Two hours later, all eight hot dogs consumed and many hands of poker played, Carter announced, "I got to take a dump Mick, try calling Vito again, will yah?"

A few minutes after Carter went into the bathroom, the phone started ringing. On the second ring Mick picked it up and said, "Carter Security can I help you?"

"Michael, is that you, its Vito."

"Yes Uncle Vito, do you have any news?"

"Is Donald also there Michael?"

"Yes he is uncle, give me a minute and I'll get him."

Knocking on the bathroom door, Mick said, "Donny Boy, my uncle is on the phone and wants to talk with you."

Carter called out, "I'll be there in a minute Mick."

When Carter came out of the bathroom and picked up the receiver he said, "Yes Vito, I'm here. Thank you for calling back."

"Donald I wish I had good news for you, but the truth is at this minute I have no idea where Miss Volasko is. She and Burnhart had dinner last night at the Palms Restaurant on Santa Monica Blvd. They left there a little before 9PM. My informant tells me that they left in Burnhart's limo and that was the last time they were seen."

"Vito, has Burnhart returned to his home or one of his offices?"

"No Donald, I'm having each of those places watched and if he shows up I will be called no matter what time."

"Vito, either Mick or I will be here at my office, please call if you hear anything."

"Get some rest Donald, I promise I will call you as soon as I hear something."

"Thank you Vito."

After Carter explained everything to Mick, he told him, "It doesn't do any good for both of us to be here. Why don't you take off and see if you can find Jimbo and give me a call later. If I hear from Vito I'll call your house and leave a message if you're not home yet. Meanwhile, see if you can find out anything about where they disappeared to."

Tossing Mick his spare keys from his desk drawer, Carter said, "Here, you'll need these to get out, I'll see you later."

"Hey Donny Boy, Don't worry about Reggie, she knows how to take care of herself."

"Thanks Mick, I know she does, but that bastard Burnhart is a violent, unpredictable asshole who has no respect for women."

32

It took only a half-hour after Mick left before Carter was snoring up a storm on the couch. Not being able to sleep each night more than a couple hours, it finally caught up to the mighty Carter with the quiet of his office, along with the comfortable feel of the old leather couch he was enjoying. He finally got a few needed winks, until the phone rang twice and then quit.

Slowly getting up from the couch, Carter shuffled his feet as he made his way to the bathroom to first relieve his kidneys and then to splash cold water on his face. Reaching into the medicine cabinet, Carter searched for the aspirin bottle and then turned on the cold water tap in the sink for a cup of water.

Brushing back his hair as he looked into the mirror, he stopped when he heard the phone ring again but decided to let the answering machine get it.

As he listened he heard, "Mr. Carter, it's Annie. I was just calling to see how everything was going around there."

Picking up the receiver Cater said, "Hi sweetheart, I'm here."

"I'm surprised you're at the office Mr. Carter, but I tried to call you at your house first and I was worried."

"Actually Annie I was asleep on the couch when you called. What's up, how's your vacation going?"

"Well I just wanted to find out how things were going around the office and see if you needed me to come back."

"No Annie, you just enjoy yourself and I'll call when it's time for you to return."

While still holding the receiver Carter heard a loud knocking on the outer office door and told Annie, "Someone's at the door sweetheart. Got to go. Bye."

As he was walking to the door the knocking continued, "Okay, okay I'm coming."

Opening the door to the steps, Carter was face to face with Det. Croft. "Sleeping in late this morning Carter, it's the afternoon for Christ-sake?"

"Yeah Croft, what the hell do you want? What time is it anyway?"

Looking at his watch, Croft said, "Its 3:20 sleeping beauty."

"So why are you here Croft?"

"You tell me Carter. I got a call from my captain at 8AM waking my ass out of bed on my day off, telling me I need to check on the disappearance of some woman named Christina Hamilton. When I asked who this Miss Hamilton is, he told me to pay a visit to you. Now what the hell's going on Carter?"

"Come on in Croft and have a seat, and I'll try to fill in some of the blanks. Just give me a few minutes to make some coffee first."

As Carter started making coffee, Croft asked, "Who is this guy Vito Terratello and how the hell does he come off calling my captain and making him jump through hoops? He's got to be related in some way to that friend of yours, Mick, Michael, whatever the hell it is?"

"Croft, I don't know what the hell is going on with the disappearance of Miss Hamilton, just that she vanished. As for, Mr. Terratello.

257

He is a man of power who has friends in high places. He doesn't push his power around or in your face, and I think that's why people respect him so much. Also, he's Mick's uncle from back east. What else do you need to know Croft?"

"Yeah I get it Carter. He's some wop mob boss who's a nice guy. Now, fill me in on what's going on."

Spending the next half hour explaining to Croft the connection Burnhart had to the deaths of a half dozen people, Carter got to the disappearance of Christina Hamilton, when Croft said, "Yeah, yeah, but can you prove any of this shit you're accusing him of?"

"Croft, this guy Burnhart is so dirty and has been responsible….."

"Yeah Carter, but can you *prove* any of it?"

"I'm working on it Croft."

Standing up Det. Croft said, "Look Carter, I'm here because my captain sent my ass here. If you get proof on Burnhart, call me. Until then, I'd be careful about what you're accusing that man of."

"So that's it Croft? You're not going to question him about Reggie?"

"Whoa! Who the hell is Reggie?"

"Sorry Croft, my mistake. Miss Hamilton and Miss Reggie Volasko are one and the same."

"Volasko? Weren't you involved with some dame named Regina Volasko a few years back involving some Russians?"

With a stare that could have melted a hundred pound block of ice, Carter said, "Yeah, same person Croft. You have a problem with that?"

"So let me get this straight Carter. This Reggie is involved in some type of scam and gets her ass in a real jam. So what! You call this mafia 'Don' to throw some of his power around, and he gets my captain to jump through hoops and rescue your girlfriend?"

"You know what? Fuck you Croft! Get the hell out of my office. I thought you had some brains, but you're just an asshole with a badge. I'll be sure and pass it on that you were such a big help. Now get the hell out."

Walking to the door Croft stopped and said, "I'll tell you what wise guy. When I leave here, I'll go and question Burnhart, and if something doesn't smell right I'll stay on his ass. How does that sound? Will that put a smile on your face?"

Carter didn't answer, but Croft got the message from the dead look on his face.

Staring at the empty doorway, and listening as the crotchety old detective walked down the outside steps, he was startled by the phone ringing right in front of him.

Picking up the receiver Carter said, "Carter Security, can I help you?"

The wise remark came back from Mick, "I don't know. Can you help me?"

Carter let out a heavy breath and said, "Hey Mick, where you at?"

"I'm at Sitton's Diner. You want some lunch?"

"Nah, stay there. I'll be there in about five minutes."

"You want me to order something for you?"

"Just coffee Mick. My stomach is doing flip flops."

"Hey boss, some real food instead of hot dogs might help settle everything down. Hurry up and I'll save you a seat before they're all taken."

Carter changed his mind once he got to the diner and had an egg sandwich and one pancake with his coffee. As he ate, they put together a plan for the rest of the day.

When Carter told him about Croft and his reluctance at first to do anything, Mick said,

"That guy can be a real ass wipe, at times. But I can see his point boss."

Surprised Carter said, "Oh, you sticking up for him now?"

"Let's see what he does first. Then I'll tell you what I really think of him."

"I don't expect too much from him or the police Mick."

33

Getting back to the office, Carter picked up a magazine and headed for the bathroom, as Mick sat at the desk and put his feet up, picking his teeth with a tooth pick. A few minutes went by and the phone started ringing. Noticing that Carter forgot again to turn on the answering machine, he picked up the receiver and said, "Carter Security, may I help you?"

The caller said, "Mick, it's Jimmy. Where the hell is Carter? I've been calling and calling but there's no one there to answer the damn phone."

"He's in the reading room catching up on the new copy of Detective Monthly. What have you been up to Jimbo?"

"Well, tell him to wipe his ass with it and get out quick, because I need to talk with him right away."

Mick yelled out, "Hey boss, it's Hudson on the phone. He says he needs to talk with you now. Wipe it and get out here quick."

The bathroom door swung open and Carter hustled over and sat down at the desk. Grabbing the receiver from Mick he said. "Yeah Jimmy, I've been waiting to hear from you, what's up?"

"Where the hell have you been Carter. I've been trying to get hold of you for the past two days?"

"Lot of shit going on around here Jimmy. Now what have you got for me?"

"Well first of all, I'm not in the Valley. I'm in fucking Pico Rivera. That foreman called me into his office yesterday and told me he didn't know what kind of shit I was pulling with the fake social security number. I made up a story that I had a lot of trouble in my past and I didn't want certain people to locate me."

"Do you think he bought it Jimmy?"

"Hell, after he stopped laughing he said, "Black man, I have a special job for you."

Next thing I know I'm in a van with two other guys picking up a few things at my place, and then driving to some industrial park in Pico Rivera. From what I gather, my new job is going to be part of their security force or the house nigger. With all these Germans around me, I don't know what is going on in their heads. Hell, I'm going to be a fucking live-in guard I think. This warehouse is filled with all kinds of art work and statues. You know that fancy shit that these rich assholes collect."

Carter asked, "Where you calling from Jimmy?"

"I borrowed the van to drive to a super market to get a few things, so I'm calling from a pay phone. Hey Carter, I didn't sign on for this shit. From what I've seen, these people Burnhart has working for him are some bad mother-fuckers. Everyone around here is carrying and they set me up with a 9mm and two clips. I don't know what they're trying to protect, but they sure ain't going to give it up without a fight."

"Look Jimmy, hang in there for a few days and enjoy your surroundings. Remember, you're getting paid by me and the Burnhart Corp. Watch your ass and call me in a couple of days and keep your eyes open for anything illegal or unusual going on there."

"Okay Carter. Listen, there's some kind of secret shit going on around here. They got three buildings here from what I see, but so far I've only been in the main building. Turn on your damn answering machine so I can at least leave a message if I need to."

"Get me an address so I can send in the Cavalry if you need help. Jimmy, watch your ass and call if it looks like trouble."

Hanging up, Carter turned to Mick and said, "He says he's in Pico Rivera, at one of Burnhart's warehouses, and he's doing some security work."

"Hey Donny Boy, you should have asked him if they got anymore openings."

Carter stared at Mick and said, "Fuck you Mick."

Mick smiled and said, "Okay boss, what do we do first?"

Sitting back in his chair, Carter said, "That asshole Croft said he would go question Burnhart this morning, but I'd like to question the bastard myself."

"Did Croft say that he would call you?"

"That's why I want to hang around the office until I hear from him Mick. I'll tell you what, if we don't hear from Croft in the next couple hours, you and I are going knocking on Burnhart's door."

"We better be careful with this guy boss."

"Yeah, I'll be careful Mick, careful that I don't leave fingerprints on his neck after I choke the shit out of the bastard until he tells me where Reggie is."

34

Waking slowly, Reggie found both her wrists taped to the arms of a wooden chair. Trying to focus her eyes on her surroundings, everything appeared very blurry. The last thing she remembered was being slapped repeatedly and questioned by Burnhart. She refused to answer any of his questions and was eventually injected with some type of drug that left her unconscious. With the side of her face swollen and the taste of blood in her mouth, Reggie looked around the room and saw that she was alone with no one guarding her.

Sunlight beams were shining sparsely through the cracked painted windows to her left. To her right she saw a doorway leading out of the room that she remembered coming in the night before. The room had only one desk and a couple of file cabinets that were pushed against the wall off to the side of the room. The sturdy old captain's chair she was in was about three feet from the wall behind her. The room smelled from dampness and mold and was extremely cold. The paint was peeling off the walls and from the looks of everything it appeared that the room was seldom used.

She shouted, "Can anyone hear me? Is anybody here?" There was no answer, but Reggie heard some movement and muffled talking before the door opened and two men appeared in the doorway.

As one guy remained in the doorway, the other walked slowly towards her and said, "Did you have a nice sleep bitch?"

Reggie asked, "Where's your boss, I need to talk with him?"

"That's funny bitch, because last night you didn't want to talk at all. What is it that you now want to say?"

"That's between me and your boss, I suggest you call him you asshole."

With that remark, the quickly agitated guy slapped her and said, "If I were you bitch. I would be a little nicer to me, since I hold your life in my hands."

Spitting the blood from her mouth onto the floor, Reggie said, "I don't think Burnhart will be very happy with you if you kill me before he finds out about the gold and where it really is?"

Grabbing Reggie by her hair and tilting her head back the guy said, "What gold bitch?"

"Call your boss and ask him asshole."

Releasing Reggie's hair with a push of his hand, the guy said, "This better not be some kind of a trick."

Leaving the room, the guy said, "Keep an eye on her, Dieter, while I make a call."

The second man walked into the office and sat on the desk across from Reggie smiling. He was studying her long exposed legs and said with a slight accent, "What a waste of a beautiful woman."

Reggie saw an opening in the remark, and said, "Dieter, is that German?"

The man smiled saying, "Actually I am from Austria."

Playing up to him Reggie said, "You seem so much different than your friend out there. What's his problem?"

"Let's just say he has a problem with strong outspoken women and leave it at that."

Smiling Reggie said, "And you don't have any problem with women like me?"

Walking over to Reggie the man removed a folded handkerchief from his pocket and gently wiped the blood from her face and said, "It's just not my way."

Walking back into the room, the first man said, "Mr. Burnhart will be here in a little while to see you bitch. If this is some kind of bullshit trick, I'm going to beat you senseless, you understand?"

"Yeah shithead, I understand. I understand that when I get out of here I'm going to kill you."

Laughing loudly, the guy said, "You think you're going to get out of here. Maybe in a box or a bag. That's the only way you'll get out of here, but it's for sure, you ain't going to walk out bitch."

35

It was five o'clock in the afternoon and Carter had still not heard from Det. Croft, so he decided he had given the detective plenty of time to call him back. With Mick stretched out resting on the couch, Carter called Croft on his private number that went right to his desk. On the fifth ring the person answering said, "Homicide, Detective Petrovich. May I help you?"

Carter remembering the detective from a few years earlier, said, "Det. Petrovich, this is Donald Carter from Carter Security, is Det. Croft around?"

"Mr. Carter, I remember you. How have you been sir?"

Carter acted cordial and said, "Fine, Detective."

"I'm sorry to tell you that Det. Croft is not in the office at the moment. Is there something I can help you with?"

"Well, Croft was going to do a little checking for me at the Burnhart Corporation. Do you know when he'll be back?"

"No I'm sorry Mr. Carter, I don't, but I can tell you he did go to see Mr. Burnhart earlier today. I haven't heard anything further on his meeting."

"Listen Detective, please give Croft my message that I called and ask him to call me at my office."

"Okay Mr. Carter, I'll pass that on to him. Is there anything else I can help you with?"

"No thanks Detective you've been a big help, thank you."

Hanging up the receiver, Carter told Mick, "Hang around here Mick. I'll put the answering machine on, but if you hear Croft call, pick it up and find out what happened when he went to see Burnhart."

Mick tilted his head to the side and asked, "And where you off to Donny Boy?"

"I'm going to do a little snooping around at Burnhart's office, maybe have a talk with the son of a bitch and find out what happened to Reggie. You might want to give your uncle a call and see if there's anything new."

"Okay boss, if you get in any trouble give me a call and I'll come running."

"I'll call you one way or another Mick. Stay by the phone."

The drive to Burnhart's office building in L.A. took about forty-five minutes with the rush hour traffic that always backed up around 5PM each day. Parking down the street with a clear view of the building entrance and the parking lot, Carter settled in and waited for Burnhart to exit the building and head for his limo.

With the sun setting a half hour earlier and the darkened skies of the forecasted rain, Carter saw the front door of the building open and Burnhart walk out holding an umbrella. The chauffeur, who had exited through a side door of the building earlier, drove the limo around to the front where his boss could get in.

Starting his car and getting ready to follow Burnhart, Carter watched as the limo pulled away from the curb and a black Mercedes slowly pulled around the corner with headlights off tailing the limo.

Carter recognized the old Mercedes as the one that had been tailing him over the past week but could never get close to. Trying not to be too obvious, Carter kept the Mercedes in sight suspecting that the occupant could possibly be a body guard for the wealthy Burnhart.

Weaving through surface streets the limo finally made its way to the 5 Freeway entrance and headed south. The Mercedes, it appeared was remaining at a safe distance and now Carter felt that the vehicle was trying not to be detected by the limo driver.

After driving south for approximately thirty minutes in heavy stop and go traffic, the limo exited on to Slauson Ave. traveling about a mile before turning onto Paramount Blvd. in Pico Rivera.

Driving only a short distance, the limo turned onto a road heading into an area which was completely surrounded by commercial buildings. Following at a safe distance with its lights once again turned off, the Mercedes parked on the side of the road. The driver seemed to watch as the limo pulled up to a barbed-wire gate in front of a large gated building compound and flashed its lights several times.

Carter who had parked his car in a small alleyway, was now on foot watching the actions of both drivers.

Only a few minutes passed when the big roll-up door at the front of the building started to open. The light from its interior and outside security lights flooded the gated area followed by a man walking to the gate and unlocking it.

Once opened, the limo drove through the parking area and into the building. The gate was again locked and the man returned through the big door closing it down. The area was in total darkness again except for a small light at the corner of the building next to a smaller door.

The driver of the Mercedes had parked out of sight of the building and was walking around in the shadows appearing to be studying the layout of the land.

Carter also was checking out the structure, looking for a window around an unfenced section of the building. There were no windows at all on the largest of the three buildings.

Keeping the Mercedes driver in sight, Carter walked slowly around the entire area looking for a way in.

The building Burnhart had entered was not a stand alone structure. It was attached to two other smaller buildings by enclosed walkways. The land it was built on was about the size of three football fields. With the main building standing around thirty feet high and the only access to the roofs being metal ladders attached to the concrete walls, it looked like the only way in would be to knock on the door.

The fenced-in area behind the number one building had a loading dock which looked very secure, but the driver of the Mercedes decided to use a pair of cutters and opened a gap in the chain link fence and checked it out.

The man had just climbed up on the loading dock when the entire area was flooded with bright lights that must have been connected to motion sensors. Two armed men appeared from both ends of the dock taking the man by surprise and walking him into a side door now opened by someone from inside.

Carter ducked behind a dumpster and watched as the man was searched before being taken into the building. Determining that there were either security cameras or motion sensors all around the building, Carter retreated back to his car to figure out his next move.

Putting his key in the ignition, Carter started the engine and then felt something cold on the back of his neck, then heard a man from the back seat say, "That's good buddy, now drive around the corner to that building you're so interested in."

The man spoke into a hand held communicator and told someone on the other end, "Fritz, come out and open the gate when you see a car pull up to the gate out front. It seems we have a snoop out here wanting to get a better look inside."

The voice said back, "We just captured someone on the back dock of main building also. Do you want the big door opened so you can drive in?"

"Yeah, better if the car is out of sight also."

Once inside the building, Carter's car was approached by several armed men. He was ordered to shut off the engine and get out.

Carter said, "Where's Burnhart?"

One of the men said, "None of your damn business wise guy."

Carter got out of the car and said, "What now asshole?"

Carter's lights went out briefly when he was hit on the side of his head by someone standing behind him. When he was able to focus his eyes again, Carter found himself seated against the warehouse wall with his wrists tied behind him next to another man who looked a little familiar.

36

With her head tilted forward and her chin resting on her chest, Reggie was unconscious with dried blood on her chin and the front of her dress. The tape that held her arms to the chair had been removed and replaced with plastic tie straps. The room she had been held captive was in, the third and smallest of the buildings. The walkway connecting the buildings had locked doors.

Jimmy Hudson in his new job had only been allowed access to the main number one building his first day. Now with his new position as a security guard, he could go anywhere in the compound without being questioned.

From what Hudson had been told and seen, the number one building contained fine art collected by Burnhart over his years as an art collector. The number two building contained statues and other fine collectables. The number three building contained mostly wooden packing crates, display cases and personal belongings of the Braumholtz family. In a secured vault there were irreplaceable items, including a vast collection of fine jewelry inherited from his parents and grandparents. Several old crates were filled with gold and silver that had been stolen from prisoners of the camp in Poland.

The two men who had been detained for snooping around the building insisted that they had no knowledge of each other.

Jimmy Hudson, who had been sleeping in his assigned quarters in a converted section of number one building, was just checking in replacing the day guard getting ready to start his night shift. As they were talking he spotted Carter and the second man being taken to a secured area in the number one building with their hands tied behind them.

Hudson, not letting on that he knew Carter, asked one of the men, "Hey Sauerkraut, what's that all about?"

The guard being replaced said, "If I were you black man, I would just mind my own business and not ask too many questions."

The two men escorting Carter, and the other man down the hallway, were both armed and one of them had his weapon out and kept using it to push Carter along by nudging him in the back.

Once inside the closed-in style office area, Hudson heard shouting and when he got closer to the door he heard, "Now, who the hell are you two and what are you doing spying around here?"

Neither man answered. Then Hudson heard, "Smack, smack, smack." Then the man asked. What are you doing here? Talk or I'll put a bullet in your ass."

Carter yelled out, "Leave the little guy alone you asshole."

Next, Hudson heard some scuffling and the sound of a chair being knocked over and then a gun shot. Opening the door, Hudson saw Carter lying on the floor still tied into a tipped-over chair. The bigger of the two guards in the room said, "What do you want nigger, get the hell out?"

Hudson saw Carter shake his head slightly and then said, "I thought you might need some help Bernard," and then closed the door and listened once again from outside.

As Hudson listened, he never noticed Carson Burnhart come up behind him until he was asked, "Something of interest in there for you Mr. Harper?"

Turning around to see Burnhart and his chauffeur Hans standing behind him, Hudson said, "Sorry Sir, I heard a gun shot and thought they needed help in there."

Burnhart said, "I'm sure everything is under control Mr. Harper. Please resume your duties and assume your position at the security monitors."

"Yes Sir."

"Thank you Mr. Harper."

Jimmy Hudson quickly went back to his post in the main security room knowing he had to get help for Carter as quickly as possible. His only hope was that Annie or Mick was at Carter's office waiting for a call, or at least Carter remembered to turn on the answering machine. If he couldn't get hold of Annie or Mick, Hudson knew he would have to do something himself.

Inside the office area, Carter and his chair were up-righted as Burnhart walked into the room. Moving closer to the two men, Burnhart said, "Well Mr. Carter, we meet again. Tell me sir, why are you here and why have you been spying on me?"

Carter just stared at Burnhart for a few seconds and said, "I didn't feel our business had been completed last time we talked, Mr. Braumholtz."

Studying Carter briefly, Burnhart then turned to the smaller man seated and tied to the chair and said, "Rabbi Simon Rubinowitz, or are you going by Simon Rubin these days? It's been a long time Jew. Are you still chasing after the heroic men of the fatherland who fought so bravely to keep their country pure?"

The little man whose face was red from being slapped several times said, "Herr Braumholtz, as long as criminals against humanities like you are still walking around free, my job will never be done."

Burnhart, with a little smirk on his face, said, "I don't think you're in any position to question my freedom, especially since I hold your life in my hands. Your search and your life could end here with just a couple of words from me, and no one would ever find your body, so I would be very careful how you speak to me, Rabbi."

37

First making sure that no one was within hearing distance, Jimmy Hudson took a chance and called Carter's office with hopes of talking to Mick. When the answering machine picked up, Hudson left a message giving his location. As quick as possible he said, "Hey Mick, Carter, Reggie and some other guy are being held and questioned by Burnhart's people. This place is built like a fortress and they are well armed with all kinds of military fire power. Be careful, but hurry! I don't know how long Carter can hold out."

Mick, who had taken a walk to the local McDonald's to pick up something to eat, returned to the office and saw the flashing light on the answering machine and said, "Shit", laid his bag down on the desk and listened to the message. Mick wasted no time and called Vito whose response was, "Michael, I will make a couple of phone calls so stay by the phone and I will call you right back."

Mick who knew his uncle would also not waste time said, "Uncle, you have the location, I'm going to go ahead and scout out the buildings."

Not happy with his nephew's decision, Vito said, "Stay put Michael until you hear from me."

"Uncle, I need to go ahead and see what we'll be facing."

"Michael, I insist that you wait. "But the last message fell on deaf ears. Mick had already hung up and was headed to his apartment to pick up his 9mm and his semi-automatic rifle with a mounted twilight scope.

It was right around 9PM when Mick drove past the buildings in Pico Rivera. Surprised by the size of the three building compound, Mick drove to the end of the street, turned around, and left the area. Parking two blocks away, Mick removed the scope from his rifle and slipped it into his jacket pocket leaving the rife in the trunk.

Dressed in dark clothing, Mick stayed in the shadows as he walked to a position across the road from the fenced in compound. Using the scope he studied the outside walls of the building and noticed things that greatly concerned him.

During the five years following his discharge from the military in special services, Mick worked for a security company that specialized in top of the line high end security equipment. Being very familiar with motion detectors, heat sensors and surveillance cameras, Mick spotted similar equipment mounted at strategic points of the structure in front of him.

Mick knew that the motion detector would turn on the flood lights, the heat sensors would pinpoint the intruders and the cameras would show them on the monitor being viewed by the security guard on duty.

Staying far enough away from the fences, Mick worked his way around the entire compound as if it were an enemy military installation. During his tour in Vietnam, Mick had been involved in several search and rescue missions of POW's from enemy prison camps. Knowing that any slip-up or mistake of being spotted could result in his own capture, he moved around the compound like a black cat on a dark night hiding in the shadows. Moving past the spot in the fence that had been cut open by the Mercedes driver, Mick saw that it had a temporary repair done to it with rope wound and twisted to close the opening.

Taking approximately thirty minutes to complete his recon of the compound, Mick returned to his starting point just in time to see the flood lights go on, the big roll-up door rise and the limo slowly exit the building.

Walking alongside of the limo a guard made his way to the gate, unlocked and slid it open and waited as the vehicle drove out, then closed and locked it once again.

Returning and walking through the roll-up door the guard stood inside looking out until the door was fully closed. Mick noticed that ten seconds after the door closed the lights went out leaving the lot in darkness except for the small light next to the smaller entrance door.

Sitting with his back against the wall across from the compound, Mick studied some quick sketches he had made of the rear of the fenced-in area and determined it would be the best place to enter the building. When the headlights of two vehicles that turned off the main road reflected on the buildings in the area, Mick watched to see if he recognized any of the occupants.

The lead car was driven by Mick's cousin Danny with Paul Conti in the passenger seat. Watching as both cars drove to the end of the cul-de-sac and turned around, Mick walked around the corner and waited for them to return after their first drive-by viewing.

Signaling Danny to pull over between two buildings down the street and out of sight of the compound, Mick walked to the car and asked, "What the hell took you so long? The main guy we wanted just left a few minutes ago."

Danny said, "Hey, cool it Mick. We had to put together a few good people and some firepower, but we're ready for anything. So what do we got here, tell me about the layout?"

"Well first off Danny, I want to talk with all your guys and let them know that we have a guy on the inside named Jimmy Hudson. Jimmy should be easy to spot. He's probably the only black guy in the whole place."

The driver of the second car, a guy that Danny has known for many years, walked over to meet Mick and find out what the set-up was. Looking like a football lineman, he held out his hand and said, "How's it goin? Name's Tony Molinaro. They call me "Tony Moe. What's the plan?"

Shaking hands, Mick said, "Thanks for coming Tony. Those three buildings you drove by are owned by some guy named Burnhart. You just missed him a few minutes ago when he drove off in his limo but he may be back. Inside are three friends of mine, Don Carter and Reggie Volasko who are being held prisoners. The third person is an under cover ex cop, named Jimmy Hudson, you should be able to spot him easily because he's probably the only black man in there, so don't shoot him, he's on our side. There's another person I know nothing about who's being held in there. I think he's some guy who has been following Carter around for some reason."

Tony asked, "How hard is it going to be to get inside, Mick?"

"Hard as a mother-fucker. They got all kinds of security shit all around the place. I checked out all three buildings and I think our best bet is to hit them at two places at the same time. Know this, the second anyone gets near the fence, the place lights up like a football stadium at a night game. Whoever is watching the monitor inside will know we're coming, so move fast and watch your asses. Any of your guy's ex-military?"

"Yeah, Sam and Bobby are both ex-vets, spent time in Vietnam, why?"

"Because this has got to be like a military operation and if they've been in combat before, it will help."

Waving to the men in the second car to join them, Tony said, "Sam had two tours in Vietnam. He's an ex-green beret."

Shaking hands with a guy that looked more like a fat pastry chef who never missed a meal, Mick asked, "You up for this Sam?"

Sticking his chest out a little and sucking in his gut, the chubby guy said, "Fuckin a, man! Don't let my looks fool you. Just tell me what you want done and I'm there."

Mick smiled and said, "Tony will fill you in."

Looking at Tony, Mick asked, "What kind of fire power did you bring with you?"

Walking over to the trunk of his car, Tony popped it open and the trunk light shined brightly on a couple of shotguns, four M-16 automatic rifles, a military issue grenade launcher that could fire a grenade with accuracy and a whole shitload of ammunition.

Mick smiled and said, "What, no bazooka?"

Just as serious as he could be, Sam said, "My buddy at the armory would have given me anything I asked for, but I thought this was enough to get the job done."

Mick said, "Only kidding Sam, this will do. From what our inside man says, they have a shit load of firepower also, so we need to be very careful. We're going to have to move fast before they know what's coming. These people are dangerous and will be shooting to kill, so we do the same. Let's go over how we're going to do this."

38

Burnhart, before leaving, gave his headman Bernard instructions to pump Carter and the Rabbi for information but leave the woman to him for when he comes back. Both Carter and the Rabbi had been beaten pretty badly before they were taken to the Number Three building where Reggie was held captive. Reggie never even lifted her head when the two men were dragged into the room. She had been beaten into unconsciousness for refusing to answer any questions.

Not knowing who or what was about to come knocking on their door, most of Burnhart's loyal followers were getting ready for a late meal in the built-in kitchen area in the Number One building.

It was almost midnight when Mick drove his car up to the front gate of the compound and blew his horn several times. One spotlight came on pointed directly at the front gate followed by the small door opening next. As one of the armed guards walked slowly towards the gate, Mick got out of his car and stood in front of it in plain sight. Walking closer to the gate, the guard said, "This is a private secured area buddy. What is it that you want?"

Faking a drunken slurred speech, "Hey, I need to talk with Chris, he's my brother and I need to talk with him now."

The guard said, "You drunken fool, there's no one here named Chris. Get the hell out of here and go sleep it off somewhere."

Mick grabbed hold of the gate and started shaking it violently yelling, "Don't give me that shit, I know he works here, he's worked the night shift in this building for years, now let me talk with him."

The shaking of the gate activated the motion sensors and the floodlights came on illuminating the entire compound as Mick kept yelling.

The guard yelled back, "Get the hell out of here you damn fool before I call the police."

Mick faked stumbling and falling over, lying next to the gate, and kept mumbling, "I need to talk to my brother. I need to talk with Chris."

Another man appeared in the doorway and called out, "Victor, what the hell is going on out there?"

The guard yelled back, "Some drunken fool keeps asking for someone named Chris. I told him we don't have anyone here by that name. Now the asshole passed out. What should I do?"

The man at the door yelled back, "Stay there and I'll send the darkie out to help you. Put him back in his car and move it away from the gate, then get back in here."

Jimmy Hudson, who had been watching on the monitor, saw everything that was going on and protested as Bernard told him, "Hey black man, go out to the front gate and help Victor put some drunk back in his car. Then get back to your post."

While the attention was on the diversion at the front gate, there was no one watching on the inside monitor. Since all the outside lights were already on and the guards were dealing with a drunk at the front gate, no one paid any attention to the rear of the building. Tony was quietly as possible using a pair of wire cutters on the rear gate leading to the loading dock. Danny waited in the shadows of the building across the street with three other men. All the men were armed and watching for a signal from Mick.

As Jimmy Hudson approached the front gate, he said, "What the fuck are you doing Victor, I need to get back to my post. They're cooking up some good food in the kitchen and I'm out here fucking around with you."

Unlocking the gate, Victor and Jimmy Hudson walked outside and lifted Mick up and walked him to the passenger side of his car. As Victor let go of Mick and opened the car door, he felt something pressing into his belly and heard Mick say, "Unless you want to die right here asshole, I suggest you just slowly get into the car and keep quiet."

With all three men seated in the front seat, and the door closed, Jimmy Hudson said, "What the hell took you so long Mick. I don't know if Carter is dead or alive?"

As Hudson started the car, Mick said, "Yeah, nice to see you too Jimmy?"

Driving around the corner, Hudson asked, "What do we do with him?"

Once out of sight of the compound, Hudson pulled the car over to the side and was quickly met by Danny and the other three men.

Victor, who decided he had to say something, said, "You'll never get away with it. They'll kill you all before you get inside."

Danny placed the muzzle of his 9mm against Victor's head, and said, "Talk quick asshole. How many men are in the buildings?"

Victor just smiled and said, "Fuck you."

Jimmy Hudson spoke up, "From what I could tell there's twelve or thirteen. At least there were yesterday."

Victor looked at Jimmy and said, "I told them not to trust you, spook."

With one clean punch, Jimmy hit Victor flush in the face, busting his nose and splitting his lip, knocking him out.

Opening up the trunk of the car Mick said, "Okay pull off his jacket and hat, then tie his hands and feet together and put his ass in here."

Danny asked, "What are you just going to do? Walk in the front door and pretend to be him?"

Mick said, "Hey, I can play an asshole German."

Danny smiled and said, "I don't know about the German part."

Mick asked, "Jimmy, are you armed?"

Pulling his jacket aside Jimmy said, "I never leave home without it."

"Good. You and I are going to walk back joking a little along the way. We pretend to lock the gate and walk in the front door. Danny, once you see us walk in, you guys come running."

Danny asked, "Jimmy, where would most of the men be right now?"

"My guess would be in the kitchen area in the back of building Number One or in the sleeping quarters, right next to it."

Mick asked, "What about the doors on the loading dock? Can we get to them easy enough?"

Jimmy Hudson rubbed his face and said, "That's a problem, you need to go down a hallway next to the kitchen to get to the loading dock area."

Mick said, "Okay! I guess our best shot is a quick takeover by surprise. What do you think Danny? We secure the kitchen area and then get our guys in from the loading dock?"

Danny smiled, "Sounds good Mick."

They all agreed so Mick said, "Let's do it."

39

Inside the Number Three building with no idea on what was about to happen, Carter twisted and pulled at his bindings trying to get free from the chair. The Rabbi, who had been severely beaten, remained unconscious as did Reggie. Calling her name over and over there was no response from her, but the yelling did bring one of the guards back into the room.

Standing in the doorway the big smiling excuse for a man said, "Stop the yelling or I'll stop you."

With a split lip and blood drooling from his swollen mouth, Carter said, I swear, I'm going to kill you before this is over."

The big man laughed and held up a roll of tape saying, "If I have to tape up your mouth, you're going to have a hard time breathing through that broken snout of yours, pig. Now shut the fuck up."

With Carter once again quiet, the big man laughed and said, "Don't waste your time thinking of killing me. You're not going to be around that much longer."

As he closed the door behind him and the sound of the heavy footsteps slowly disappeared, the room fell into a dead silence.

With his head hanging down and his chin almost resting on his chest, Carter's eyes were closing as he thought of revenge against the big German. His eyes could barely focus and his mind was playing tricks on him when he heard a huge explosion from somewhere in the distance.

Mick and Jimmy had just walked in the small front door of the Number One building with plans of quietly making their way to the loading dock. The plan was to open the doors and let Tony, Sam and the rest of the rear assault team in. The explosion they heard told them their quiet walk to the rear was not necessary. Tony figured out his own way to gain access through the loading dock.

Two men appeared in the narrow hallway armed with automatic weapons. It was obvious to them that they were under attack from some unknown force, so they fired at Mick and Jimmy. Mick dropped to the floor and opened fire on them, as Jimmy stood his ground close to the wall also returning fire.

The sound of the automatic gunfire in the hallway was deafening. Hudson was hit in the leg by one bullet but the two men who were shooting at him were hit in far more critical areas and fell to the floor dead.

With all the gunfire, the hallway was filled with smoke making it hard to see to the end of the hall. The doorway the men had come through with the automatic weapons was quickly filled by a slamming metal door. At the end of the hallway several men came through another doorway and positioned themselves for an attack, so Mick and Jimmy pushed their way through a doorway leading to the warehouse for safety.

The men at the other end of the hallway were quickly taken out by Tony and his crew coming up behind them with one man throwing down his weapon saying, "I surrender, don't shoot anymore."

At that point the body count was five dead or severely wounded and if Jimmy Hudson was correct in his assumption, there were still at least seven or eight men remaining in the compound.

After Tony and Sam secured the kitchen area, Jimmy was carried in there to check out his injured leg. The bullet that hit him had gone through the calf muscle slightly striking the bone and exited leaving a fairly clean wound but one that bled profusely. Ice from the freezer and towels from the closet made good bandages that would slow down and coagulate the blood.

While Jimmy was being patched up, he explained to Mick and the others how the three buildings were connected and a rough layout of the offices and warehouse space. Mick knew that Burnhart's men were also going over their defensive plans and would be ready for any assault.

Sam asked, "Are the loading docks on the other buildings the same as the first one?"

Jimmy thought a few seconds and said, "The number two building is exactly the same. The number three building no longer has a loading dock. That area has been closed in to make a storage room for the maintenance department."

Mick asked, "What are you thinking about Sam?"

Sam scratched his head, looked at Mick and said, "It only took one grenade to blow the shit out of the first dock door, so why not try it again?"

Tony said, "What about hitting that Number Three building with a couple of guys and nailing them from both sides?"

Mick said, "They'll be waiting for us to hit them again. Besides, I think I got a better idea."

40

While the buildings were under attack by the unknown source, Burnhart's top man, Bernard, was on the phone trying to get hold of his boss. The three phone numbers he had all went to answering machines, which was no help to him at that moment.

While the big man was on the phone, Carter sat semi-conscious in the next room, where he could hear the sounds of gunfire and it brought a slight smile on his face. In a startling surprise, the door to Carter's room burst open and three men entered walking quickly towards Carter. Lifting his head slowly, Carter said, "Sounds like you have company coming?"

Bernard walked behind Carter, grabbed a handful of his hair, yanking his head back, and asked, "Who are they?"

Carter still with the smile on his face said, "Fuck you big man."

Before Bernard could inflict any further pain on Carter, an explosion appeared to come from outside the building followed by flickering lights and then total electrical blackout.

Hearing someone yell out from down the hall, "Shit," Bernard said, "Stay where you are, the lights will come back on as soon as the emergency generator kicks on. Everyone hold your positions."

Just as the big man said, a minute later the generator did kick in and as the lights started to flutter, a second explosion was heard and they were once again in total darkness.

With nothing more than a couple of cigarette lighters, Bernard and his sidekicks left the room quickly, leaving the door open as they ran to find out what was happening.

A few minutes passed and Carter could see lighted beams from flashlights shining side to side in the hallway. As one of the lights shone through the open doorway and flashed on Carter, Mick called out, "Here they are Jimmy."

Carter slurred out the words, "Now that's an entrance. Check on Reggie, Mick. I know she's still breathing but she's been unconscious for hours."

Jimmy Hudson came in the room while Tony and one of his men stood guard at the door and asked, "Who's the little guy in the other chair?"

Carter said, "He's some old Rabbi who's been following Burnhart for some kind of shit he did in the Second World War. Untie him will you Jimmy?"

Checking the Rabbi for a pulse, Jimmy said, "His following days are over Carter, the old guy's dead."

Mick cut the plastic ties holding Reggie's arms to the chair as Jimmy removed the tape and rope that was holding Carter to his chair.

As Carter tried to stand he found his legs were weak and he fell to his knees. Mick lifted Reggie out of the chair and said, "Jimmy, help Carter, we need to get the hell out of here before the police show up or those assholes regroup. I'll carry Reggie."

Before exiting the room Mick called out, "Everything clear out there Tony?"

Tony yelled back, "Yeah Mick, clear. I don't know where the hell they went, but I can't see them. So let's get the hell out of here quick."

Getting closer to the passageway that connected Building Number Three and Building Number Two, all was still quiet. When Jimmy slid the big metal fire door open, the sound of gunfire and ricocheting bullets made him slide it closed again. Mick asked, "Is there another way out of here, Jimmy?"

"Yeah Mick, there's another fire door on the other side of the warehouse, but we need to make our way there around a lot of shit."

"What kind of shit?"

"I only had a quick look yesterday, but it looked like hundreds of display cases, you know, the kind you see in department stores."

Mick said, "Okay, that's the way we go." Then he turned to Tony and said, "We need to get word to Danny and your guy Sam to clear out."

Tony said, "Let's get our asses out first, then I'll get to the other guys and get one of the cars so we can get the lady to the hospital."

Carter said, "Mick, you better tell those guys to gather up all their weapons and clear out before the boys in blue show up. There's going to be a lot of questions about all the dead bodies around here."

Mick said, "Already taken care of Donny Boy."

Making their way through the maze of glass display cases, more gunfire could be heard coming somewhere in one of the other buildings. When they got through the piles of display cases and boxes, a chained and locked door was the only thing separating them from freedom.

Handing Reggie to Jimmy Hudson, Mick asked, "You okay to carry her?"

Jimmy said, "Yeah I got her Mick."

It took a couple of shots from Mick's 9MM to blow open the lock and they were out into the cool air on the far side of the compound.

As Tony, Sammy and their buddy Dino worked their way around the rear of the buildings, Mick, Jimmy, Carter and Reggie headed for the gate in the high fence on the side of the property.

Paul had been waiting in his car looking for any sight of Mick or Carter when he saw Danny and Tony come running across the street to the parked cars. Tony called out, "Paul, follow me."

With a seven foot chain link fence surrounding the entire compound, there was no easy way out to the street. Once they reached the side entrance gate that had an unused rusted padlock, Mick said, "Step back."

Two shots later, they were all walking through the gateway to the street that was illuminated only by a street light at the end of the block. Looking back at the three buildings, Mick saw plumes of heavy black smoke coming from the rear of the number one building and the maintenance area behind number three building, and said, "It won't be long before the fire department arrives so I suggest we get as far away as we can and watch for Tony's car."

Carter asked as they walked, "How many guys did you bring Mick?"

"Danny and Paul showed up with six guys and a shit load of fire power."

"Everybody make it okay?"

"That remains to be seen boss. Hudson caught a bullet through his leg and I think one of Tony's guys got hit also."

A few minutes went by and there was still no sign of Tony's car, but sirens could be heard in the distance and they were getting closer.

Walking quickly they heard an explosion behind them and a large fire ball could be seen as they all turned to view the number two building completely engulfed in flames.

With their flashing lights reflecting off the windows of surrounding buildings, two fire engines pulled up in front of Building Number One followed by two police cars. A couple more minutes went by and Tony and Paul pulled up in their cars one block away and Tony yelled, "Get in quick."

Carrying Reggie once again, Mick said to Tony, "Drive around the block to the right and you'll see a big parking lot where my car is parked. Drop me off. Then get the hell out of here before we get spotted. Get directions from Carter and I'll follow you to the hospital."

Back on the I-5 Freeway heading north, Tony asked, "Okay so where's the closest hospital Carter?"

Un-expectedly Reggie spoke up, "Just get me back to the hotel, I don't need a hospital."

Carter said, "Reggie you're pretty beat up, I think you need a doctor."

"Carter, what I could use is some water and then my own bed. No doctor! Got that? They ask too many questions. Believe me, I'll be okay. Vito will take care of getting a doctor to the hotel room."

Tony asked, "So what do we do Carter?"

Carter didn't like it but said, "Head for the hotel Tony, the Beverly Hills Hotel."

Carter asked, "Did all your guys get out okay?"

"One of them didn't make it."

"How are you going to handle that Tony?"

"That's something you don't have to worry about Carter, I'll take care of it. My guys knew going into this that anything could happen."

"You know I really appreciate what you and your guys did."

"Hey, anything we can do for Danny and Mick we're right there. Vito and our boss go way back so don't worry about it."

"Tony, I'll be sure to let Vito know what a good job you did and someday, somehow I would like to show my appreciation."

"Carter, you're welcome. But the truth is, after I drop you and your girlfriend off at the hotel, you'll probably never see me or my men again."

"Tony, we owe you our lives, do you really think I'm going to forget or not repay you back in some way?"

"Look Carter, that's the way it works. If our services are needed again, Vito Terratello will know how to contact my boss.

Meanwhile, you owe us nothing except your friendship."

"Thank you Tony. Just know that if the time comes you need my help, you know how to contact me."

When they arrived at the hotel, Carter, Reggie and Jimmy got out of the car and Tony drove off without another word spoken.

41

Sitting in Reggie's suite at the hotel, Carter, Mick, Jimmy, Danny and Vito were waiting to hear what the doctor had to say. Just as Reggie had said earlier, once they were back at the hotel, Vito contacted a doctor he knew and he was there in just a short time.

Carter's first call had been to Vito and the second was to Det. Croft. Carter's call to Croft was answered by a desk sergeant who told him, "Det. Croft is out of the office at this time, but I will pass on your message to him. Leave your number and I'll have him call you back when he comes in."

Becoming a little un-glued Carter asked the officer's name and said, "Sergeant Coyle, I suggest you get hold of him real quick and tell him I have the proof he was looking for. He'll know what I'm talking about. Also, let him know that I can give him information about that big fire and shooting in Pico Rivera late last night."

The desk sergeant was silent for a few seconds and asked, "Sir, are you saying that you are withholding information about a shooting and a warehouse fire scene?"

"Sergeant, it's important that you listen carefully. Det. Croft needs to be contacted immediately and I don't give a damn if you have to wake him up from his beauty sleep. MY name is Donald Carter. He can call me back at 555-5000 or he can sleep in and call me at my office. He has my office number but by the time he calls there, it may be too late. You got all of that, Coyle, or do I have to repeat myself?"

"I've got it, Mr. Carter. I'll pass your message on to him. Have a good night sir."

The doctor completed his exam of Reggie and suggested that she be admitted to a local hospital for additional tests, but she refused to go. Even after the doctor's insistence that she go to the hospital Reggie said, "Look Doc, I'm not going to any hospital. Right now all I want is some sleep, so if you have some pills in your little black bag to help me with that, I'll be fine. In the other room there are two men who need your help more than I do, so please, just let me get some sleep."

The next job for the doctor was Jimmy Hudson's bullet wound on his leg. Because the bullet went completely through the calf muscle, just nicking a bone, the doctor gave Jimmy a tetanus shot, stitched up the wound and gave him a prescription for an antibiotic.

When Vito was told of Reggie's decision, he shook the doctor's hand, gave him a few hundred-dollar bills and said, "Thank you for coming doctor. If you'll write the prescription for the lady, I'll be sure and have it filled."

The doctor very quietly said, "Sir, you do know that I am supposed to report any gunshot wounds that I treat? If word ever got out that I didn't report this type of wound, I could lose my license."

Vito put his hand on the doctor's shoulder as they walked to the door and said, "What's to say it was a gunshot wound? I think he may have gotten injured climbing over a fence. Treating an injury of that type wouldn't have to be reported. Am I correct in that assumption doctor?"

As Vito handed the doctor a couple hundred dollars more, the doctor said, "The wound did appear more like a puncture than a bullet wound."

Once the doctor was gone and Reggie was sleeping comfortably, Carter Told Vito that he was heading home to take a hot shower and change his clothes. Since three hours had passed and there had been no word from Det. Croft, Carter called the police station again. Talking to the same sergeant he spoke to earlier, the officer said, "I'm sorry sir but I was unable to contact the detective."

Carter said, "Fine sergeant, I'm leaving my present location, so I'll be in touch with Det. Croft later today. If he comes in, he can call my office for an appointment."

Giving Vito and Danny a handshake and a hug, Carter said, "Thank you my friends for all that you did. If ever you need my help, I am there for you."

Mick also hugged his uncle and said, "Thank you Uncle. I'll call you later so we can make arrangements to have dinner together."

Jimmy Hudson held out his hand and said, "Thank you Mr. Terratello for having the doctor fix me up. It was very nice meeting you."

Shaking hands, Vito said, "I understand Mr. Hudson, you were once a police officer?"

"Yes Mr. Terratello that's true."

"Please call me Vito. May I call you Jimmy?"

Hudson smiled and said, "Of course sir."

"Jimmy, I want to thank you for helping Michael, Donald and Miss Volasko and keeping them safe."

"Sir, just like Carter, if ever you need my help, all you have to do is contact me."

Vito patted Hudson on the shoulder gently, "Thank you Jimmy. I always value good friends and you have proven your worth."

As the three men exited the hotel, Mick asked, "So where the hell did you leave your car boss?"

"Last time I saw the car, Mick, was when I drove into that building. Next thing I knew I woke up strapped to a damn chair in that office."

"Boss, when they check the registration they're going to tie you into the shooting in that warehouse, so they will know you were there."

"Yeah, well I'll deal with that later Mick. For now, I just need to get some rest before I have to talk with Croft."

"Well I'll tell you what, how about I drop Jimmy off at his place and then I drive you home?"

"How about this Mick, drop Jimmy off and then take me over to one of the car rental places at the airport so I can have a way to get around until I get my own car back?"

Carter asked Jimmy, "Since your cover is blown working for Burnhart, how about meeting me at the office later today after we catch up on some sleep."

"You know what Carter, my leg really feels like shit, how about I meet you there tomorrow sometime in the morning?"

Shaking hands, Carter said, "I never thanked you for what you did Jimmy."

"Yeah Carter, don't go all soft and mushy on me, I won't know how to act."

"How about we meet at Sitton's Diner around ten tomorrow morning and I buy us breakfast?"

You got it Carter. I'll see you at ten."

42

Driving west on the Ventura Freeway, Carter was heading home in the Oldsmobile Cutlass he had just rented and was starting to feel the effects of the lack of sleep.

It was a few minutes after 7AM when he pulled into the driveway at his house in Chatsworth. Slowly getting out of the car he walked to his front door and fumbled with his key before he entered. The thought of a nice hot shower and a change of clothes was the only thing on his mind after a very hectic night.

The stairs leading up to the second floor to his bedroom were draining away his last bit of strength when he heard his phone ring.

With a deep breath and a quickened step, Carter entered his bedroom and answered the phone after the third ring, "Hello. Oh, hi Annie. How are you?"

"Mr. Carter, are you alright?"

"Sure sweetheart, are you still at your mother's house?"

"No Mr. Carter. I'm back at the office. I came in early. There are so many messages on the answering machine for you. I got here at six this morning and that detective; you know the one, the guy you don't like. Well, he was parked in the lot when I got here. I'm sorry Mr. Carter if I sound shaky."

"It's okay Annie, just take a deep breath and then tell me what he said."

"He said he has a warrant for your arrest, Mr. Carter, and wanted me to tell him
where you were. He told me that if I didn't tell him where you were he would arrest me for not cooperating with the police."

"Everything will be okay Annie. I'll call him as soon as I get off the phone with you. Now what else did he say?"

"He said you and a bunch of other men broke into a warehouse somewhere, shot the guards and then started the building on fire. Is that true?"

"No Annie it's not true. Look sweetheart, I'm glad you're back. Go through the messages on the machine and make the return calls as needed. I'll be there after I take a shower and put on some fresh clothes. Don't worry, everything will be fine."

Ending the call Carter called Det. Croft's number and after several rings he heard,

"Homicide, Det. Croft may I help you?"

"Croft, this is Carter. What the hell is going on?"

The detective said boldly, "Where are you Carter? I have a warrant for your arrest."

"My arrest? You damn fool! Burnhart should be the man you need to arrest. The man is responsible for kidnapping and torturing three people and killing one in the process."

"That's not the way Mr. Burnhart and his many witnesses tell the story Carter. You need to get in here now because a warrant by Judge Haskell has been issued for your arrest and there is a pick up and detain out on you."

"That's ridiculous Croft. Burnhart and his henchmen kidnapped Miss Volasko and a Rabbi named Rubinowitz and tortured both, killing the Rabbi. When I followed Burnhart to the Pico Rivera location, I got my ass captured and they beat the shit out of me."

"Look Carter, I told you not to screw around with Burnhart. Whom do you think the DA and the Police Commissioner are going to believe, a well respected land developer and businessman, or a PI who can't keep his mouth shut or ass out of trouble?"

"This is all bullshit Croft. As soon as I take a shower and call my lawyer I'll be there and we'll straighten this out."

"Look Carter, don't screw around, get your ass in here as quick as you can."

"Yeah right Croft. Where the hell were you when I was trying to get a hold of you early this morning?"

"Hey Carter, I'm not your personal protector, just get in here or I'll come out there and drag your ass in here myself."

Carter decided to call his lawyer first and told him what his plan was. His lawyer, John Baldwin, told him to get out of the house immediately and meet him at the police station. He also told him it will look better to a judge while asking for bail if he turns himself in rather than being picked up on a warrant and arrested.

Carter said, "John, I'll meet you at the Van Nuys Police Department. I'll be with Det. Croft of Homicide."

Carter next tried calling Mick, but after ten rings he finally hung up. He splashed cold water on his face and brushed his teeth to get rid of the taste of blood in his swollen mouth. His shirt and pants were stained with blood so he had to change his clothes also before taking off to Van Nuys. The freeway was fairly empty so the trip to Van Nuys only took about fifteen minutes, then another ten minutes to find a place to park.

Carter walked into the police station and asked the desk sergeant for Det. Croft and was told to have a seat. After about five minutes the detective came through a doorway behind the desk sergeant's desk and said, "Follow me Carter."

Halfway down the hallway Croft turned left into a small office and said, "Have a seat Carter, I need you to give me your statement. Oh by the way, where's that sidekick of yours, Michael Terratello?"

"As far as a statement, you'll get that once my lawyer gets here. What the hell do you want Terratello for?"

"Your buddy Terratello is also listed in the warrant by the judge."

Carter pulled his chair closer to Croft's desk and asked, "Just what in hell are we being accused of Croft?"

Walking through the doorway John Baldwin said, "I'd like to know the answer to that also detective."

Det. Croft said, "And who might you be?"

"My name is John Baldwin, I'm representing Mr. Carter, and the question still remains, what exactly are the charges against my client?"

"Well counselor, your client has been charged with trespassing, breaking and entering, discharging a weapon, attempted murder, arson and fleeing a crime scene."

Carter said, "Are you out of your fucking mind Croft?"

John Baldwin said, "Don't say anymore Donald. First thing we need to do is arrange bail."

Det. Croft said, "Well counselor, that's something you'll have to take up with Judge Haskell, but your client will be remaining in custody until the judge tells me different."

Carter started to protest but his attorney advised him to hold his words and let him do what he was being paid to do.

While Carter was being detained in custody, John Baldwin met with Judge Haskell trying to arrange the release of his client on his own recognizance. Baldwin explained that the charges were entirely fabricated and in reality, Mr. Burnhart should be the man behind bars.

Judge Haskell became outraged at the accusation that a fine citizen and businessman like Carson Burnhart would be accused of any wrong doing. The judge told John Baldwin, "I am setting the bail on your client at one hundred thousand dollars and I will see you both in my court room at 2PM this afternoon. Now, I suggest you go and talk with your client and inform him of my decision. Goodbye counselor."

By the time John Baldwin had a chance to speak with Carter again and inform him of the judge's decision, Mick and Jimmy had arrived at the police station. They both decided to hold back giving statements as to what happened the day before until they spoke with their attorney. The two men were being represented by their own attorney, Paul Conti. Vito Terratello had instructed Paul to put up the bail money for Carter, Mick and Jimmy.

With John Baldwin at his side, Carter asked Det. Croft, "What have you found out about the Rabbi?"

The detective sat back in his chair and said, "Carter, none of the people from the warehouse know anything about this mysterious Rabbi you're talking about. You'll have your chance in court to tell your story."

"Croft, you're a damn fool."

Once out on bail, Carter, Mick and Jimmy met with Vito and both attorneys who advised them to just sit tight and not add anything that would cause complications.

Vito told Carter, "Donald, trust me, this case and the charges will be dismissed, just give me a little time to work on it."

John Baldwin spoke up, "With all due respect, Mr. Terratello, I feel that Mr. Carter needs to prepare for his defense."

Vito said, "Mr. Baldwin, you along with Mr. Conti will follow through with all procedures that are expected of you. When you are informed that all charges against these men have been dropped, I would like you to submit your bill to me personally."

John Baldwin looked at Carter and asked, "Is that what you would like me to do Mr. Carter?"

"Yes John, that is what I want you to do."

43

It had been three weeks since the incident in Pico Rivera. Reggie had moved out of her suite at the hotel and moved in at Carter's house. Only a couple of small bruises and discoloration on her face remained that she could not cover with make-up. Vito had flown back to New York to take care of business that required him to be there in person. The last conversation with Vito, Carter was told, "Don't worry, all will be fine."

Not hearing any news about a trial date or if in fact there would be a trial, Carter had taken on an investigating assignment at an electronics firm that had him working under cover. Mick was working as his assistant and things were progressing smoothly.

Annie was taking care of things at the office and Carter would stop by each day to find out if there was anything that needed his attention. One morning around 10AM as Carter walked into the office, Annie said, "Mr. Carter, there was a message on the answering machine for you from that Det. Croft. He wants you to call him as soon as possible. That man never sounds very happy."

Sitting down at his desk Carter called Det. Croft's number and after the third ring it was picked up. "Homicide, Det. Croft. May I help you?"

"Yeah Croft, it's Carter. You called?"

"I don't know how you pulled it off Carter, but I was informed about an hour ago by the DA that all charges against you and your two buddies have been dropped. Mr. Burnhart has decided that you and your friends are not responsible for the damages to his property. A new investigation is underway that does not involve you and your friends. I don't know what's going on Carter, but I damn sure intend to find out."

"Well, how about that Croft? Now I have a question for you. Did you ever check on that Rabbi I told you about?"

"We are still trying to locate that Rabbi. We have not been able to get any information on him."

"He's dead Croft. Burnhart's man killed him. We checked him for life signs and I'm telling you he was dead."

"All we have is your word on that Carter, and no body to prove your claims."

"Bullshit Croft. Mick, Reggie and Jimmy Hudson all gave you sworn affidavits about the Rabbi's condition."

"Their statements are still under investigation Carter. So my advice to you is, don't make claims you can't prove. As far as I'm concerned, no body, no murder. You got lucky on this one Carter. My advice to you is to just back off and stay away from Carson Burnhart."

The detective hung up the phone and Carter said softly, "The son of a bitch got away with murder, again."

Once off the phone with Croft, Carter called his attorney, John Baldwin, to inform him of the charges being dropped and to his surprise, John Baldwin already knew it.

Carter asked, "When did you find out John?"

"Actually Donald, I received a phone call from Burnhart's attorney about fifteen minutes before your call."

"And what reason did he give for dropping the charges after his threats of burning me at the stake?"

"There was no explanation, only a statement of the charges being dropped against you and Michael."

"Well thank you John for all that you did. Please send me the bill and I'll get a check in the mail ASAP."

"No need Donald. My bill has already been taken care of by Vito Terratello."

"Thanks John. I'll be calling you sometime in the future, I'm sure."

While explaining both conversations to Annie, the phone rang and Annie answered, "Carter Security. May I help you?"

"The caller said, "Sweetheart, you can help me anytime you want, you know I only have eyes for you."

Annie handed the receiver to Carter and said, "It's that hot blooded friend of yours, Mick."

"I was just about to call you Mick. Did you hear from Paul about the charges being dropped?"

"Yeah Donny Boy, I guess they figured out just whom they were dealing with."

"Yeah, right Mick. What do you think it's really about?"

"I have no idea, but I think I'll give my uncle a call and see if he can put any light on it. What do you say about lunch at Sitton's around one?"

"Sounds good, I got a few things around here I need to take care of. I'm going to give Reggie a call and have her join us. She's just been hanging around the house trying to figure out something to do. I caught her yesterday doodling caricatures of bleeding figures lying on the ground and when I asked her about them she said, "It's a dream I've been having about Burnhart and one of his men." Then she looked at me straight on and said, "Some day I'm going to kill both of them."

"Sounds like the lady is formulating a plan Donny Boy? See you at one."

Reggie was glad to hear from Carter and couldn't wait to get out now that her bruises were disappearing. Her drive from the West Valley after a little cosmetic cover-up took her only fifteen minutes. Stopping at Carter's office, she picked him up and then they made their way to Sitton's Diner.

Arriving at the restaurant about ten minutes early, Carter asked for a table in the back room to the left of the front counter. After ordering coffee, Carter told the waitress that they were waiting for another person to join them.

Before the coffee was poured, Mick came walking in and said, "Make mine iced tea sweetheart."

Taking Reggie's hand in his, Mick kissed it and said, "If that guy can't keep you satisfied Darling, you have my number."

Reggie smiled and said, "Right Mick, I'll keep your number under my pillow in case of an emergency."

Carter said, "If you two are through? Mick, did you talk with Vito?"

"My uncle, who is back in San Francisco along with Danny and Paul, was out playing golf with one of his business associates, so I did talk with my cousin Danny. It seems that Uncle Vito has been busy collecting on some favors from an old friend in San Francisco. Get this. His name is Tommy "Stogie" Rico. He was a big time mob boss in Chicago back in the forties. After a bout with cancer ten years ago, when he almost lost his life, he relocated and moved in with his daughter and son-in-law in San Francisco. He and Vito go way-back. From what Danny told me, he owes my uncle big time."

"Hey Mick, I can't wait to hear more of the family history, but to tell you the truth, I still don't see what it had to do with our charges being dropped."

The waitress came back to the table and asked, "Are you folks ready to order yet?"

Carter said, "We need a few more minutes please."

Mick went on, "Danny told me that Uncle Vito was checking on some rumors about the disappearance of some old lady that ran a vineyard in Napa Valley. It seems that the woman had driven into town to get her hair done at one of the beauty shops but never arrived. Since my uncle knew that the woman happened to be Burnhart's sister, he wanted to express his concerns."

Reggie smiled and said, "Stogie kidnapped that old bitch?"

Mick said, "Now, now, let's not jump to conclusions Reggie, that's not what the facts are. Uncle Vito simply called Carson Burnhart. He volunteered his services to try to help locate his missing sister. Vito also told Burnhart that he could guarantee that once the kidnappers were found, they would get what was coming to them. He assured him that his sister would most likely be found in a short time."

Reggie said, "So that explains about the charges being dropped?"

Mick said, "Well you know sweetheart, Uncle Vito just loves to help people in distress."

Reggie laughed and said, "Yeah, I've known him to help many people back east in the same way, and he always seems to be rewarded in some way."

After their meal, Mick went to Carter's office to spend a little time with Annie and find out what new assignments were coming up. Carter and Reggie decided to take some private time and drive down to San Diego and spend a night away from the Valley and hopefully to get her mind off of Burnhart.

Bella Fisher had been found by an alert highway patrolman who had stopped at a roadside café just outside of San Francisco. When the patrolman spotted her, he noticed that she appeared disoriented. After a short conversation with her, he discovered that she was under the influence of some type of drugs, so he called in to his dispatcher and she was taken to a nearby hospital for observation.

With a week going by since the return of Bella Fisher to her Napa Valley vineyards, and the local police questioning her to try and describe her kidnappers, she insisted that she had been drugged and blindfolded and had no idea who they were.

With no positive ID of the kidnappers, the detective who had been on the case for several days had no other choice but to say, "The case will remain open and continue to be under investigation."

Returning after a couple days in San Diego with Reggie, Carter was sitting in his office reading the newspaper article about the kidnapping of the vineyard owner in Napa. He was smiling when Mick walked in and said, "I got a call from my uncle this morning. Danny was killed in a car accident two nights ago driving from Vegas heading to LA."

"Oh shit Mick, how'd it happen?"

"So far all Vito knows is that Danny's car was involved in a collision with a semi and his car was totaled."

"Was anyone in the car with him when it happened?"

"There was a woman with him, but she still hasn't regained consciousness yet. She's in the ICU at some hospital in Barstow."

"Barstow?"

"Yeah, they were about five miles out of Barstow when it happened."

"How's Vito taking it Mick?"

"Not good. He was just notified this morning and he'll be arriving in LA this afternoon. He already contacted his friend Salvatore Lazamo who owns Lazamo Funeral Parlor in the Valley to pick up Danny and fix him up a little before he sees him. I guess the accident messed Danny up pretty bad."

Carter said, "I need to call Reggie and let her know what's going on."

"Let her know Donny Boy that all the arrangements have been made for the limo and hotel. Vito said he will call once he arrives at the hotel."

When Vito and Paul arrived that afternoon at the hotel, there was a message waiting for him at the front desk from Salvatore Lazamo, that simply read, "Vito, please call me, we experienced a problem with the Coroner's Office in Barstow. Salvatore."

After speaking with his old friend Salvatore, Vito called the Barstow Police Station to speak with the detective in charge of the investigation into Danny's death and was told Det. Martinez of Homicide would be with him in just a few minutes. After several minutes a man came on the line and said, "Mr. Terratello, my name is Det. Martinez and I apologize for the wait. I'm sorry sir for your loss, how can I help you?"

Vito said, "Thank you detective for your kind words. I understand that there are complications in the investigation into my son's death?"

"Yes sir, our county coroner while examining your son's body, noticed a wound to the side of his head that was not caused by the accident. The wound sir was a bullet wound, and after x-rays confirmed the coroner's findings, the traffic accident fatality became a homicide investigation."

You're saying detective, that my son was shot in the head and then the vehicle he was driving was run off the road by a semi-truck?"

"Yes sir. We're still trying to locate the truck and the driver who was involved. The incident took place at approximately 4 am in a very remote area on highway I-15. Unfortunately there were no witnesses other than Miss Carol Marino who was a passenger in your son's car. As of the last report I received on Miss Marino late this afternoon, she has still not regained consciousness."

"Detective, how soon can I make arrangements to pick up my son's body?"

"Sir, I know this is a difficult time for you, but your son will have to remain at our facility here until our investigation warrants his release."

"Detective, I thank you for all your information, but if you would be so kind, I would like to speak with your captain."

"Sir, Captain Jenkins is out of the office right now on an investigation, but if you leave a number where you can be reached, I will give him your message."

44

Sitting in the coffee shop in the hotel, waiting to be joined by Vito after his phone calls to the Barstow Police Department and Salvatore Lazamo, Mick, Carter and Reggie were in a very somber mood as they sipped their coffees, waiting.

When Vito entered the coffee shop along with Paul Conti, his step and outward appearance was that of a much older beaten man. Vito was just two weeks short of his seventy-fifth birthday, but with his extremely bloodshot eyes and the slight growth of gray whiskers he appeared more like eighty-five and very tired.

With the passing of his much younger wife who died of cervical cancer several years earlier, and now the death of his son, Vito for the first time in many years was searching for a direction to follow. The man, who for almost forty years controlled a major crime family on the east coast and had to make decisions where it sometimes meant the liquidation of lives, had to now pull everything together and find out who was responsible for his sons death.

The large circular table at the rear of the coffee shop was fairly secluded. When Vito had finally sat down after a warm greeting of hugs by everyone expressing their sympathy, he said, "Daniel's death was not an accident, he was murdered."

Carter asked, "Do you have any idea who was responsible, Vito?"

"I have no proof Donald, but I feel it was Burnhart, in retaliation for the kidnapping of his sister. I would like you and Michael to find out if I am correct."

"Vito, if Burnhart is responsible, you need to let the police handle it."

"Donald, If Burnhart was behind the death of my son, I will handle it in my own way. And if there is someone else who is responsible, I need to know. I will not have you or Michael involved after you provide me with the information I am seeking. Your help will be completely appreciated and neither you nor Michael, nor any of your employees will ever be mentioned after the guilty have paid for what they have done."

As Vito spoke, it was obvious that Paul Conti was very uncomfortable with what Vito had been saying. Being an attorney he knew it was a crime for him to hear and not report any plans to take someone's life, so he excused himself saying, "Please excuse me, I'm having a small problem with my hearing and I also need to use the restroom."

Vito looked at Paul and said, "I understand completely Paul, I hope everything turns out okay. I'll see you at the cabana."

A few minutes after Paul's departure, the assistant manager of the hotel walked over to the table and said, "Please excuse the interruption Mr. Terratello, but there is a call for you. Would you like me to bring an extension to the table?"

"Yes Ricardo, thank you."

Answering the phone, Vito said, "Yes, this is Vito Terratello. Thank you Sheriff Jenkins for returning my call. I was hoping there might be additional information about my son's death? Yes Sheriff, Senator Roberts is a fine man. I had no idea he would contact you Sheriff. Yes, I'm glad you enjoyed your conversation with the Senator."

As Vito spoke with the sheriff, he was writing notes on his paper napkin, until Reggie slid a small note book across to him. Several more minutes passed, when Vito hung up the phone and said, "We have some leads. There was another witness who came forward with information on the truck involved in the shooting."

After giving the information to Carter, Vito said, "Sheriff Jenkins told me that he would be releasing Daniel's body within forty-eight hours. The woman who was with Daniel at the time of the shooting died of her injuries early this morning. All the information gathered has been turned over to the District Attorney for a follow up investigation. Paul and I will be remaining in Los Angeles until after the funeral, and then Daniel's body will be flown home to the east coast for burial in one of the family plots."

Mick, who had been very quiet until this point, said, "Uncle Vito, we will find out who is responsible and get you the information as soon as possible."

Getting up from the table, Vito was hugged by everyone and said, "Please excuse me, I'm feeling a little tired. I will hopefully see you all tomorrow."

Once Vito had left the coffee shop, Carter said, "We need to find out who the son of a bitch is that did this."

Mick said, "Donny Boy, if we find out that it's Burnhart, just leave me alone with him and disappear."

Looking at the notes that Vito gave him, Carter said, "According to the Sheriff, the truck belonged to some company named Kindle Produce, Inc. in Watsonville."

45

Over the next week, Carter and Mick were checking information about produce companies in the Watsonville area. Using the phone company and other produce suppliers, it was discovered that there was no company named Kindle Produce. They had taken two trips to Watsonville and questioned employees of other produce companies in the area and it had all turned into dead ends.

Carter had printed up flyers announcing a reward for any information about the Kindle Produce truck, knowing that people in the area were mostly unemployed and money hard to come by.

Carter Security received dozens of calls over the following two weeks, all from individuals with information that could not be verified. Some said that they saw the truck going through town, but could not even give the color of the vehicle. Others said they knew the owner of the vehicle but refused to give a name without being paid first. All leads were checked out by Carter and Mick. Reggie even traveled to Watsonville to find out that the calls were bogus. In time the calls about the truck's location dwindled off, but Carter would continue for as long as it took.

With many new companies seeking the services of Carter Security, Carter saw his small business expanding and he knew he had to do something about it. With business picking up and being far more than Carter could handle himself, he felt it was time to take in a partner, and there was only one choice, Mick.

A week earlier, Reggie, had confided to Carter that she was homesick for New York. She needed to go back and work out some doubts and decide once and for all if she was ready to commit to a permanent position at Donald Carter's side. It was hard for Carter to accept but he agreed, or possibly he would lose her forever, because she was leaving.

Carter had many things to keep his mind occupied over the next few weeks and even hired Jimmy Hudson and another ex-cop named Ed Smith to work full time.

With the new help and experience, let alone some connections with people who knew how to extract information from those not willing to talk, a legitimate lead was gathered by Ed Smith in Watsonville.

A man who worked as the mechanic at a produce company years earlier, who had been fired because of excessive drinking on the job, remembered the truck well. His boss had purchased vehicles from out of state and he had the job of fixing them up. He decided to speak with the investigator from Los Angeles and try to get the reward money that was offered. Not only did he know the correct color of the vehicle, but also a year earlier he had the job of driving the truck to an auction where it was sold to a vineyard in Napa Valley. After some persuasive conversation, tequila, and a nice fresh hundred dollar bill, the man remembered many details about the truck, like being dark blue and "Kindle Produce Inc." on the doors. The truck was originally from another state, so the name Kindle meant nothing to the local people in Watsonville.

When Ed Smith returned to Los Angeles, he headed straight to the office and gave Carter all the new information. After talking with Mick, Carter made a phone call to Vito and told him about the new discovery.

After a few seconds of silence, Vito said, "Donald my boy, I had my suspicions about Burnhart being behind it. I thank you and your men for proving my suspicions correct. I will see you soon. Thank you again Donald."

One of Carson Burnhart's fourteen-story office buildings in the West Valley had been completed, and an official grand opening party was scheduled for the upcoming weekend in two days. Invitations had been sent out to many of the big wigs on Burnhart's list of supporters, including politicians, judges, potential renters and close friends.

Although the building was listed as a fourteen floor office building, the entire top floor was the new office and residential home while Burnhart was in town. The living area included a partially covered swimming pool, guest rooms, a game room, complete with a fully stocked bar and a heliport landing area.

The grand opening of the building would include a ceremony to show appreciation for the hard work and extra effort by the employees of the construction company.

Reading the newspaper announcement about the big celebration each day as the event neared, just didn't sit right with Carter.

Vito told Carter as they were dining at one of his favorite Italian restaurants in Los Angeles, "Donald, you must understand something, people like Burnhart always get what they deserve. Sometimes it happens while they live and sometimes it happens after they are dead. The good Lord makes sure that people like Burnhart burn in hell and if I can assist in any way, I am always ready to help. I need you to promise me that you don't do anything foolish. Please keep your distance from that man."

Carter was quiet for a few seconds and then said, "Vito you have my word. I will stay away from that man and as you say, I will let the Lord work his miracles, with your help. But one day, if the Lord doesn't take care of that bastard working for Burnhart, a man named Bernard, the man who beat Reggie and me and killed the Rabbi, I will lend a hand and make him pay for what he did in his lifetime."

"Be patient Donald, I'm sure all will be taken care of in time. You have my word."

The following morning, early, Carter received a call at the office from Mick, who told him, "Hey Donny Boy, pack a bag for a trip to Vegas. My uncle has reserved a suite for us at Caesar's Palace for the next four days."

"What are you crazy Mick, with all the work we have lined up. There's no way in hell we can take off for four days."

"Look Donny Boy, Vito wants us out of town for the next four days, and he wants us to be seen in Vegas. He told me to tell you that he's calling in one of those favors you told him you owed him. I'm just the messenger and he insisted we go."

Carter sat quiet for a few seconds, then said, "Okay Mick, get hold of Jimmy and fill him in on what he has to take care of around here. I'll explain to Annie when she gets into the office. Who's driving? You or me?"

"Neither one of us, boss. We got tickets waiting for us at Burbank Airport, where we will be seen boarding a plane for Vegas. All we have to do is get there. Vito arranged for us to have a limo at our disposal while we're in Vegas."

"Well, he thought of everything didn't he? Okay, pick me up in an hour at my house. I can call Annie from there. I got some cash at home in my safe that should be just enough for a weekend."

At 3PM that afternoon, Carter and Mick were taxiing down the runway on their way to a four-day weekend compliments of Vito Terratello.

46

With the streets blocked off at 6PM around the new luxury office building in the West San Fernando Valley that would be known as the "Burnhart Tower", the security was posted in full force. Having no reason to suspect that he was in any danger, Burnhart himself stood by the elevator doors and welcomed the first twenty to twenty-five guests as they arrived for the grand opening.

The mayor and his aide arrived accompanied by a councilman and his aide. The Chief of Police along with a lieutenant and a sergeant mingled with the crowd adding flavor to the conversations with some of the snobbish visitors. About a dozen high-end real estate agents arrived along with prospective renters from the surrounding areas. One of the most influential agents from Beverly Hills arrived and was accompanied by none other than Vito Terratello. When Burnhart recognized Vito, he excused himself from the group he was standing with and quickly walked over to greet him and the agent.

Burnhart offered his hand to Vito, who declined the gesture as he showed his gloved hands. "Skin disorder Carson, I must avoid physical contact with other people."

Burnhart now shifted his attention to the agent at Vito's side. Offering his hand saying, "I don't believe we've met, Mr. Sheffield, but I am familiar with your agency and your reputation for leasing high end properties. I believe you handled the Hunter property in Toluca Lake last year?"

Shaking hands with Burnhart, Mr. Sheffield said, "That's correct Mr. Burnhart, the *sale* of the property was a very lucrative endeavor for all involved. I hope, with your permission, to arrange some top of the mark renters for this beautiful building."

Burnhart smiled and placed his hand on Mr. Sheffield's shoulder and said, "I believe you and I need to have a private meeting after all the hoopla of this weekend."

When Burnhart turned to face Vito he noticed that he had walked to the bar and was ordering a drink. Vito's intention was to send a message that he had nothing further to say to Burnhart at this time, and it had been fully received.

Overall, there must have been at least two hundred people by 8PM on that penthouse floor, eating, drinking and making promises they knew they couldn't keep. Burnhart made his way to a make-shift stage and dais. He then tapped on a microphone with an oversized ring on his hand and asked for everyone's attention.

After thanking everyone for attending, he then directed the remainder of his speech to the mayor, conveying how he would be helping the community with the addition of this building and several more in the planning stages, just from the additional funds the city would be receiving in taxes. He then called two of his employees to the stage for some personal recognition for their contributions relating to the early completion of the construction of the building.

After introducing Mark Foreman as his head of construction and Bernard Weise as the director of land procurement, Burnhart said, "First, after a little investigative work on my part, I was able to find out one of your loves in life was bass fishing. So Mark, for a job well done I would like to present you with the keys to a brand new Ford pickup truck along with a custom sport bass fishing boat."

Once the applause died down, Burnhart said, "Next, to the man who without his strong perseverance in obtaining property in this beautiful section of the valley, I want to say thank you to Bernard Weise. Bernard, you have been my close friend for many years and a very loyal and hard working member of the Burnhart family. It is my great pleasure to present you with the keys to a Mercedes SL 500 Convertible. Please drive it and enjoy it in great health my friend." Applause followed Burnhart's presentations. "Now, I would like to thank everyone for coming tonight. I hope you all enjoy yourselves and I promise there will be no more speeches by me tonight."

As he left the stage the applause and hand shaking went on for several minutes. It seemed like everyone wanted to congratulate this wonderful man for all that he had contributed to the West Valley.

Somewhere around midnight, the crowd had dwindled down to about ten people.

Those who remained, were either too drunk to stand and walk, or they just wanted a private audience with Burnhart. A cleaning crew had been hired to clean up after the party, but they remained out of sight until they were given the word to move in and start working.

Approximately 1AM, everyone had cleared out except Burnhart and his chauffeur-bodyguard Hans, who were sitting enjoying the quiet of the moment. Being approached by the head of the cleaning crew, Burnhart gave them permission to start their work.

As a half-dozen people from the cleaning service moved in to commence their cleaning, Burnhart told Hans, "Hans, I'm going to my quarters to change into my swim suit, I'll be back shortly."

Once Burnhart left the area, a woman who had been cleaning in the cabana stood smiling in the doorway of the cabana and called out for Hans to possibly give her assistance with something she had found on a table.

With a little macho in his step, Hans walked to the cabana door. As he cleared the doorway and the door closed behind him, Hans felt something pressed against his back and was told, "Don't make a sound or you're dead."

The man behind him was holding a shotgun tight against the bodyguard's back and pushed him towards a couch on the right side of the room. As Hans turned, appearing to sit, he made a move to disarm the man with the shotgun. In his attempt of doing this, the woman who was off to his left, fired two shots from a silenced gun dropping the big man to the floor.

Walking over to Hans, who was laying on the floor, the woman very coldly bent down, placed the gun against the back of his head and fired two more shots just to make sure.

Unaware of what had transpired in the cabana, Burnhart came out of his private quarters wrapped in a large red robe and called out for Hans.

A man wearing a cleaning crew uniform stepped quickly in front of him and pointed a gun in his face. Burnhart asked, "Where's my man Hans? And who the hell are you?"

Ignoring the question, the man said, "Listen close asshole. You will do exactly as I say, or I'm going to put a bullet in your head. Now sit your ass down in that chair."

Burnhart yelled out, "Hans. Hans. Get out here now!"

The man smiled and said, "Hans won't be joining us, but you may be joining him soon."

"What do you mean by that? Do you know who I am? I'll have you locked up by morning."

The man, Tony Moe, said, "Yeah right."

The other members of the cleaning crew were standing guard except for Tony's female assistant who was now holding the shotgun pointed at Burnhart. Tony told Burnhart to stand and put his hands behind his back. Using a pair of handcuffs, Tony cuffed his wrists together.

Seeing what might possibly be in store for him, Burnhart started yelling for help. After yelling the word help twice, Tony's female assistant produced a roll of duct tape and covered Burnhart's mouth.

Trying to run, Burnhart was tripped by Tony and fell forward hard to the ground on his chest and face. As Tony sat on Burnhart's back, his assistant ran tape around both of the old man's ankles several times.

Removing a small plastic case from his coverall pocket, Tony opened the case and removed a hypodermic syringe. Removing the protective cap over the needle tip, he then injected the contents into Burnhart's arm.

Once unconscious, it took three of the men to load Burnhart into a large laundry cart.

Hans' body was also loaded into a second cart and both were rolled to the service elevator.

As the cleaning crew exited the penthouse floor, Tony put on a pair of gloves and removed an envelope from his pocket and placed the contents on a table near the pool. Next he walked to the door, turned out the lights and locked the door behind him.

After loading both laundry carts into a waiting truck and watching it drive away, Tony along with a couple of his men walked through the hallways to the front lobby.

Leaving the building, the rest of the crew was joined by the security guard at the main entrance who had been put in place after most of the guests had left the building. The real guard had been drugged and placed in the janitorial closet down the hall.

While Burnhart and his chauffeur were being dealt with and removed from the building, several of Tony's associates had been assigned to follow Bernard Weise and Mark Foreman, so they could also be dealt with quickly over the next few hours.

Mark Foreman, real name Marcus Frauman, was responsible for many deaths. His hand and orders were responsible for the death of property owners and fellow employees of the Burnhart Corporation who didn't cooperate. His passion for bass fishing and the gift of a new truck and fishing boat brought him to Castaic Lake at 6AM the next morning. Although slightly hung over, he couldn't resist the temptation of going out on the lake with his new toy.

Spending five hours on the lake and catching a half-dozen fish, Foreman hauled his new boat out of the water and headed for a local country bar that he knew. Parking in the big lot around back of the bar, far from the other vehicles, Foreman went into the bar and found a seat. It was about three hours later when he staggered out of the bar, unlocked his truck, and then climbed in and fell asleep.

The next morning, a sheriff's deputy pulled up next to the truck and boat in the lot. Seeing no one around, he got out to take a closer look. First looking into the cab, he saw no one, but noticed an envelope on the seat. He then walked around to the side and looked into the bed of the truck. Looking in disbelief, the deputy saw a nude body of a man gutted down the middle like a fish.

Calling for back-up the Deputy waited for the Sheriff to arrive. First putting on gloves, the Sheriff opened the door of the cab and retrieved the letter. The letter on the truck seat gave the Sheriff information about Mark

Foreman and his connection to the Carson Burnhart Corp. Also in the envelope was a copy of a statement implicating him to the killing of several previous property owners in the West San Fernando Valley?

The Sheriff next contacted The Homicide Division of the LAPD and informed them of his discovery.

47

Bernard Weise enjoyed sitting in his car at the beach with a bottle of Jack Daniels at sundown. His joy was watching that big golden ball descending into the ocean as he sipped the Jack. When all was right with him, and he was lucky enough to snag a little company, he had a hooker by his side with her face buried deep in his lap doing what came naturally in her profession.

Sitting in his favorite parking space in his new Mercedes convertible at 3AM, with no hooker and only his bottle of Jack Daniels, Weise was looking out at the ocean when he decided to take a walk on the beach. Walking down to the water's edge, he looked out and thought about how good his life was progressing. He was startled when he heard someone walk up behind him and say, "It's a beautiful night. You better enjoy it asshole, because it's the last one you'll ever see."

Turning around, Weise said, "Who the fuck are you?"

The two men standing behind him looked like two big mountain men, each probably tipping the scales around two hundred and eighty pounds and standing around six foot five.

Weise, a big man himself, was not intimidated, so he turned and asked again, "I said, 'who the fuck are you assholes?' "

Both men slowly lifted their weapons from their sides and one of them said, "You can call us the grim reapers, mother fucker, and it's time for you to pay for some of the shit you been doing."

Trying to figure a way out of the predicament he was in, Weise said, "I have no idea who you think I am, but you guys are on the wrong track."

The one big guy looked at the other and said, "Did you hear that Sammy? He says we're on the wrong track, I guess he forgot about beating that Rabbi to death and damn near killing Reggie? It's payback time shithead."

As an airplane was coming in on its approach to LAX flying over the beach, the sound of the jet engines drowned out the gunshot to Weise's kneecap that dropped him down onto the sand.

Sammy said to his partner, "Why did you do that Bobby? Didn't you hear him say that we were on the wrong track?"

Bobby looked down at Weise and said, "That one was for Carter, you remember Carter, don't you shithead?"

Weise knew he was not leaving the beach alive after hearing Carter's name, so he tried jumping up and tackling one of the men and getting his gun. As the two men rolled on the sand another airplane was starting to make its approach over the beach. Seeing an opening Sammy fired a shot striking Weise in his other leg and he stopped his attempt to disarm Bobby and screamed in agony.

Sammy said, "That one asshole was for Reggie, you know, that pretty woman you slapped around so much."

As Bobby got up and brushed off the sand on his clothes, he swung his hand with the gun in it and smacked Weise in the head, knocking him out, saying, "Shit, I just got these pants back from the cleaners."

When Weise regained consciousness, he was spread-eagled and tied to a large boulder still at the beach but near the road about twenty feet down the hillside. He had lost a lot of blood but was still very much alive when Sammy leaned over him and asked, "I heard you were a Nazi lover. Is that true asshole?"

Weise laughed, spit at Sammy and started yelling something in German. Sammy quickly stuck a small piece of driftwood in Weise's mouth, held up a straight razor and said, "This is for the Rabbi, asshole."

Weise tried yelling as Sammy carved a swastika into his chest, and cut his throat from ear to ear. Bobby had taken the car keys out of Weise's pocket for the Mercedes, removed the piece of wood from the dead man's mouth and stuffed the key into it, leaving the Mercedes tag dangling from his lips.

Before leaving the scene, Sammy removed an envelope from his inner jacket pocket and carefully removed the contents and dumped it on the front seat of the Mercedes.

As the sun came up that morning, Weise was found by some people walking on the beach as the crabs and birds picked at his flesh.

When the police arrived and cordoned off the area and the detectives and crime scene crew showed up, the Mercedes was searched and the contents bagged as evidence.

The letter that was left on the Mercedes seat identified Weise as an employee of the Carson Burnhart Corp. He was also identified as a Nazi war criminal supporter wanted for the slaughter of many people, both in Poland and here in the United States.

48

Carter and Mick, not knowing what was going on in Los Angeles, spent Friday night checking out several casinos before finally heading back to Caesar's Palace and trying their luck at the Black Jack tables. Somewhere around 5 AM the two amateur gamblers returned to their suite a little lighter on cash but with a better understanding of the saying, "The house always wins when you drink too much and think you can beat the pros."

Vito had arranged for a 1 PM starting time at the Desert Inn Golf Course for Carter and Mick. They couldn't wait to play the famed golf course even though a little hung-over and only with rented clubs. They stood at the first tee with the temperature hot enough to fry an egg on a sidewalk. Carter smiled and said, "Can't get any better than this, right Mick?"

Lifting his sunglasses exposing his bloodshot eyes, Mick said sarcastically, "Oh yeah, I'm enjoying the shit out of this experience Donny Boy, I can't wait to thank my uncle."

Because of slow play, and the starter overbooking tee times, it took them six hours to finish eighteen holes. Rather than heading back to their room at Caesar's, they decided to take a cab downtown and try their luck at some of the old established casinos and eating at the great buffet at the Golden Nugget.

Once again, the day and night seemed to disappear with over-drinking, gambling and the belief they could beat the odds, so they returned to Caesar's around 1 AM on Sunday morning. After a couple hours more of blackjack and winning back some of their money, the hotshot gamblers returned to their room around 3:30 AM.

When Carter sat down on the edge of his bed, he noticed a red light flashing on the telephone. The little flashing bobble was letting him know that there were calls waiting while they were out and messages that were left.

The first message was from Annie, who said, "Mr. Carter, it's Annie. Please call when you hear this message. The police have been calling and need to talk with you. I don't know if you heard the news about Carson Burnhart, but he disappeared from his penthouse early Saturday morning."

The second message was from Vito, who said, "Hello Donald, I hope you and Michael are enjoying your short vacation in Las Vegas. I look forward to seeing you on Sunday night when you return to Los Angeles. Please call me when you and Michael get in so we can have dinner and enjoy some after dinner conversation.

After listening to the messages, Carter decided to make a call to Det. Croft first. Removing Croft's card from his wallet, Carter turned it over and called his private home number.

On the third ring a woman answered and said, "Hello."

Carter said, "Hello ma'am, I hate to bother you at this late hour, but I need to speak with Det. Croft if that would be possible."

The woman asked, "Who may I say is calling?"

"Would you tell the detective that it's Donald Carter and it's very important that I speak with him?"

In the background Carter could hear Croft's voice say, "Okay, give me the phone." Then Carter heard, "Carter, what the hell are you doing calling me at home at this hour?"

"I heard you needed to talk with me Croft."

"Where the hell are you?"

"Not that it's any of your business Croft, but Mick and I are in Las Vegas on a short vacation. Now what the hell is it that you wanted to talk to me about?"

"I suppose you've heard the news about Burnhart, you wouldn't know anything about that would you?"

"The first I heard about it was fifteen minutes ago when I checked the messages on the phone in my room."

"When do you expect to be back in L.A., Carter?"

"Mick and I will be on a plane out of here this afternoon."

"I want to see you and Terratello in my office after you get back to Los Angeles, you got that?"

"Look Croft, I'm tired and I need to get some sleep. We'll be in to see you on Monday morning, you got that?"

"If I need to I'll have you picked up for questioning Carter as soon as you arrive at the airport."

"Fine Croft. I'll have my attorney right there with me, is that what you want?"

A few seconds of silence, then the detective said, "Monday morning Carter, first thing or I have you picked up for not cooperating with a police investigation."

"Hey Croft, turn off the lights and go back to sleep or your wife is going to be pissed off at you. We'll see you Monday."

49

Carter and Mick had checked out of Caesar's at 10 AM Sunday morning, but decided to enjoy breakfast there before their 2 PM flight back to L.A. Sitting in a back corner booth away from other customers, they were able to talk without being overheard.

After ordering their breakfast, Carter told Mick, "You know Croft is going to assume we knew something about Burnhart?"

"He can assume all he wants Donny Boy, but he can't prove shit, because we don't know anything about it."

"Well Mick, I hope Vito has covered all his bases."

"Knowing my uncle, I'm sure he has thought of every angle."

"Okay Mick, enough said. Let's chow down and head for the airport. I want to pick up something for Annie in one of the gift shops. The kid has been great through all of this."

At 2:10 PM, Carter and Mick sat in their seats as the plane taxied down the runway bound for Los Angeles. The flight would only take forty-five minutes and they would be circling Burbank Airport preparing to land very soon.

Once back on the ground and parked at the terminal, Carter and Mick sat back and watched as the plane emptied. Being the last to deplane, the men slowly walked into the terminal. When Carter saw who was standing just inside the door, he said, "Shit! Look who our reception committee is."

Det. Croft stood with his young sidekick, Det. Petrovich, who said. "Welcome home gentlemen."

Carter, not thinking this reception was funny, said, "What the hell are you doing here Croft? I told you we would see you Monday morning, so why are you here?"

"You know what Carter? I thought that was a great idea, but my captain thought otherwise. After he got through reaming my ass out and reminding me that this was a murder investigation, and that the big boys were watching every move we make, he simply told me to get my ass down here and bring you both in for questioning."

Carter, not amused, said, "Croft, unless you're prepared to cuff us and arrest us with some bullshit charge, I suggest you get the hell out of our way."

"If that's what it will take Carter, I'm ready. Your choice!"

Carter looked at Mick, shrugged his shoulders and said, "You believe this crap?"

Croft not taking his eyes off Carter asked, "Well Carter?"

"Okay Croft, but I need to make two calls before we go with you."

"You can call from the police station."

"If you don't mind, I'll call from here?"

Not happy with Carter's statement, the detective said. "Okay, make your damn calls."

Carter called Annie, while Mick used another phone to call his uncle and let him know that they were being taken in for questioning. Vito asked where they were being taken and told Mick he would have an attorney there to meet them.

Once they were both off the phones, Croft asked, "Do you have a car here or were you preparing to take a cab?"

Mick spoke up, "I have my car here in the long term lot. I'll pay the bill and we can follow you and your sidekick."

Croft said, "Carter you know how it works. I prefer that you both come with us."

Carter smiled and said, "Look Croft, we're tired and we want to get this bullshit over as quick as possible, and then get home. Mick is driving his own car and I'm riding with him. If you want to join us, it's up to you."

Croft and Carter were in a stare down for a few seconds. He then said, "Yeah, that's okay."

Looking at his partner, Croft said, "Go ahead Petrovich, we'll meet you back in Van Nuys."

The drive to the police station only took twenty minutes, and as they walked in they were approached by a man they didn't know. The man handed Carter a business card and said, "Mr. Carter, my name is Tony Russo, and I'm an attorney. I will be representing you and Mr. Terratello during your questioning until your other attorney arrives.

Now it was Croft who said, "What kind of bullshit is this Carter?"

Mr. Russo spoke up, "Det. Croft, this is only to make sure that Mr. Carter and Mr. Terratello's rights are not abused, nothing more."

Croft, appearing a little annoyed said, "Fine, let's get this over with."

50

Three hours later, Carter and Mick walked out of the Van Nuys Police Station. They were a lot more tired but much more knowledgeable about several homicides that took place while they were enjoying their trip in Las Vegas. Because of the now late hour they made a phone call and headed for the Beverly Hills Hotel for dinner with Vito as planned.

A private room had been reserved by Vito and the large table was set for ten with place cards on the plates. Carter and Mick were early but they were led to the private room by the assistant manager and told that

376

Mr. Terratello would be notified of their arrival.

As Carter walked around the table looking at the names on the place cards, he told Mick, "I don't get it. Does this make any sense to you Mick?"

Before Mick had a chance to answer, Carter heard Vito say as he walked in, "Donald, Michael, welcome home."

Vito was accompanied by Paul Conti and two men Carter didn't know. After a few hugs and handshakes, Carter and Mick were introduced to the two men.

Vito said, "Michael, Donald, I would like you to meet a very good friend of mine who lives here in Beverly Hills. 'Don' Luis Franco and his associate Antonio Scanuto."

After handshakes all around, Vito said, "Please, everyone, be seated. Our other guests will be here shortly."

As they all sat, engaging in conversation, another man quietly entered the room, nodded to Vito and took his position near the door. Ten minutes later as everyone sat talking and sipping wine, there was a knock at the door.

The door was opened and two women entered, followed by Gino Vochelli.

Everyone at the table stood and were introduced to both women, whose names were Joan and Gerti.

After the introduction, they all sat and resumed talking. Carter asked one of the women whom he continued to stare at, "Joan, you look very familiar. Have we met before?"

The woman, who was dressed very elegantly said with a smile, "Perhaps Mr. Carter, I should have brought my shotgun with me and tied my hair back in a ponytail."

Carter smiled and said, "My God. Nice to see you again Miss Unger."

Vito looked at Carter and said, "I'm sorry Donald, I thought you recognized Joan. She had told me you visited her at her home in Acton several months ago."

"Yes Vito, but when I last talked to Miss Unger, I had no idea there was such a beautiful woman hidden under the dust of the desert."

Everyone laughed, and then Vito said, "On a sad note Donald, without your knowledge, you were familiar with Gerti's husband before he died several months ago. Her husband was the late Rabbi Simon Rubinowitz."

Carter sat back in his chair, more confused about the two women and eagerly waited for an explanation.

Vito, who sat with the two women at his side, said, "Joan and Gerti are sisters. They, along with Simon, were family to me and Gino when we were kids growing up back in New York." Looking at Gino who smiled and waved his hand, Vito continued. "Growing up in the Depression years was very hard on everyone, with money and food extremely hard to come by. Gino and I had a knack for finding things when we were young boys, but sometimes the local police weren't very happy with us. At one point we were wanted for questioning for a crime we did not commit but couldn't prove our innocence. Simon, whom we both knew from the neighborhood, had an uncle who owned a farm in Flemington, New Jersey, about sixty miles away. The late Mr. Myron Rubinowitz took both Gino and me in, gave us jobs working on the farm for two years, and showed us that there was a better more honest way to live."

Carter asked, "May I ask, what about your own parents during that time?"

Vito smiled, "That's quite all right Donald. Gino's father and my father were killed in a gangland execution. Gino's mother came to

Flemington with us and I'm sorry to say my mother passed away from cancer just before we left New York. Gino and I have always stayed in touch with Gerti and Simon, but until recently we had not talked with Joan. Now enough with reliving the past, we will be able to clear up several other matters as the night goes on. Let's enjoy a fine meal and we can talk later."

After a wonderful meal and lots of small talk around the table, Vito, Carter and Mick were standing on the outside balcony enjoying their Cuban cigars, when Carter said, "Vito, I want to thank you for getting us out of town while a big liquidation was taking place."

"Donald, both you and Michael were in danger of being set up for the actions that were taken this past weekend. 'Don' Franco is the one you should be thanking for being far away and not possibly a suspect in the past weekend activities.

From what my sources say, there was a full disclosure supplied to the authorities with each of the victims when they were found. As you must have already heard, Carson Burnhart has disappeared. Not admitting that I had any personal involvement in his disappearance, I have heard that Mr. "Braumholtz" will be eliminated from the list of most wanted WW2 war criminals being hunted by the Simon Wiesenthal Center in Los Angeles. Where he is today, I have no idea, but I do know that his soul will rot in hell while his victims can smile at his passing. I feel personally that justice has been served, but I do not assume any responsibility in the actions taken."

Carter held out his hand and said, "Still, I want to thank you for all that you did to protect us from harm."

When the three men re-entered the room, there was one new person who had come in to join the party, Reggie. When she walked over to Vito, she kissed him on the cheek and said, "I'm sorry I'm late, but the flight out of San Francisco was delayed."

Looking at Carter, Reggie said, "Hello Carter, nice to see you again. Hello Mick?"

As Carter stood quiet, Mick walked to Reggie and hugged her. "You look great Reggie, are you in town for a while?"

"That depends on how things work out Mick, we'll see."

Vito said, "Let's all sit and hear what news Miss Volasko has for us."

Once everyone was seated and after dinner drinks had been served, the waiter left the room. Vito said, "The table is yours Miss Volasko."

51

Reggie cleared a spot on the table and placed a folder in front of her but spoke without opening it, "First, I want to apologize for not being here at the start of this gathering of old friends. Unfortunately, I had no control over my tardiness. From previous meetings I am familiar with everyone in this room and want to thank you all for including me in this reunion. As instructed by Mr. Terratello, I was visiting the Napa Valley in Northern California to present his proposal to Mrs. Bella Fisher, the sister of Carson Burnhart. The proposal was to offer Mrs. Fisher a fair amount for her ownership in The Fisher Holtz

Vineyards. After an outburst of profanity by Mrs. Fisher, she asked me to be seated while she prepared a statement she wanted me to read to the prospective buyers."

Opening the folder in front of her, Reggie removed a typed statement and read, "To Whom It May Concern, I am not now, nor will I ever be in the future, willing or ready to sell my vineyards to anyone, especially to some Wops from New York who think they can push me around or threaten me. If you make any attempt to pressure me or my employees, I will contact my attorney and press charges against you. I know your group of people are responsible for my brother's disappearance and when he is found you will be prosecuted by the law. I wish no further contact with you. Bella Fisher."

Passing the typed statement to Vito, Reggie said, "I'm sorry to have to be the one to bring you this information in this way, but it was done at her request."

After several seconds, Vito said, "Thank you Miss Volasko. I am sure you handled your meeting with Mrs. Fisher in a professional manner and presented our offer with all good intentions. From this point on, there will be no further talk of Bella Fisher or The Fisher Holtz Vineyards. I would like to look at the matter as being closed. But, if for some reasons, negotiations should start again, I'm sure our offer will be accepted."

Vito nodded his head slightly to 'Don' Franco and Gino Vochelli, and then said, "'Don' Franco if you and Gino would be so kind as to join me in my suite, I believe we have further business to discuss in private."

As the three men stood up, Vito said, "I want to thank you all for coming this evening. Please enjoy yourselves as long as you wish and I will talk with you all tomorrow."

Carter stood quickly and approached each man to shake hands as they started for the door, and said, "Thank you very much Vito, it was a pleasure to be invited to this special gathering, and I do very much appreciate all that you have done on my behalf. 'Don' Franco, it was an honor to meet you sir."

The 'Don' held out his hand and said, "Mr. Carter, Vito has spoken highly of you, and it is my pleasure to finally meet you. Please remember that my door is always open to friends of Vito and Gino. Since we are fortunate to live so close, I would enjoy an occasional visit if you find the time."

"It would be my pleasure 'Don Franco'."

Once the men exited the room, Carter and Mick walked out onto the balcony to relight their cigars and discuss what their next move would be for Carter Security. One of the things they had talked about while they were in Las Vegas was hiring an additional experienced investigator. When Mick brought it up again, Reggie who was standing in the doorway of the balcony asked "Have you considered hiring an experienced woman for the job?"

Carter stared quietly at Reggie for a few seconds, then turned away looking out at the view.

Mick asked, "Why? Are you applying for the job Reggie?"

"Well, since I decided New York just ain't the place for me anymore, I thought I'd give California a try again, on a more permanent basis."

"So what happened with New York, Reg? I thought you loved living there?"

"I did, but something was missing and no matter what I did, I just wasn't happy being there anymore."

"So what was missing?"

Reggie nodded towards Carter. "Some asshole I fell in love with, and now I can't get him out of my head."

Carter turned around, looked at Reggie, and then walked past her back into the room.

Reggie said, "Come on Carter. What do you want me to do, beg for your forgiveness?"

Antony Scanuto and Paul Conti got up from the table after overhearing some of the conversation. "Well guys, Reggie, I think it's time for the rest of us to leave."

Mrs. Rubinowitz and Mrs. Unger looked at each other and decided it was time to turn in for the night. So they thanked everyone and said goodnight.

Mick smiled at Carter, then Reggie, and said, "You two have some issues to work out, I'll be down in the bar when you're ready to go."

Two hours later, Carter and Reggie walked into the cocktail lounge, and Carter said, "Okay Mick, take us home."

Mick smiled and said, "Take us home? Is that my home or your home, boss?"

Carter said, "My home, wiseass."

Reggie spoke up, "I can drive us Carter, I have a rental car, and besides, Mick looks like he needs a pot of coffee before he drives anywhere."

"Hear that Mick? We'll see you at the office in the morning."

On the ride back to Carter's home, there was very little conversation, and then

Reggie said, "What's the matter Carter, you all talked out?"

"No Reg, just thinking about how Vito is going to handle Mrs. Fisher."

"I wouldn't think about it Carter, I'm sure we don't want to know."

52

Two days later, the body of Carson Burnhart was discovered at a Jewish cemetery in Glendale by a grounds keeper. The body clothed in the typical striped garment that had been worn by Jewish prisoners in the Concentration camps in Poland, was staked out on the ground in front of a memorial for the over six million Jews who died at the hands of the Nazi guards. An investigation into the millionaire's kidnapping and murder was stepped up, and a promise by the police to find the guilty parties was issued in a statement given at police headquarters in Los Angeles.

The private funeral service for Carson Burnhart was held at the Forest Lawn Cemetery in Glendale, California. The service was attended by many high ranking politicians, selected employees and several unexpected mourners.

Keeping out of sight, but close enough to hear the spoken words of the Monsignor who was presiding over the service, Vito Terratello and Paul Conti waited for Burnhart's coffin to be lowered into the ground before moving in closer.

One by one, the mourners walked up to Bella Fisher and offered their condolences. When there were only a few people remaining, Vito and Paul walked to the grieving sister of Burnhart. As Vito started to speak, Bella Fisher stood up and said, "You son of a bitch, how do you have the nerve to show up here? You get the hell away from me before I have you arrested."

Turning to the man standing behind her, Bella Fisher said, "Wilhelm, please remove these men from my sight."

Vito said, "That won't be necessary. We're leaving.

One thing before we go Mrs. Fisher, when all of this is over, I would still like to discuss purchasing the vineyards, but now is not the time."

As the men started walking away, Bella Fisher said softly to herself, "We'll do business alright you wop bastard, but my kind of business."

One week later, after enjoying a meal together, Vito, Paul, Mick, and Tony Scanuto were coming out of an Italian restaurant in Woodland Hills. They were walking through the parking lot when shots rang out and everyone searched for cover. When the shooting was over, Paul Conti and Tony Scanuto lay dead in the parking lot. Vito had been shot in the back. Mick somehow avoided the mass of gunfire and was able to yell to some passers-by, "Call 911 and get the paramedics here quick, there's been a shooting."

The fire station that was close by had a paramedic unit and fire truck on the scene in just a few minutes. Vito was stabilized and taken to the closest hospital. Once the police arrived, and the bodies of the dead were examined by the coroner and crime scene investigators, the bodies were removed and taken to the morgue.

When Mick finally got hold of Carter and told him about the shooting, he then said, "My uncle got his answer from the woman up north, but I don't think she's going to like his response once he's able to retaliate."

Mick gave Carter the information about which hospital Vito had been taken to, and told him, "You and Reggie keep your eyes open, they may come after you next."

Carter asked, "Mick, where are you, are you alright?"

"Yeah, they missed me Donny Boy. I just finished answering a shit-load of questions for the police, now I'm on my way to the hospital, I'll see you there."

53

Six weeks had gone by since the shooting in Woodland Hills. Vito Terratello had returned to New York and the comfort of his own home and care of his personal physician. With his wound healing at a slow pace because of his age, Vito still felt fortunate to be alive. Reflecting back to the death of his son Danny, and the death of Paul Conti, Vito found it hard to find enjoyment in life around him, no matter what his surroundings were. Tony Scanuto, who was a close friend, would also be missed and it brought much sadness to his heart.

Back in North Hollywood, Annie Dugan, sitting at her desk, answered the phone on the second ring. "Good morning, Donald Carter Security, may I help you?"

The caller said, "Hello sweetheart, it's Vito Terratello, is Donald in?"

"Hello Mr. Terratello. Mr. Carter and Miss Volasko have not come in yet, but they should be here any minute. How are you doing sir, I heard about what happened?"

"I'm feeling fine sweetheart, thank you. How about my nephew Michael, is he in by any chance?"

"Actually sir, he's downstairs talking with the owner of the truck repair shop. If you'll hold on for a minute I can run down and get him for you."

"Thank you sweetheart, it's really important."

"Two minutes later, Mick was upstairs sitting at his desk talking with his uncle. When he got off the phone, Mick asked Annie, "Where the hell is Carter?"

"He'll be here any minute Mick, he and Reggie are on the way."

Five minutes later, Carter and Reggie walked in laughing, both looking like they were enjoying life to its fullest. In truth they were, they had been closer than they had been when they lived together many months earlier, and their attempt of cohabitation years ago.

When Mick saw them, he said, "I just got off the phone with my uncle. Boy, have I got some news for you guys."

Carter asked, "How is he doing Mick?"

"He's doing fine. He said his wound is healing and he'll be back out here in a couple more weeks to celebrate the purchase of his new vineyard up in Napa Valley. The new vineyard will be called Terrachelli Vineyards."

Reggie asked, "Is it anywhere near that Fisher Holtz Vineyard?"

"Funny you should ask Reg. It seems that for some reason, Mrs. Bella Fisher had a change of heart and decided to sell the vineyard to the newly formed corporation. The new vineyard is owned by my uncle and Gino Vochelli. The Vineyard will be managed jointly by Mrs. Rubinowitz and Mrs. Unger. How's that for a surprise?"

"How the hell did he pull that one off?"

"Well, from what he told me, he had a couple of shrewd negotiators who would not take no for an answer. I guess it's just in the way the offer is presented."

Carter said, "That is a surprise. I wonder what Vito had to do to persuade that old witch?"

"He told me that after he offered her an extremely large amount of money, he threw in a long extended cruise out on the ocean, with a promise that they would never have to do business again with each other."

Laughing, Carter said, "Ya know Mick, somehow I always knew your uncle would get things his way, but to have Gerti and Joan running that vineyard, that's a bonus."

54

The half day fishing boat, 'Charley's Dream,' that left the dock at the Ventura Marina each morning at 6 AM, made its routine stop at the bait dock before going out for a six hour fishing trip. With eighteen anglers aboard, the captain and his crew had plans of going out to a known location where fishing was plentiful. They picked up chum, live bait and frozen bait, things that were needed to help the happy high paying fishermen have a good day out on the ocean. The other things were the liquid refreshments that the fishermen had to supply for themselves, or pay the high prices the crew would charge.

The live minnows were kept in a bait tank and the squid and chum were frozen and had to be thawed out. The squid was sometimes sliced into strips or used whole depending on what the fishermen were going after. The chum was sometimes packed in five, ten or twenty-pound packages, frozen solid and placed in five-gallon buckets to be ladled out onto the ocean to attract fish when thawed out.

Charley's first mate was ladling out chum while the boat was sitting about ten miles off the coast of Ventura. As he performed this duty, he spotted something shiny in the bottom of the chum bucket. Reaching in with the ladle the crewman scooped out the object that appeared to be a crunched and twisted band of gold.

Rinsing the band off with clean water, he then looked at it carefully and saw that it had writing on it but couldn't make it out. Putting the ring in his pocket, he continued to ladle out the chum and watched as his work attracted fish and seagulls.

His plan to look closer at his find after they returned to their dock would keep him curious the whole morning. It was three hours after they had returned to the dock that afternoon, and the boat had been washed down and prepared for the next morning's trip, before the crewman could check out his find.

After everyone had gone home for the day the crewman sat in the boat's galley with a magnifying glass and looked at the partial inscription that read, 14K Bella & Wil.

There was no way the crewman could have known that it had been an entire year since the disappearance of Bella Fisher and her foreman Wilhelm Gruber. The story in a Napa Valley newspaper a year earlier said the couple were returning home after signing papers for the sale of Fisher Holtz Vineyards in San Francisco. Bella Fisher's attorney, who had overseen the signing of the papers and acted as a witness in the presence of a Notary Public, passed away from a heart attack only hours after the transaction was completed.

The speculation about Mrs. Fisher and Mr. Gruber was that the two lovers took the cashiers check for the four million dollars and disappeared to a life in hiding.

The documents for the sale of the vineyards had all been recorded with the state, and everything had been approved pending validation. Copies in the possession of the new owners, had been checked by handwriting and signature experts and proven to be authentic.

Back in Woodland Hills, a statue had been erected at the site of the Burnhart Building in memory of the land developer. To this day, the statue is covered in graffiti and bird droppings but no one seems to care. The man who tortured and killed so many people in his life is finally getting what he deserved.

Carter Security had become a well respected investigative service and was prospering. With Mick and Annie working the phones in the office most of the time, Jimmy Hudson and Reggie were handling much of the investigations. Carter was working on his sobriety one day at a time, attending AA meetings and keeping his drinking in check. As the days went by the future looked much brighter for Donald Carter.

THE END